Recent Books by Mignon G. Eberhart

Two Little Rich Girls
Murder in Waiting
Danger Money
Family Fortune
Nine O'Clock Tide
The Bayou Road
Casa Madrone
Family Affair
Next of Kin
The Patient in Cabin C
Alpine Condo Crossfire
A Fighting Chance

A Fighting Chance

A Fighting Chance

Mignon G. Eberhart

Random House · New York

All rights reserved under International and Pan-American Copyright
Conventions. Published in the United States by Random House, Inc., New
York, and simultaneously in Canada by Random House of Canada Lim-
ited, Toronto.

Library of Congress Cataloging-in-Publication Data
Eberhart, Mignon Good

  A fighting chance.
  I. Title.
PS3509.B453F53   1986   813'.52   85–25596
ISBN 0-394-55082-X

Manufactured in the United States of America
9 8 7 6 5 4 3 2
First Edition

All the persons and events in this book are entirely imaginary. Nothing in it derives from anything that ever happened.

A Fighting Chance

One

"Then she is still in love with him."

"Oh, yes. I'm sure she is. A murderer! It really seems too bad. She won't look at another man."

"It's been five years. She was only eighteen."

"I was married at eighteen and it was a happy—a very happy marriage." There was a slight pause.

"Yes, I know." It was Blanche Surton, her voice gentle now.

"Blanche, tell me honestly. Do you believe Jim Wingate shot that awful Walker man?"

"No. Delia, I must go."

"How is your mother?"

Voices of themselves, rid of facial expressions, eyes, smiles, anything, take on their innate meanings. Julie knew that Delia's face would be smiling in a friendly way; her voice was perfunctory, merely polite.

Blanche's voice, on the other hand, was uncertain, troubled. "I don't know, Delia. I think . . . I know that she is feeble. She still pretends she is fine. She always says, 'It's been a splendid day.' Or the times I was not at home, 'I was fine, don't bother about me.' Something like that."

"Dear Blanche. You can't send her to a nursing home as long as she's in full control of her mind."

"Oh, no! I couldn't possibly do that. But she's had such a hard time. Such a long period of invalidism. She is courageous always."

"I wish I could help you."

"You always help just by being you, Delia. I must go. Good night."

There were sounds of the door to the street opening, vague murmurs of goodbyes, the door closing again and then Delia stuck her head, blond- and silver-colored, into the little room. Once, probably, this had been a ladies' cloakroom, but Delia had affectionately converted it into a workroom for Julie, complete with desk, typewriter, filing cabinet, bookshelves and an easy chair.

By this time Julie Farnham was sitting almost huddled at her desk, her hand on the stack of galley proofs she had been reading when she heard the voices outside in the hall, and all at once, tears she thought she had learned to control were streaming down her face.

Delia, a raincoat over her arm, saw Julie and a wave of embarrassed color surged into her plump but still very pretty face. "Oh, Julie! I didn't hear you come in. I didn't mean to talk about Jim, but that was Blanche."

Julie nodded. "Yes, I heard—"

"Oh, my dear child! Truly, I didn't mean to discuss you or—"

"It's all right, Aunt Delia." Julie mopped her face with the backs of her hands and sat back. "You were talking about Jim, of course. And, yes, I'm still in love with him. Five years . . ." Julie put her hands flat and hard on the desk, made herself speak forcefully and honestly. "It would have been a much harder five years if you hadn't helped."

4

But Delia was still apologetic. "I didn't notice your rain-coat until after she went home. I thought you were still out. I wouldn't have talked to Blanche about—well, you know, about him, but she brought up the subject and I—"

"Never mind, Aunt Delia. It's simply one of those things one must try to live with. John always says that."

"John Wingate ought to know." There was the slightest trace of sarcasm in Delia's usually soft and pleasing voice. She went on briskly, however, "And John has told me over and over that I must not bother you when you're working. I'll just hang up your raincoat. It was on the chair behind the door."

"I'm only reading galley proofs."

Delia eyed the stack of proof sheets rather nervously. "It looks like work."

Julie fiddled with the proof sheets and risked a question. "Has Blanche heard from Jim?"

"Oh, I wouldn't think so! But she doesn't believe he killed Alben Walker."

"Yes. I knew that. I expect I ought to have come out and spoken to her, but—Aunt Delia, do you suppose she has any idea where he is?"

"My dear, I shouldn't think so. The plain fact is, Julie, that he would have been arrested on suspicion of murder and then probably indicted. He was simply the only suspect. That would have meant a trial and there was just no other evidence that could have saved him."

"Jim didn't murder that man."

"Oh, I know that!"

Julie had traveled all the possible paths of speculation and reasoning during the five years since Jim had disappeared. To put it more bluntly, he had run away. The certain outcome of his situation would have had to be that Jim was accused of killing a man named Alben Walker; then, later, tried by a jury of his peers, he would have been pronounced guilty and removed to prison until the judge pronounced a mandatory sentence for murder.

Delia smoothed down her neatly designed, pinkish-brown dress; expensively designed, too, Julie knew. Her hands, plump and white, sparkled with the diamonds her husband had lavished on her; Delia cherished his memory and resolutely followed what she believed to have been his precepts as if he were still alive. He had been devoted to her, as she was, now, to his memory.

She sighed. "Poor Blanche! She's had a very hard life, hasn't she? That mother! Left with only enough money to live on, nothing but that and the little house in Brookboro. I still don't understand how Blanche got through university and law school and was able to work so hard—yes, and so brilliantly—that she not only earned a great deal of money but also became the youngest partner in Sturke, Bridge and Smith, I believe, that there ever has been. A prestigious—I do hate that word, but I can't think of another. However, the firm does have a long history of respect and—yes, prestige. She was young, only in her thirties. But then"—Delia looked triumphant—"we do have a beautiful young woman on the Supreme Court now, don't we!"

"Blanche is beautiful," Julie said slowly, "in spite of a kind of mantle of rigid professionalism. Somehow I can't think of her as having very strong feelings of her own."

Delia nodded. "You mean love affairs. Good heavens, child! When would she have had time for a love affair? She was too busy building up her practice, caring for her mother. I'm glad she's earned enough to give herself a little freedom."

"You mean that apartment in the city!"

"Well, she's got to have someplace where she can get away from her mother, that hospital atmosphere, and work, of course, her time to relax, to go to the theater." Delia sighed. "I've always guessed—well, known really—that she liked John."

Julie said, "Passion, love, Blanche?"

Delia frowned. "Don't get carried away by the romance in your own writing! However, it is true that she rarely lets herself go, so to speak. In all the years I've known her, I've never . . . Oh, well, it doesn't matter now. To get back to Jim. Seems too bad that he just vanished that way."

"Would you rather have seen him be indicted, tried, almost certainly sent to prison in the end?"

"No!" Delia was getting flustered. "That is, no! Certainly, I didn't want him to go to jail. But this way, why, poor Jim can't make himself known anywhere. He has had to wander the earth like . . . whoever it was." Delia said more calmly, "Blanche wanted to see you, Julie, but I didn't know you had returned from your walk. She said to tell you that she had read your book. She wanted me to be sure to tell you she had bought it, because, according to her, the sweetest words to any author are 'I bought your book.' She also said she liked it very much and sent her congratulations, and I told her you had almost finished another. I told her John Wingate had made you work."

"John has been great. And you, Delia, you took me in, and Peter too, long ago when we were alone. You acted as if you were our own—"

"Don't say mother," Delia intervened. "Say strict, cranky, firm aunt. After all, your father was my brother, and your mother was like a young sister of mine. Besides, Peter is my godson. Now, there. We'll not think of that. But aunt, yes."

"Aunt or anything," Julie said warmly. "You were and are wonderful. Even after Jim had gone, you helped me."

"What else was I to do? Now, get back to work."

But she leaned over the desk, gave Julie's shoulder a loving pat and whisked out of the little room.

Julie leaned on her elbows, tried not to think and failed. It did not surprise her that she could still cry about Jim; a person could love steadfastly and forever as painfully at eighteen as at twenty-three. Twenty-three, she thought dismally; five years without Jim, and without any word at all of him, where he was, or if there was ever any possible chance of his return. She mopped at her face again, settled her red sweater over her shoulders, for the October dusk was growing chill, and made herself return to the stack of galley proofs.

This was to be her second novel. After John Wingate had all but forced her to try to write, helped her with the hard spots, encouraged her, had in the end taken the manuscript to his own publisher, she now felt the need to repeat the first moderate, yet to her highly satisfactory, success of her first book.

"It's the second one that proves you," John had said. "A successful first book could be just a fluke. It's the second one —get at it, Julie."

John Wingate was a famed and admired author; he had been on a trip in South America (actually in Bolivia) when Alben Walker was murdered. It had taken a long time to find John, and when he finally arrived, Jim had already run away. That was not like Jim. Yet that was what he had done five years ago.

Later, when John saw that life had lost its special meaning and zest for Julie, he had told her she had to do something, something hard. When she had protested about writing, he had said only, "You never know whether or not you can do anything until you try it."

Good John Wingate, but perhaps not always communicative John Wingate about his own affairs. They were his own business, Julie reminded herself, and reminded herself also that there was urgent work on her desk; she turned back to the galleys and the little sheet of printer's marks she had learned to keep beside her. She found one sentence, which during her walk she had decided to change. Luckily it was at the end of a paragraph, which was not so tiresome (or unwelcome) a change as it would have been had it occurred in the middle of a paragraph. Nevertheless, she counted the letters and spaces she was removing (indicated with a reasonable facsimile of a mark that meant "delete") and compared them with the characters—the letters and spaces—of the sentence she wished to introduce in their place. Finding that the final count was only two spaces over, she wrote it in the margin with the correct mark showing where it was to be incorporated in the text.

Everyone said it must be great to write; she sometimes, if rarely, felt like saying, Why? It was, as John had promised her, exhaustingly hard work. But it had in fact given her life; not only energy but some kind of goal. She couldn't have Jim, but she could have work.

John Wingate had given her all the advice he could; one bit recurred to her then: "The reader is led by a silken thread."

Yet she could not help reviewing the scraps of conversation she had overheard. She had had no idea that Blanche was in the house when she returned from a walk in the light autumn fog, which would soon turn to rain. She had gone up the two steps that led directly up from the sidewalk and supplied a very discreet entrance to the narrow, red brick house. All the entrances to the houses were alike, white doorways and almost unknown except to residents or their intimates.

Perhaps the two steps leading to the Van Clive house were a little whiter and the brass knocker a little brighter than those at the entrances of neighboring houses, but if so, that was due to Aunt Delia's adopted Dutch views of cleanliness and solid determination to fight off New York's inevitable dust and soot.

Her ownership of the house derived from Delia's marriage to the descendant of an authentic Dutch ancestor: Pieter Van Clive. Her husband had been born in that house and had died there, leaving it to his widow.

Julie had inserted her key in the door and entered the

house quietly, not deliberately but merely because during her walk she had had an idea that seemed constructive. So she had gone directly to her workroom.

In the past, Aunt Delia always accompanied Julie to her own home in Brookboro. But Brookboro had changed for Julie the day Jim disappeared. Delia scolded her, but Julie couldn't help shrinking from the usual little round of pleasures. Brookboro was by no means a large Connecticut city, yet it was big enough to possess a good yacht club on the river, and a pleasant country club and golf links out on Brookboro road. When Peter, Julie's seventeen-year-old brother, was not at school, both Delia and Julie felt they had to make a real home for him. Julie had sincerely tried to follow Delia's advice to go anywhere any time she could; but now that Jim was gone, whenever Peter returned to school she found little satisfaction in anything but her dog and the hard work of writing. So she and Delia had left the pleasant, very New England white house, with its generous rooms and gardens and trees and, for Julie now, far too many memories of Jim—meeting him at the door, going out for a walk or just sitting before a fireplace in the evening, watching Jim, listening to him and—at last wondering what he could see in her, little Julie Farnham, but unbelievably happy so that each morning she awoke thinking of Jim, thinking of the day ahead when she would see him, thinking of her whole world, which *was* Jim.

All at once there were too many memories in the Brookboro house. It had been left to her and her brother jointly; the trustees had retained a kind of combination caretaker-gardener-chauffeur named Ollie, who loved the dog and would see to him as well as to the house and grounds. From the time of Jim's departure she had lived almost all the time with Delia in the city.

Jim's flight (she had to admit that's what it was) was not in character. Yet it had happened. She shook herself mentally. It was darkening; there was a slight patter of rain as the fog, so near the East River, changed to a shower. It was time to stop brooding and try to ease the ache in her heart, straighten up her desk and herself and join Delia in the living room.

Two

But first she must try to remove the marks of tears on her face. She went into the tiny and amazingly old-fashioned lavatory which had been wedged in the side of the room, washed her face in cold water and took the brush to her hair.

"Your hair is not quite the color mine was," Delia had told her. "Mine was more golden brown. My husband called it honey brown. That is, before I managed to get these whitish streaks in it. Yours is not quite golden," she added with a touch of the young coquette. Then she added generously, "But your hair has a kind of wave in it. Mine hasn't. And while your eyes are blue, too, I think they are more like your mother's than mine. Her eyes were very dark. My husband called mine a good clear Dutch blue."

Somehow through the years, Delia had lost what must once have been a youthful slimness and grace. But as her figure increased, so did her kindness. Her intense loyalty had always been there.

Julie pushed the brush through her hair, which was in an obedient mood because of the rain; when the weather was very dry, her hair preferred standing out like a furious cat's tail. She added a trace of lipstick, shrugged her red sweater around her, made sure that her white collar was straight and went out to the living room.

Delia was waiting amid the massive, highly polished tables and chairs, the brightly shining brasses of the fireplace, the heavy red curtains, open now in order to let in the last of the warm, blueish twilight.

"All finished?" Delia said.

"I think so. At least I hope so. Oh, Delia, why didn't John warn me against writer's nerves?"

"There, there! You needn't worry about that."

Julie sat down and tried to relax. "John told me he always had nerves. He said he always has writer's block, too—every morning before he goes to work."

Delia shrugged that off. "Never mind, let's have our drinks."

"I'll mix them." Julie went to the bar; this was a concession to modernism on Delia's part, set in the far end of the dining room. Everything was there, ice, glasses and promising decanters. She poured carefully, put the glasses upon the silver tray which Delia, a very proper housekeeper, kept on the bar, and returned to Delia. "What's for dinner?"

Delia brightened. "You won't believe this but I don't know. She needs no telling."

"She's a wonderful cook. You do use magic to keep her. Cheers!"

Delia's pretty, round face, a little middle-aged as was her blond hair, neatly waved and touched with a silvery shine, dimpled. She said firmly, "Money magic. The only way. But wages are scandalous. Well—yes, cheers!"

Julie sipped her drink. The rain was now streaming down the windowpanes and made a pleasant, soothing murmur.

Julie watched it; Delia watched it. Both drank slowly and thoughtfully; probably both were thinking of Jim. There was an appetizing odor coming from the kitchen below. The dinner would be sent up by way of a remarkable dumbwaiter set in the wall of the dining room. Everything about the house was old-fashioned except some completely mandatory things like heat, plenty of hot water at any time of day, and a vacuum cleaner to each floor. The stairs were steep. The supply of vacuum cleaners was one way of keeping a three-times-a-week maid for cleaning. Few people would cheerfully attempt work in a house that required one vacuum cleaner to be dragged up and down the stairs.

Shad Cove was itself an enclave of tall, narrow houses, surrounding a large and beautifully tended garden. All the residents combined to pay for a skilled gardener, so that even in the middle of an October rain the garden was still charming and thriving.

"Autumn showers," Delia said absently.

Julie said, "Yes. Aunt Delia, where do you think Jim is?"

"Oh, darling! How can one know! I have thought, I suppose, of someplace where we have no extradition treaty— where—" she shook her head, then lifted a defiant chin. "But wherever he is, Julie, he still thinks of you."

Yes, Julie was sure of that. Or, in dark moments, was she sure?

"Did Blanche say anything about George?"

"George Wingate?" Delia sighed. "Blanche said that he is trying to get some roles in winter stock now—summer stock later. Anything to do with the theater. Of course John Wingate will never try to stop him. His own son."

Both women were silent. The room itself seemed to listen, with all the gleaming old-fashioned mahogany listening, too. It would not have seemed unreasonable if the yellow piano in one corner of the room let out a musical note of inquiry, for it was an important part of Delia's life. It was indeed a fabulous piano; not as large as a concert grand, but large. It was enameled in a cheerful yellow, festooned by painted and really charming bouquets of flowers; it had gilded and enormous legs. The big triangular top, however, was always down, and below their lid, the keys covered with a strip of felt. Delia and her husband had seen it in Harrods in London, during their honeymoon. Noticing her admiration, he had bought the piano for her, and it was one of Delia's most cherished and guarded possessions.

Delia herself was no musician; she kept her Thursday night box at the opera, but she never touched the piano. Once a year a little man (with suitably large ears) came to tweak the piano strings, tune it, deliver a kind of précis about heat and humidity, and depart. After that Delia closed the piano firmly; she didn't even wince at the cost of its insurance, although she was always careful about money. So much so that before promising to join any philanthropic board, she was known for first asking to see its financial statements. Still, she was by no means ungenerous, and the yellow piano did make a lovely spot of color in the rather dark and heavy room.

Delia put down her glass as a shrill whistle blasted from the basement kitchen. The fabulous cook had proved herself a fabulous whistler but an impatient one. Both women jumped to their feet; the whistler was not to be irked in the least degree.

They went in to dinner and Delia pulled herself together; obviously the conversation with Blanche and also with Julie had rather shaken her usual calm. Julie and Delia almost never talked of Jim. To Julie it was too tragic, too painful, too reminding; Delia was tactful and understanding. They talked of the book on her desk; they talked of Peter; they talked of the weather; they talked of the whistling cook's superb chocolate mousse and, moments later, of the equally superb coffee she had sent up—after Julie had placed all the dinner dishes, as neatly as she could, in the tray on the dumbwaiter and sent it down with a spirited punch at the electric bell. This was another concession of Delia's to the present age; there were still usable ropes, however, although largely a reminder of the past. Delia had made other concessions in the basement kitchen: once dark and dreary, it was

15

now brilliantly lighted by long tubes across the ceiling; every appliance electricity could provide was there. Delia honored her husband's memory, but she was also sensible.

The only approach from the kitchen to the upper regions of the house was a narrow, steep stairway, which not only the whistler but other cooks had refused to negotiate. There was, of course, a small door to the outside from the kitchen; it was even more discreet than the main house door, and hidden, discreetly too, by shrubs.

"You look tired," Delia said. "Better go to bed early."

Julie said perhaps she would finish some work first; Delia nodded and went upstairs. But first Delia saw to the locks and bolts of the street door; the big French doors into the garden were always bolted.

Not, however, that there was much fear of their neighbors.

Shad Cove was an extremely choice block in Manhattan; it lay on the very edge of the East River and was old—older, its owners claimed, than Turtle Bay, and much older than Kips Bay. But certainly it had fewer modern conveniences. Delia loved it and took such delight in following Pieter Van Clive's ways that she had become almost more Dutch than Pieter. In truth, she was Julie's father's sister and a Farnham of Boston, New York and Connecticut. But she adopted every manner of Dutch housekeeping, cleanliness and quiet force. Perhaps she had always believed in the power of money—not an enormous fortune, but enough.

Presently Julie heard the subdued murmur of the TV from Delia's room. She did not hear the subdued departure of the whistler.

Shad Cove was occupied mainly by celebrities, or at least by people who did not care for their comings and goings being noted and reported. A once famous movie star lived quietly in one of the houses. A former opera singer in another. A retired but, it was said, wildly rich stage manager in another, and a retired somebody important in government in another. There was scarcely an owner in that tightly con-

16

trolled little group who had not a completely unassailable name. The discreet entrance doors, leading directly from the sidewalk, were therefore valuable and much sought by people known to the public and wishing only for privacy.

It was, however, privacy with comfort. The houses were narrow, the stairs were steep, but privacy was there and rigidly maintained.

Because she had said she was going to work, Julie went to her workroom. Not, she had said with determination to everyone who asked, *not* her den. Small though it was, it gave her that valued sense of privacy that was not only a desideratum of Shad Cove but of a writer, even a beginning writer. On her rare visits to Brookboro now, she worked in a large onetime bedroom. John Wingate had always said it didn't matter when or where one worked; it was only important to work.

From being at one time a mild and unassuming young man around Brookboro, John had leaped into fame as a writer on travel and politics. Brookboro was slow to accept this but began to accord him a certain respect. After his first book he wrote others; then a godfather died, leaving him (so Brookboro said and believed) a very substantial fortune.

In his youthful days he had married Elaine. Julie was too young to remember Elaine; she had left Brookboro and John Wingate before he came into what was literally fame plus fortune. Delia had once described her. "She was a fool. Pretty, stupid, and . . ." Delia had finished icily, "she drank. She left John, of course. That was when he was sort of mooching around, everybody said, making very little money. Elaine took their boy, James George Wingate, with her. Elaine died. And George came to Brookboro."

To the violently interested mind of Brookboro, it was a puzzling story. The sum of it was that Jim (James) had been installed as John's son. A year or so later, when George turned up with all his proofs of his own identity as John's son (and again, observed by the violently interested Brookboro citizens) John simply, quietly, explaining nothing, took on both young men as if both belonged to him.

Brookboro, or what Julie knew of Brookboro, had subsequently made up its mind. Jim was John Wingate's son, deserted by Elaine; George was also his son, but here there were a few reservations. If he was Elaine and John's son, and Elaine, in what Delia called her completely scatterbrained way, had in fact been pregnant when she left John, then George was the result and thus was truly John's son, as Jim was.

Or, and this was whispered, Elaine had met some other man; George was *his* son. This, however, was problematical and barely hinted at. In any event, Brookboro decided to accept John's decision and merely agree when John claimed both young men as sons.

Julie was aware that no one but John knew the whole story. Julie didn't care, for by the time she was eighteen she knew she loved Jim; Jim, twenty-three but sure of himself, had decided that this girl he had thought of as only a neighborhood friend was in fact the only girl for him.

After unbelievably happy days, which Julie now remembered far too clearly, they were actually planning marriage. John had consented. Delia had consented. Everybody smiled at the two young lovers. Eighteen; Julie often thought and wondered how she could have been so sensible, so deeply aware of happiness and what her life was to be, at eighteen. But as Delia had reminded Blanche, Delia herself had been married at eighteen and it had been a lifelong love as far as Delia was concerned and, after her husband's death, she still treasured the great memories of love and constancy.

So, Julie had been sure, it was to be for her. The plans for the wedding were made; the time was almost settled, only depending on John Wingate's return from his present trip for material for another book. Her wedding dress was ordered, expensively, by Delia. The invitations were agreed upon but were awaiting the date of John Wingate's return. In another year Jim would graduate from M.I.T. John had volunteered the handsome wedding gift of covering their living expenses until then. Even Judge Munger, a close family friend, standing almost in loco parentis as Julie's father (or perhaps grandfather; he was far from young even then), was to give Julie away. Everything was in order when the happy world, the dreams of the future, were shattered.

For then, oh then, a man named Alben Walker was murdered. Jim was not formally accused or formally indicted but almost on the eve of that certain process of law, Jim had gone. No one knew where or admitted it if they did. Jim had not been heard from since, at least not by Julie.

Jim had come to see her, late, the night he went away. She was sitting by the living-room fire, thinking only of Jim's danger, when she heard his soft knock at the door. She ran to the door and he came in, caught her up in his arms and whispered, "Don't call your aunt. I have to talk to you. I'm getting out."

"Oh, Jim! You couldn't have killed that man!"

"I didn't kill him. But all the evidence involves me. I did go to his house when he phoned me. I hardly knew him, but he said he had something urgent to tell me. Something, he hinted, about my mother. I went to his house, rang the bell and opened the door when he didn't answer, and went into the living room and"—he gulped a little there—"there he was. Flat on the floor. Blood all over and—I thought only of trying to help him, phoning for help, something, and started toward him— But you've heard all this."

"I wish you hadn't picked up the gun."

"So do I! But I was so stunned, so horrified—to tell you the truth I hardly knew that I had picked it up. I stumbled over it and just as I got up from kneeling beside him, his neighbor Bill Hamilton came running in. He had heard the shot. By that time I had recognized the gun. It was one of my father's. Bill was scared. He took it out of my hand. Brave, really. Then he called the police. Well, you know how

19

it's been ever since. Today the police questioned me again. I'm minutes away from arrest on suspicion and indictment and a trial and—oh Julie, I didn't kill him but I can't prove it, so—"

"You must find a way to prove it!"

"I've tried. I can't. There is simply no other evidence. There was I, like a fool, standing there with the gun in my hand. Since then, Julie, everybody in town thinks I killed him. So—so I'm leaving."

"But your father!"

"No, I'll not tell him. Nobody has advised me. Nobody has told me to get out. But I'm getting out. For now. It's very hard, Julie. I'd rather stay and fight but, just now, I haven't a fighting chance. But—" He took her hard in his arms. "I'll be back. Remember that. I'll come back."

That was all. He left her standing in the hall. He ran down the steps and disappeared into the darkness and in all those five years she had not seen or heard from him.

The hubbub in Brookboro the next morning rose like a whirlwind and flourished, as if fed by a sweeping fire, through the entire county. Brookboro was a small town in a small county, and everyone in it seemed to know of John Wingate and his two sons.

Delia, almost instantly, took Julie into her own home. She could fight off any intruder, any questions, anything at all there, she said, confident of her own power.

Of course there had been a certain continued hubbub. But Delia had coped with canceling all the wedding arrangements. After what seemed a very long time, the interest died away, probably for lack of further fuel.

In the first months of Julie's stay with Delia, both Blanche and John had come and talked, but said very little; both were sad and gravely troubled.

Later on, two others had managed to get past Delia's firm protection. They were together, Maude Munger and George Wingate.

Maude Munger was a remote connection of Judge Munger's and apparently had either been foisted upon him or taken over, charitably, by him; in any event, she was determined to be an actress and so, prudently, she changed her name. She didn't want to bother to change it legally, but by dint of charm, force and deadly patience she induced others to call her Lisa Carlyon. It would look better on programs, she said, which was probably true. But her call with George Wingate was not entirely to show Julie sympathy, although she did say sadly, "Deserted practically at the altar. Poor Julie."

Julie could have slapped her but, probably wisely, refrained.

George too was all sticky sympathy—his brother! "No real brother of yours," Julie thought; he and Jim could not have been less alike. However, again she stifled her thoughts, accepted their expressions of sympathy until Maude—that is, Lisa—got around to the real purpose of her visit, which was to find out just where Jim had gone. She had always shown great interest in Jim, and Julie knew it. When she told them that she did not know where he was, neither seemed to believe her.

Delia showed them out a little briskly and once they left, she gave a ladylike snort but still a fine snort. "That girl! That Maude Munger! Had to change her name. Lisa whatever-it-is."

"Carlyon."

"Wouldn't have thought she had the sense to read Thackeray's *Vanity Fair*." Delia was on the warpath. "She wanted Jim, always honeying around him. Like a—a vampire," said Delia with a flight of fancy that astonished but secretly satisfied Julie.

"As if Munger isn't a good name! The Judge—"

"Yes, Delia. But honestly, 'Lisa Carlyon' would look better on billboards and programs."

"Oh, she's got her eye fastened on billboards all right. Oh,

Julie, I wish that—that awful thing had never happened. Or at least," said Delia, recovering from her moment of weakness, "I wish it hadn't involved Jim so —" She paused and said only, "Involved Jim."

Once dear Judge Munger had come; he asked no questions of Julie; he was as always only kind and affectionately interested in her welfare. John came often as the time went on; he made her finish college and get decent grades. He made her try to paint; this did not work out at all; he gave her the dog, Beau; after some time, he suggested a cooking school. This did not work out either. After a few weeks in white sauces (thin, medium, thick) and various other dull facts, Julie lost what fleeting interest she might have been able to summon up. At last John told her to try writing. "You never know whether or not you can do anything until you try it," he insisted. She had tried writing.

So she kept on writing. The editors had seen the present book; it had already been copyedited. "A book is never finished," John had said, "until it is in print. Like a play is never finished until it has concluded its Broadway run and is on the road."

Yet all the time, secretly in her heart of hearts, she remembered Jim's saying, "I'll come back."

Oh, she remembered everything. And actually, as if summoned up by her remembrance, the telephone on her desk rang.

She moved quickly to pick it up. There was an extension in Delia's bedroom and Delia just might have tired of her TV and gone to sleep.

She said, "Hello."

"Julie! Julie! It's me."

"You—" her voice choked but she got out an incredulous word. *"Jim—"*

"Do you still love me?"

"Jim! Oh, yes!"

It seemed an adequate reply.

"Then put on your coat. I'm coming to get you. Be there in ten minutes. Too bad one can't kiss over the phone but just wait—" Jim said jubilantly.

Three

She had a fleeting impression that someone beside him had said something; then there was only the click of his telephone.

Her knees were shaking. She was shaking. Come with him —where? But it was Jim at last. Then she thought, oh, he shouldn't have come back. There was still that unfinished terrifying suspicion of murder. It was dangerous for him to come anywhere near the scene of Alben Walker's murder.

Oh, dangerous! But it really was Jim. Her heart was thudding so hard that not only did her knees shake, her hands shook as she thrust open the neatly arranged coat closet across from her workroom and snatched the first coat that met her fingers, which happened to be, as a matter of fact, a most elegant sable coat belonging to Delia. Nothing mattered just then. Jim was back from wherever he had been and he was coming to get her.

There was a tiny shelf and a mirror set efficiently on the inside of the closet door. Delia did not approve of going out anywhere without a last look at herself in that mirror. Julie took the brush that lay on the shelf and tried to make her hair extra neat.

She must tell Delia that Jim had returned.

She could not think with anything like logic. Her ears were attuned to the arrival of a taxi. Jim had said ten minutes.

All at once, through the pounding of her heart, she heard the smooth, polite arrival of a car stopping just outside the door.

It had to be Jim. She opened the door, half afraid that she had been dreaming, but Jim flew into the hall, kicked the door behind him and gathered her into his arms all in one motion.

After a magic, fantastic, magnificent moment, she heard him speaking, rather oddly, huskily but happily, she was sure of that, and snuggled her head closer against his shoulder.

"I was afraid! All that time! I was afraid some other man —Oh, Julie!"

She locked her arms around him. She almost had to convince herself that it was really Jim, yet she knew it by every instinct, every nerve and pulse beat in her body.

He said after another magic moment, "Blanche is waiting for us. She wants to talk to you."

That got through the haze of thankfulness; Julie lifted her head. "Blanche!"

"She is waiting for us. At '21.' Come on."

"But Blanche didn't tell Delia—or me—"

"She told me that you hadn't begun to—to be interested in any other man. She's been talking to me. She wants you to hear too — oh, come on, darling. Now, don't flip your wig, but there may be a chance. Come on."

She had the presence of mind to snatch up her handbag with the house key in it. It was no taxi politely panting across the sidewalk. It was a long, luxurious limousine with a uniformed driver who attentively sprang out to open the door for them.

She sat as close to Jim as she could and he, understanding, slid an arm around her and held her even closer.

"Jim, have I changed much?" Eighteen to twenty-three— she must have changed.

Jim had a moment of prudence; he reached for a button, the glass between the driver's seat and their own slid silently upward, and Jim said, "You, never. You look just the same. I hear you've grown famous—"

"Not famous!"

"Blanche says you've been writing. Had success with a book. It hasn't changed you?"

"How could anything ever change the way I feel about you?" Julie answered and Jim snuggled her closer in his arms.

Magic, that's what, Julie thought. Magic.

Jim said, "You have questions. First, where have I been? A number of places but most recently Tanzania. Jobs are easy to get there."

"Did Blanche know where you were?"

"No. I couldn't take the chance. She's a lawyer. Bound to inform the police of any of my letters. I phoned her from Paris just before I took the flight home. She couldn't have stopped me. So she met me at Kennedy. I wasn't sure about you until Blanche said she had seen your aunt and she was sure you were still—"

"Oh, Jim! Of course I still— How could I help it! I can't believe you are here."

"Well—" After another magic moment, Jim laughed. "You believe I'm here now?"

"Oh, yes. Yes! But Jim—" Some kind of common sense touched Julie. "It's dangerous for you. An arrest. Indictment. A trial!"

"I'll explain. Blanche will have to listen. That's why she wanted you to meet us at '21'."

"Jim, you've got to tell me. Where else have you been?"

This stopped Jim in the act of lowering his face to her own

again. "All right, here it is, such as it is. I was low in my mind about the very likely possibility of a trial and the only verdict I could see that a jury could reach. Even an appeal would mean months of waiting for me. But mainly I didn't see how any jury could fail to convict me with the only evidence being against me."

"Who phoned and asked you to come to Alben Walker's?"

"Just as I told you. Told everybody. It was Walker himself. When I got there—well, you know all that. He had been shot. A gun was on the floor. I recognized it, one of my father's. I picked it up, like a fool, and Bill Hamilton came bursting in, struggling into his clothes, saying he'd heard a shot, and of course there I was, standing with a gun in my hand. You know all the evidence there was. I was apparently caught in the act."

"You went away the night you came to me—"

"Yes. To say goodbye. But I told you I'd come back. Remember?"

"Oh, yes. I remember."

"I couldn't write to you. I had a notion, probably foolish, but still a notion that the police might take an interest in your letters. I got the midnight train to New York. I had some money I'd been saving for our wedding trip, so I used that. I took jobs wherever and whenever I could and finally wound up in Tanzania. They are in the vortex of change, so when I heard of all the work to be had there, I drifted in. I knew enough engineering to pass. They were kind enough not to ask too much of my history and put me to work."

"I thought of everything. I even thought that Blanche or your father had persuaded you to leave."

"Here we are."

The car, under the driver's skillful hands, glided to a pause. The driver jumped out and opened the door. At the entrance to the "21" Club, guarded by two well-known statues, a doorman came to meet them. The chauffeur said to Jim, "Miss Surton told me to wait. Right?"

"If Miss Surton says wait, one waits." Jim was exuberant.

Once inside, they were guided by the smiling captain to the flight of stairs that led up to what had for years been known as the Celebrity Room. Blanche, chic and slender in black, her gray eyes brilliant but her face too set, took Julie's hand. "We had to do it this way," she said. "I don't want even Delia to know. I hoped you would talk Jim out of what he is determined to try to do. But don't look like that, Julie! For heaven's sake, sit down. I've ordered champagne."

"Wow," said Jim and held a chair for Julie, who slipped off Delia's fine coat and, briefly, rather wished she'd worn anything but the red sweater and gray tweed skirt. Blanche, as always, seemed composed and smartly, appropriately dressed.

The champagne was a celebration of Jim's return, but Blanche was very solemn. "We'll hope for Judge Munger's friendly advice."

"He's got to give me that chance," Jim said.

Julie swallowed hard. "I don't know what you mean. Is Jim really safe in returning?"

"Yes!" Jim cried. There wasn't time to explain anything to Julie. "Go ahead, Blanche. And believe me, if this works out, you're going to be the finest lawyer—"

"I may charge you the finest retainer, too." But Blanche did not smile.

Julie said, rather dizzily, as if the champagne had already gone to her head, "How *can* Jim come back without being in danger of—of arrest— everything?"

Blanche took a long breath. "Jim will tell you. But first, will you order something to eat? They make the most delectable watercress and ham sandwiches here. You've had your dinner, Julie?"

Julie nodded.

Blanche began as the waiter to whom she had nodded took Jim's order and retired. "A principal argument has always been lack of motive. Jim scarcely knew Alben Walker. But when Alben Walker phoned him—you were always sure it was Walker, Jim?"

"Sure. I hardly knew him but I recognized his voice. When he said it was Walker and it was urgent, I thought I might as well see what it was all about."

Blanche lifted her glass and put it down again. "Jim, you had no conceivable motive for shooting Walker."

"There was no other suspect," Jim said under his breath, but Blanche and Julie heard.

"None. Of course, Alben Walker was not really known in Brookboro. A newcomer. He seemed interested only in his painting—"

Jim interrupted with something like a growl. "I saw some of his work. He invited a lot of people to what he called a private showing. Oh, I don't know why, but I went. Then I aroused a rather serious dislike on Walker's part." He turned to Julie. "You see, I looked at those—whatever they were he had hanging around—and I said, to Bill Hamilton as a matter of fact, 'Is that art?' and I rather think Walker overheard me."

"That couldn't have been any reason for a quarrel and—and your shooting him," Julie said.

"Oh, no," Blanche said abruptly. "I expect he had heard that whenever he got up the sheer nerve to show any of his paintings."

Jim broke in again, "But it still is a fact that nobody could find a motive."

Blanche said, "I'll have another glass, please, Jim. And that's a point. Jim simply had no motive for shooting Walker. As you both know, nothing much was discovered about Walker. He had arrived, rented that little house, then spent his time either painting or going to art school in New York. Remember, his whole house was searched minutely. There were no papers, nothing to suggest his circumstances, his past life."

"As if he had come out of an egg," Jim said dourly.

"People don't come out of eggs. He had to have some kind of past."

Blanche nodded. "As I recall, his bank account was found, his banker interviewed. He had gone to a bank there at Brookboro, started an account. Not a large one. He added something to it from time to time, nothing traceable to anybody as far as we could discover."

Jim interrupted again, "Remember, Julie, he always gave the impression that he had been a stockbroker and got tired of it and had always wanted to paint, so now he had a small house in a quiet town and was painting. He was certainly dabbing all kinds of color on every canvas."

"Blanche," Julie began hesitantly. "I have always wondered if somebody—"

"Framed Jim?" Blanche picked it up at once. "Yes. We all thought of that, but Jim was sure that it was Walker's voice over the phone. He saw nobody but Walker—"

"Stone dead on the floor." Jim gave himself a shake. "I'll never forget that . . ."

Julie said, hesitantly again, "The one person who could perhaps hope to gain eventually by framing Jim was . . ."

Blanche again nodded. "Oh, yes. George Wingate. But George had an alibi. He and Maude—I mean Lisa, as she insists on calling herself—were both taking some course in dramatics and that night were performing in a revival of *The Man Who Came to Dinner* in New Haven. There simply was not time during the play for George or Maude to leave the theater, drive to Brookboro, shoot Walker and get back to the play. If you'll read the play you'll see what I mean. I suppose neither of you has ever seen it," Blanche said with a touch of indulgence. "But I did. I have to admit that what I saw was also a revival. I only wish I had been old enough to see the original Whiteside."

Julie said absently, "Perhaps that's where George got the idea of a beard?"

Blanche nodded. "Wait till you see George, Jim. He's got

a flowing reddish beard. Not very becoming. But he does get short jobs in stock here and there. So does Maude—I should say Lisa. Oh, really!" Blanche said with exasperation. "That girl is sure she is going to be the world's greatest actress. So her own name, Maude Munger, isn't good enough for her. She must be called Lisa Carlyon."

Julie, with a rather mean reluctance, felt obliged to set Blanche straight. "You see, we were in school together, you know, and Lisa liked acting. She was very ambitious. The girls called her Maude the Mugger, or just Mud the Mugger. Only teasing, of course. Schoolgirl humor. But Lisa didn't think it was funny. One can see why, when her eyes were fixed on the stars."

"Billboards," Blanche said shortly, as Delia had said, but absently.

"Well, it wasn't very kind of them, and I think that is why Lisa determined to change her name. Gradually everybody began to call her Lisa Carlyon. It makes sense."

"In its way," Blanche said, "but she ought to have been proud of bearing Judge Munger's name. She is only a distant cousin of the Judge's, but he did help her, gave her a home and paid for her schooling. He's old, but he's a fine man. He dreaded a trial for Jim. He dreaded the only verdict a jury could have given. And after that verdict he would have been horrified by the necessity of pronouncing a sentence upon you, Jim. There might have been an appeal, even bail. But Jim wouldn't wait for all that. He thought he saw a way out."

The sandwiches came, delicate and delectable, as Blanche had said. Rather to her own surprise, Julie eyed them with interest. "I didn't eat much dinner." She took two. "You see, Blanche, I overheard you and Delia talking there in the hall today as you were leaving. But isn't this dangerous?"

"It is very dangerous," Blanche said soberly. "I have tried to talk Jim out of it."

"Impossible," said Jim around a mouthful of sandwich.

"I know." Blanche linked her hands and looked at them.

"You see, it's this way, Julie. I'll try to put it simply. Just over five years ago a law was passed that was intended to give assistance to various people who were suspected of certain crimes but not proven—"

"Also murder," said Jim.

"No. No," Blanche said firmly. "It did not include murder specifically. It did supply a statute of limitations for certain crimes. But not murder. You must understand that, Jim."

"I can't give up." Jim munched on his sandwich. "Or, rather, I *will* not give it up! I've held on to this chance for five years."

He took out his wallet and produced two copies of newsprint, carefully laminated in a transparent material. He put them flat on the table. Blanche only looked at them. Julie seized them and read and read and read. She lifted a startled gaze to Jim and then to Blanche. "But these say—why, they sound as if anybody can come back after five years and claim a statute of limitations!"

"That is what I plan to do," said Jim.

Blanche almost paled. "But, Jim, I've tried to tell you that can't be—"

Julie broke in, reading from the clippings. "They say— why, they say, in five years—any crime—"

"No," said Blanche firmly. "Not any crime."

"I don't care what you think, Blanche, one of them says that after five years anybody can shout from the city hall and say I-dun-it and nobody can arrest him. I happened to see those articles in some very good Connecticut papers. So it seemed to me, then, a way out. Take a chance. So I did. As fast as I could." Jim picked up another sandwich.

Blanche said, "No. There cannot be a statute of limitations for a capital crime like murder. You see, Jim, that particular, and brief, law was not worded to exclude murder. It was intended only to include other crimes or even misdemeanors after five years because a witness would find it hard to prove any sort of alibi for, say, a particular date and crime. The law was meant to protect. It is an example of the expression 'good facts make a bad law.' Oh, never mind all that. The plain truth is that you must give up this plan—"

"I'll not give up," said Jim. "It's been like a lifeline. Oh, Blanche, don't you see, at least it gives me a fighting chance!"

"No, Jim, you must acknowledge plain fact."

"Dear Blanche, I cannot stay away from Julie and home and—and everything forever. I am determined to prove somehow that I didn't kill that guy."

Blanche lifted her gray eyes. "The evidence being what it was, a jury could have come to only one decision."

"I'm going to try," Jim said. "I've got to try. I'll be a—test case—"

"You'd be that, all right, Jim," Blanche said. "You'd never get a jury to accept this limitation. Not with murder."

"But I didn't kill the guy!"

Blanche looked at her hands. "No, Jim—"

"Come on, Blanche, you know you'll do your best for me. But I am going to find out who killed Walker."

Four

Julie remembered that tone in Jim's voice. He meant what he said. And that, too, was dangerous, wasn't it. "Jim, no—"

He looked at her with a spark of something very like anger in his eyes. "You are going to say 'Let sleeping dogs lie.' I'm not going to."

Blanche was very grave. "All right," she said after a moment. "I'll do my best for you, Jim." It was like a vow.

"I do have to clear my name, Blanche. I want Julie to marry me. She can't—I'll not let her take a name that people associate with murder. And I want to clear my father's name. I must do that," said Jim. "Any coffee in this joint, Blanche?"

"Yes, certainly." Blanche barely lifted one hand; instantly a waiter arrived, took the order for three coffees and departed. His alacrity was so marked that Jim grinned good-naturedly for a change. "Why, Blanche! You've got everybody running around."

Blanche smiled. "I've had a small apartment here in the city for—oh, since I could afford it, really. Merely for convenience. No, not entirely for convenience. I got a little bored

34

with phone calls any old time of night in Brookboro telling me that Sam this or Harry that had got into trouble speeding, or drinking, or with drugs, and would I get him out. Of course, I have very definite obligations to the firm. Also to my mother. She is very—very feeble, you know. But I've been lucky in getting nurses for her, so there are occasional times when I can get away. An answering service says I am out of town but will take any messages. Nine times out of ten, whoever called got Ralph Elwell to see to whatever the trouble was about. Ralph is young but a very good and upcoming lawyer. Jim is staying in my apartment tonight, aren't you, Jim? There's a small extra room."

Jim frowned. "Why, yes. That is, yes, thank you. I had intended to motor up to Brookboro tonight and see my father."

"You'll come back with me to Brookboro," Blanche said quietly but firmly. "Now, Julie dear, whatever happens, there will be trouble. It's true, that law was a little imprecise in its phrasing. But there cannot be a limitation—"

Jim broke in. "Never mind all that." His eyes had a determined, hard-as-steel look, which Julie knew came only when Jim had made up his mind and intended to stick to his decision. She remembered every look, every tone in his voice as if he had never been away from her.

Blanche sighed. "Jim, I trust you not to make a police force of yourself. Don't invite danger from—from any direction. If you'd only wait."

"I've waited too long. Whoever killed him removed all the papers that might have given information about him."

Blanche nodded. "Yes, the cleaning woman said he kept a locked briefcase. That was gone. But Jim, remember, it *has* only been five years. They seem to be getting a little restless here. Perhaps—"

Jim got up. "I'll take Julie home. Then—yes, thank you, Blanche, I'll come back to your apartment, and tomorrow . . ."

"We'll both take Julie home." Blanche took Julie's hands. "It's not going to be easy, Julie. Sometimes it really is better to let sleeping dogs lie. Now, our waiter has been peering rather anxiously at our table. Everyone else is gone."

"The car—your limo, Blanche? It must still be waiting. Costing a bundle."

Blanche smiled. "I think I can afford it." She rose. The waiter all but bowed them out. Julie had a swift impression that their leaving was not really the occasion for such exquisite courtesy; more likely it was because Blanche was well known. She had become a very successful and rather rich lawyer indeed.

Julie, in Delia's magnificent coat, and Blanche, in her own fine Russian broadtail, were handed into the limousine. Blanche gave the address to the driver, who didn't quite bow but looked especially respectful.

The lights of the city had changed during their long talk; there are always lights on in New York City, but the remaining ones were mainly from storefronts or, as they crossed town, a few scattered lights from apartment houses and their entrances. It took only minutes to arrive at Shad Cove and Delia's door.

Julie gave a kind of frantic clutch at Blanche. "Oh, I hope it will be all right—"

"Good night, dear Julie." Blanche sounded sad.

But Jim got out and went up the two steps to the door, which then opened. Delia, clad in sweeping pink silk and her hair in curlers, cried out, "Jim!" She didn't quite scream, but Blanche said, from the car, "Shut up now, Delia. Julie will have to tell you all about it. Come on, Jim."

Jim lingered, however, to kiss Delia softly on her cheek and take Julie tight in his arms and kiss her. He was gone then, back into the car, which smoothly moved away.

Delia stood as if turned into a pink marble statue with one curler dangling free from her pretty hair. "That was *Jim*!"

Julie closed the door behind her. She took off Delia's sables and Delia still stood, her pretty mouth open, staring at Julie with utterly confused eyes.

"That *was* Jim," she said. "Where did he—why did he—see here, Julie! Sit right down. You are white as a sheet. Except"—Delia was very observant even in moments of shock—"you look as if somebody has been kissing you. Well, of course, somebody was! Jim . . . but how did he . . . sit down. Tell me everything."

So Julie told her what there was to tell. They sat in the long living room. At some point in the telling Delia suddenly rose and closed the red curtains over the big windows. She muttered, excusing herself, yet intelligently, "No need to let anybody see us in this state. Obviously so very dégagé—now then, go on, Julie. Is there really such a law?"

"Jim thinks he has a chance. He's in a fighting mood."

When Delia had heard all that Julie knew, she sat for a time, brooding over it. Delia was no fool. Finally she said, "This could be very dangerous to Jim. Because of the law. Or the real murderer."

"He thinks there is a chance! He is determined to take it."

"Oh, I was thinking mainly of Jim's determination to ferret out Walker's murderer. It is like tweaking a tiger's tail. Now, that is dangerous. We'll go out to Brookboro tomorrow morning, Julie. You want to, don't you?"

"Yes. Oh, yes."

"It's your home. And I intend to go with you. But—" Delia shook her becurlered head. "But Blanche is right. This is dangerous."

So they went back to Brookboro. They got rather a late start; there were always things Delia felt she must do before leaving the house. And Julie must pack the galley proofs of her novel, to take them with her to Brookboro and mail them back to the publisher. She crawled out of bed, tossed a cashmere dressing gown over her shoulders—a gift from Delia (her royalties had not yet amounted to enough to indulge in cashmere)—and crept down the stairs, holding the railing instead of sensibly turning on lights and possibly waking Delia. However, in her study she had to turn on a light, and as she gathered together the two stacks of proofs and added the few notes she had made, the telephone gave a small but definite tinkle. So Delia was using it. Julie had no qualms whatever about carefully lifting the receiver in time to hear Delia say, "—of course, I'm sorry, Blanche, at this hour. But I had to talk to you . . . Well, you can go back to sleep again. What is all this about Jim returning? I think it is very dangerous, myself . . . Oh, I can see Jim's point of view. But it is dangerous just the same. Somebody killed Walker and he'll kill Jim if—"

It really was against all good manners to eavesdrop on a conversation like this, but Julie dismissed that notion and kept her ear glued to the telephone.

Blanche said firmly, "Don't talk like that, Delia. I can't tell you any more now. Julie will explain—"

"She did, but there are so many questions that I—"

"You'll just have to wait."

"I'm coming to Brookboro in the morning. Julie is coming with me."

"Not now, Delia."

Delia paid no attention.

"Blanche, is this possible? Could Jim really go free owing to that five-year commutation? It doesn't seem reasonable."

"It is not at all reasonable. I have told him that. Murder is never actually forgotten or the punishment commuted. The best we can hope for, as I see it, is arrest on suspicion and a trial."

There was a rather long silence. Then Delia said, "I suppose Jim is hellbent on returning to Brookboro."

"Oh, yes." Blanche sounded tired. "He says he didn't murder anybody at all, ever, and must clear his name."

"That means, in a way, John Wingate's name too."

"Well, yes. Oh, go to bed, Delia. I'll see you tomorrow, I suppose. If I can't stop you."

Unbelievably, Blanche simply hung up. Nobody ever dared treat Delia like that. Julie was sure she heard a muttered strong word or two. Then Delia's own receiver banged in Julie's ear.

She put the phone down thoughtfully. Delia didn't miss much. But she didn't say much either if she thought it best not to speak.

Julie automatically gathered the proofs on her desk into their box, wrapped and addressed them. Then she went back upstairs and crept past Delia's closed bedroom door.

She hadn't had any scruples about listening to the conversation between Delia and Blanche; she couldn't have stopped herself. Jim had come back, and there might—oh, there *might* be a chance!

There was no time to lose in the morning. The whistler arrived by way of the small kitchen door and rather grudgingly brought up breakfast herself. Delia, with her usual efficiency, gave the whistler a check (Julie wondered absently why they never thought of her by her real name), and told her to take a few days off; she'd let her know when she, Delia, returned. This seemed to please the cook, who disdained the dumbwaiter and trudged up the stairway again to bring fresh coffee.

It was Delia who had already telephoned Ollie, telling him to open the house and send a taxi to meet the train.

"Is the dog all right?" Julie asked over her second cup of coffee.

"Of course, he's fine. Ollie would have let us know the instant he sneezed."

Ollie's full, rather stylish name was Oliver Wendell Atherton; he was known all over the town of Brookboro as Ollie. He was slow, dependable and equipped with a New England accent, which ensured him a place in Brookboro. He was not a real gardener, he was not exactly a caretaker, he was not exactly a veterinarian or housekeeper for dogs, but he was a most reliable blend of all.

Brookboro was the county seat, but Brookboro County was not a big one. Everybody knew everybody in Brookboro; only the newcomers did not, and there were few of those, for it was not easy to commute to the city or even to Stamford, Norwalk, Danbury, or other cities that had grown up with astonishing rapidity during the past few years. Consequently it was not in the least what used to be called a bedroom community. It was Brookboro, thank you, and had its pride.

It also had a propensity for talk.

Time ran short while Delia closed the house and both of the women hurriedly packed their suitcases. They made it to the train, and it was just after noon when they arrived in Brookboro and saw the straight white steeple of the Congregational church, which had been there, it was said, since the 1700s. It had been remodeled and repaired, but the white steeple everyone knew had remained the same, as had God's Acre, a triangular plot of still green grass surrounded by always green rhododendron. Julie and Jim had planned to be married there.

A taxi was waiting for them. "Hi," said the driver, Hank Wilson, with true Brookboro democracy. He did take their suitcases, but it was done more as a favor than a duty.

"How are things?" Julie asked.

Hank got into his seat. "Huh! Whole town is about to boil over. Guess who came back this morning."

He shot a shrewd glance in his rearview mirror. "Guess you already know who."

Delia said snappily, "We just got here."

"Huh," said Hank. "Thought you'd know. Everybody knows about it by now. All the phones in town going, I'll bet you. That Wingate boy, of course. The one that killed that guy. Back here. And they do say—"

"Look out," Julie cried. "You turn here."

Hank gave a rather strong word of exasperation. "Durned if I almost didn't notice. Right. You're going to the Fan'um place?"

Everybody in Brookboro called it the Fan'um place. Julie said yes. Hank grunted. "You got a new cat."

"Cat? What do you mean?" That was Delia.

"Sure. That big dog of yours seems to have taken to the cat. And the cat just took to your place." He turned a corner and added, "Ollie likes the cat, too. Him and the dog. Here we are.

"And there's your cat." Hank stopped at the terrace steps to the white New England house where Julie was born; she had arrived so swiftly that there was no time to get her mother to the New Haven hospital where a room was waiting for her. It had been Julie's and her brother Peter's home always. Their parents had lived a happy, rather daring kind of existence. It was one of life's ironies that they had been traveling at a sedate speed, merely going home from the theater, when the accident occurred that left Julie and Peter in Delia's care.

"That cat," Hank went on as he hauled out their suitcases. "Acts as if he owns the joint. You'd think that dog of yours would have a claim to his top place in the pecking order. He was here first. But—that cat!" There was a kind of admiration in Hank's voice.

The cat sat with terrific dignity on a terrace step; she did look as if she owned the place. Brilliant blue eyes shone from a black mask; black paws were placed firmly on the stone step; a long black tail had a decided kink in it.

"Why, she's a Siamese!" Julie said.

"Don't know what she is," Hank said. "But she sure acts important. Hi, Ollie! Here's your women folk."

Delia was eying the cat with no favor; she was far too finicky a housekeeper to feel real admiration for a creature that might shed and might sharpen claws on everything that took her fancy. The dog wasn't so likely to offend. John Wingate had given him to Julie as a puppy, a tousled, elegant French poodle who had been christened Beau, as a matter of fact, by Peter, after he had read *Beau Geste*.

Beau had a happy nature and needed only a word or a look to understand and instantly obey.

At that moment Beau himself came galloping gracefully around the corner of the house and flung himself on Julie, uttering sounds which could readily be interpreted as "Where have you been so long? Why didn't you take me with you?"

"There, there—" Julie bent down to caress him and couldn't help the tears coming to her eyes, as his cold nose pressed against her and his tail wagged like mad.

Ollie came into view, grinning and trying not to. He believed in being severe and gruff and adored all animals. He wasn't so sure about adoring people, but animals, yes. However, he did accord Julie a kind of friendly . . . not respect, but consideration.

"That dog," he said sternly but with a sparkle in his deep-set eyes. "He's been fussy all morning. Knew you were coming. Don't know how he knew, but he knew. Now, Beau, down."

Beau gave a conspiratorial glance at Julie, as if to say, "Oh, well, we must humor Ollie," obeyed and sat down.

The terrace had been swept clean. The wide door was open.

"Told you there was a cat," said Hank cheerfully and shoved the suitcases onto the terrace. "All yours, Ollie."

Julie paid Hank; Delia drew slightly away from the cat. John Wingate appeared in the doorway, smiling and holding out his arms.

Five

"Oh, John!" Julie ran up the steps. He held her, kissed her and turned to kiss Delia's cheek.

John was just the same, an older edition of Jim. They were so alike that in Julie's mind there was never the slightest question of Jim's parentage. There were touches of gray now in his black hair. His smile was, as ever, warm and affectionate and, for Julie, always loving and encouraging. "Oh, John," she cried again. "You've seen Jim."

"Yes. You'd better come in."

The house was the same, too.

There was the wide hall, with a stairway climbing against the wall. There were the old Oriental rugs, worn thin, and the familiar smell of furniture polish and fresh air and potpourri, which were as familiar to Julie as the gray and white figured wallpaper, the glimpse of the dining room on the left, and the big living room on the right, shining with polished mahogany, old and out of date and loved by Julie. Her mother's portrait hung over the mantel. Her father's portrait was beside it. They still offered comfort to Julie.

But Delia had never failed her or Peter. Delia had been there when the murder occurred.

John Wingate drew them into the house. "I hope you don't mind my taking over, Julie, but I wanted to be the first to see you when you arrived. There's a fire in the library. Getting coolish these days. Frost coming. Thanks, Ollie."

Ollie had already deposited both suitcases in the rooms Delia and Julie always used and was happily clumping down the stairs. Beau came to Julie's side, nosing her hand. The cat nonchalantly strolled into the room.

Delia said, low, "That cat!"

The cat might have heard her for she paused to give Delia a cold sapphire-blue glance.

Julie swallowed a giggle. "What's the cat's name, Ollie?"

"Call her Pie."

Delia lifted her eyebrows. "Custard? Mince? What kind of pie?"

John laughed. "Pye for Pyewacket. Remember the play?"

Delia remembered. *"Bell, Book and Candle*—right, John?"

John nodded. "Before your time. But I remember it. Suits that cat, don't you think?"

Delia clearly had doubts as to thinking that anything would suit such a remarkably self-assured cat.

From the doorway Ollie said apologetically, but as if his heart wasn't really in it, "Got a lot of dignity, that cat. Found her, just sitting on the terrace as if she owned the place. Couldn't send her away. Thin, hungry—you wouldn't have liked that, would you, now?"

He addressed Julie, who said, but rather doubtfully, no. Pye gave her a long, blue, thoughtful look.

John said, "There, now. Ollie and I made coffee. Not much for lunch but if you're hungry—"

"We are," Delia said positively, and started for the kitchen.

"Oh, I'll see to it," Ollie said and disappeared.

John had already gone to the cabinet where such liquor as was the custom to keep in the house was arranged in neat rows. Glasses and an ice bucket stood on top of the cabinet.

"Whiskey?" John said over his shoulder. "Vodka? Sherry?"

Nobody at that juncture seemed to feel that sherry was quite adequate. Even Delia took a wallop of whiskey without much soda before she leaned back in the big leather-covered armchair, fixed John with her determined pale blue eyes and said, "Where is Jim now?"

John had returned to stand before the fire, holding his drink, which also seemed rather dark in color.

"Well, actually, at this moment I believe he and Blanche are in Hartford. Julie, my dear, I may as well come to the point."

"Yes. Fine." But Julie's voice wavered.

John's gaze softened. "My dear, I do realize what it means to you—Jim's return and the hope that— But I've got to be honest. I am very much afraid that Jim is sadly mistaken."

Delia sat up, splashing her drink. "Go on!"

"I can't think there is any chance for him. Blanche and he got here early this morning. We hashed the thing over and over. Then Jim said he had to see Judge Munger himself, so he did."

"What did the Judge say?"

John frowned. "I gather he was astonished and altogether discouraging. He did say something about a trial but that he'd have to think it over. Jim was not at all daunted. After that he and Blanche took my car and went to Hartford. Blanche is doing her best. She always does."

"What do you think?" Julie asked tautly.

"Obvious. To my mind there is simply no interpretation of any law which could condone murder no matter how many years after it occurred. A murder case is never closed until the murderer has been brought to justice. That onetime law about limitations has been rescinded—as it was originally written, anyway. I talked to the Judge later, too. He said that he knew of no case where it had been brought into dispute. He was . . ." John swirled the liquid in his glass. "He was upset about it. Jim must simply face the thing. Murder is a very grave crime," John said with a tight smile. "I'm sorry Jim came back. But it's great,"—his face softened— "really great to see him again. But, Julie, my dear, I am afraid this will be a terrible disappointment to you and Jim and all of us."

"Then you mean there's not even a chance of hope," Julie said. Beau heard something in her voice that the dog seemed to know required comfort. He came close, took one of her hands very carefully in his mouth and pushed against her.

John said gravely, "I suppose it is possible that Jim may gain just a little time—"

Delia, never slow to grasp an idea, sat up. "Time! You mean that with time Jim *may* be able to discover some evidence—"

John nodded. "Jim is very optimistic. He swears that he didn't murder Walker. I am sure he didn't. But as to being able to uncover any evidence leading to Walker's murderer after this length of time—" John shook his head. "I can't really count on that."

"But Jim is so hopeful. So am I—" Julie didn't start to cry. Delia would never have permitted that. But again Beau heard that trouble in her voice and shoved his head upon her knee. She absently patted his lovely white pompadour.

"So," Delia said thoughtfully. "That's the way you think it stands, John."

"Oh, Delia, I can't help having just a shred of hope. I was so thankful, so glad to see Jim again. My son—" John clearly thought he was getting too emotional. He turned away, took a shining brass poker and thrust it into the flames.

There was a long pause. Beau kept his head on Julie's knee as if he knew she still needed comforting. The cat watched them all, rather skeptically perhaps, but with interest.

Delia said presently, "John, you'll forgive me, I've never said this to you, but I could never understand why on earth you took in both those boys. One of them, that is George, is really your son, but Jim—"

"Jim," said John, his eyes steely, "is my son. I can take in both of them if I want to, can't I?"

Delia quite seriously considered the question. "I suppose nobody could stop you. But the cold fact must be that one is your son and the other a boy you happened to find and like."

John shook his head but smiled. "Oh, now, Delia, don't you suppose that all our friends in Brookboro have come to the same conclusion? Some believe that Jim is in fact my son, the son Elaine took when she left me. And some believe that George is a later son, Elaine's and mine. It is possible that Elaine did not know she was pregnant with George when she left me."

"It's also possible—" Delia began and stopped, a wave of crimson sweeping up over her face.

But John only nodded. "Oh, yes. The thought has occurred that perhaps George is in fact the son of some other man."

"Don't you know?" Delia cried.

John smiled again but not mirthfully. "George does slightly resemble Elaine. He had proofs. Elaine's marriage certificate to me, our divorce certificate, some jewelry (well, really trinkets, I didn't have the money for real jewelry, but nevertheless I recognized them). No, the plain fact is that both of these boys—that is, young men, I must say now—are—could be—my sons. So I treat them as sons. Why not?"

Delia sighed. "And I thought you believed us when we just accepted your calling each of them your son as a mark of—"

"Chivalry? No. I don't think so. In any event both Jim and George have behaved very well about it. There was only a year between George's arrival and Jim's involvement in murder. Just now, if there is anything to help clear Jim, I'm for it. I understand Jim. He feels he can't go through life with people thinking he's an escaped murderer. We will have to proceed as best we can. Come on, now, finish your drinks. Ollie will be upset if we don't eat his lunch. We'll all meet at dinner at my house, Delia. If you'll accept my invitation. Let's try to make Jim's homecoming as warm a welcome as we can!"

Delia shook her head but rose. Ollie, in the doorway, said glumly that there were scrambled eggs.

The cat preceded them into the dining room. Beau walked courteously beside Julie.

There was time, that afternoon, for Julie to go over in her mind all she knew of the two young men whom John had accepted into his life. During her years of growing up she had known in a general way that John had all but moved heaven and earth to find his son Jim. There were references to his continued efforts; Delia, Blanche and John had mentioned some of them. Once, John had made a quick and, to Julie, mysterious trip to Switzerland. He had returned disappointed. "Elaine," Delia had said to Blanche in Julie's hearing, "Elaine may not have much sense but she is very wily. Sly as a fox."

"Vixen," said Blanche, staring at the rug.

There was a slight pause during which Julie was suddenly struck by a new idea. Julie was older then, more aware of nuances in her elders' words. Surely Blanche was not in love with John; they were merely good friends.

Delia pretended to be adamant as marble; in fact she had swift perception and a heart like sugar. "Oh, my dear Blanche!"

"I know. You see it. But Delia, believe me, John is still in love with Elaine. Always was in love with her. If she were dead he'd still—cherish—" She was on the verge of tears but managed to say, "Never mind, Delia. I'll get along."

"But John depends upon you, his best friend. Along with me," Delia added.

"That's exactly what it is. He likes both of us and depends upon *us*. Not me alone."

Delia bristled. "I hope you are not implying that John—I mean that he is interested in me!"

"Oh, Delia! No! Everyone knows of your devotion to the memory of your Pieter. You wouldn't dream of another man. But as for me—oh, well," Blanche said. "I may as well give up."

At this interesting point Delia remembered Julie and told her crisply that it was time to do her homework. But Julie departed slowly and heard Delia say, "All that money out of John and then Elaine disappears and he still has not found his boy."

Julie knew from some conversation that John had inherited money; she didn't know how much, but clearly it had been enough to send a sum to Elaine; clearly then Elaine was to tell John where Jim was to be found. Clearly too, Elaine had failed to keep her part of the bargain.

Time went on slowly as it does with a maturing child, yet Julie knew, again in a general way, that John had acquired a certain fame through his successful writing career but had never ceased in his efforts to find his son. As she grew older, she did listen with sharpened interest whenever John spoke of Jim.

"I know every consulate in Europe," he had said once. "Through every change in all these years. Nobody has ever been able to give me any facts. But she's got to know where that boy is." He had put his head down in his hands at that point. "Time is going, he's a young man by now."

But then Jim was found in an unexpected way. John's career had been the subject of a television interview, during which he had said that he had a son somewhere, but didn't know where. The interviewer had tried to cut him off, and a time limit to the interview did stop the discussion, but not before, as the TV interviewer had said sadly, John Wingate had let himself in for a siege of letters and inquiries from young men of about Jim's age.

Those which were patently false were easily ruled out. Blanche had helped John see to that. The stream of inquiries had rather quickly petered out. But then Jim had written to John Wingate; he had said flatly that he didn't want anything, but he had no family, no father and knew nothing of his mother. He said also, very firmly, that he didn't need money, he only would like to see Mr. Wingate if Mr. Wingate cared to see him.

Something about the letter had made John take to it as a fish takes to luscious bait, Delia had said crossly. John had gone to see Jim, who was working his way through a rather small college, had liked him, had, in short, decided that Jim was his son. He had brought him back to Brookboro, had told everyone that Jim was his son and had overcome Jim's sincere resistance to the offer of money for education and had got him into Harvard.

Jim was working hard for his degree when John received notification of Elaine's death. This had come from some sanitarium in Italy but when John replied, his own letter was returned, unanswered.

"Poor Elaine," Delia had said.

"Poor!" Blanche's eyes had an angry flash. "She almost ruined John's life!"

"No, Blanche, he has Jim. And— Oh!" said Delia impatiently. "If he'd only use his eyes—his head—"

"Never mind," Blanche had said. "Alive or dead she's still the girl he loved. Forget it, dear Delia."

But then George had arrived, bringing all his proofs of identity. Plus, according to Delia, a convincing likeness to Elaine.

So John had simply accepted both young men and treated them equally as his sons. Could anybody question his right to do that?

All seemed peaceful until some months later. Alben Walker was murdered and suspicion fell upon Jim.

Nobody seemed to have known much of Alben Walker. He was a newcomer to Brookboro, not a particularly well liked newcomer; however, he said that he was trying to paint, something he had always wanted to do.

Delia said more than once that Alben Walker's past, whatever it had been, must have caught up with him. No one, however, could find anything discreditable about him; indeed, the police could find very little information at all. That, in itself, was suspicious, according to Delia, according to all Brookboro.

But it came down to proven facts. Jim was there. He admitted holding the gun. In spite of every effort, there was simply no other evidence anybody could discover.

The night before his almost certain arrest on suspicion of murder, Jim had vanished.

Now, Jim was determined to find the person who had, in fact, shot Alben Walker.

The tranquil October twilight faded to a deep purple dusk. Beau had stretched out on the rug beside Julie's bed. He stood, stretched and nudged Julie, who pulled herself from the well-worn ways of thinking for five long years, showered and dressed herself as attractively as she could. The previous Christmas, in a spirit of defiance or something like it, she had bought herself a charming red dress, a party dress, a very expensive and feminine dress. She had told herself she was still young; she must make an effort to enjoy anything she could enjoy. She had worn the dress once and hated it.

Now it still hung, in its neat plastic cover, in the closet of her room. She got it out happily; this was what it was for! She looked at herself with a certain approval and went down to meet Delia, who also showed approval. "Thought you'd get around to wearing that little number," she said tartly, but was obviously pleased. She added, "I do hope things go smoothly tonight."

Dinner might certainly provide a volatile situation; under John Wingate's control it could not explode because John simply would not permit explosions.

Julie smiled thinking of John, for there was something about John Wingate that dominated any situation. It was not his manner, which was quiet and kindly; it wasn't his tall, well-built figure, which did suggest a certain muscularity if he ever went into action, but it was almost unthinkable to consider John Wingate in a position that he would ever be called upon to use, say, some strong fists. Jim was so like him that their relationship proclaimed itself; both tall, firm, good-looking. True, John's face had sobered during those five years; subtly, not only had he become older, but a kind of cloud seemed to have settled over him. His dark gray eyes could still sparkle with courage and even laughter; his mouth could smile but, too often, became rather stern and set. But Jim had now changed, too; he had matured in an indescribable yet natural way; he had certainly become more sure of himself. Yet he was the same man, only older and stronger.

Anybody who deserved it could always count on John's backing. George might not really deserve it; Julie had never quite trusted him. George would be present that night, since he lived in John's house, Jim would be there, also probably Blanche, and Delia was very likely to make a rather pointed remark or two. And, of course, Maude (no, Lisa) just might be present. Oh, yes—Julie set her lips—Lisa would not fail to want to see Jim.

She was right.

When Julie had explained her dinner engagement to Beau, who consented with a tail wag but anxious eyes, she got out her small car and drove herself and Delia to John Wingate's house. When John himself had led them into his booklined living room, Lisa was kissing Jim, holding her arms around his neck.

Losing no time, Julie thought coldly. However, Jim did not appear to be resisting with any degree of vigor. A voice at Julie's elbow said, "Julie, darling! How splendid to see you again! Forgotten me?"

She had certainly not forgotten George Wingate. Still she looked at him a moment, trying to associate the rather plump, red-bearded young man with the thinnish, weak-chinned one he had once been. Five years changes anybody. Certainly George looked even more like the few photographs she had seen of Elaine. Elaine had had a youthful prettiness that had certainly engaged John's love at some time, but she had not cared to cope with poverty or any exigency that required backbone.

"Of course not, George."

He took her hand and pressed it tenderly. "My dear, how wonderful you look! Being a successful author must agree with you."

She didn't reply, for John Wingate came to her side. "Julie, there's a phone call. The Judge wants to see you. I'll tell them to hold dinner. He seemed urgent and— What is it?" He turned to a properly aproned servant, probably the cook.

"Mr. Wingate, the doctor phoned, too. He says Miss Fan-'um—he says to tell her—"

"What on earth—" John began and the cook continued, "It's Ollie, Mr. Wingate. He broke his leg. Or something. Anyway, he's in the town hospital. He wants to talk to her—" she nodded to Julie.

So, as it happened, there was no dinner party.

Six

Delia said decisively that Julie must go first to the Judge. There was nothing just then she could do for Ollie. The doctor and nurses would be busy seeing to whatever was broken. There was a hubbub of voices, questions to which the cook had no answer. She disappeared in the direction of the kitchen.

Jim came out of the hubbub. "Julie, I'll take you to the Judge. Delia's right, you can't do a thing for Ollie just now."

"I'll take her," said George. "This is a dinner party to celebrate your return, Jim." It was said in a most friendly manner—too friendly? Julie thought coldly.

Delia decided. "I'll check in with the hospital, Julie. They wouldn't let you see Ollie now, anyway. You take your own car and get over to Judge Munger—"

Lisa intervened. "But he's *my* cousin! What does he want? I'll go—"

Blanche interrupted. "The Judge has been sick, Julie. Everybody knows that. But Jim and I went to see him for a few minutes this morning before we went to Hartford. The Judge may want to tell you what he told Jim but, Julie, the Judge is really very frail. Can't you send word that you'll see him tomorrow morning? He'll be rested then and—oh, all right." Blanche always knew when to give in. "Here's your coat. But do take it easy, Julie. Don't get him upset. I mean, just agree with him. That's best."

Delia had whisked out Julie's fur jacket, which Julie had bought for herself, extravagantly but rather relishing the fact that she had earned the money to pay for it and also wishing in her heart that Jim, wherever he was, could have seen her in the flattering fur.

Now, Jim took her arm and went with her out to her car. "Julie dear, don't let the Judge discourage you. He's an old man, set in his ways. Like a—" Jim hesitated and said, unexpectedly, "like a leaf about to fall. But he's got a mind as sharp as a razor. So don't let him discourage you. Remember, it's not only my name. It's my father's name. So I've got to do what I can."

She hugged her furs around her, got into the driver's seat, leaned out for Jim's swift kiss, turned on the lights and the engine, did not say, "Why did you let Lisa kiss you?" and left.

Probably, the Judge would give her a discouraging view of Jim's situation. She would not accept that! However, he had asked for *her.*

It had seemed bitterly ironic that the Judge, who had never failed in friendship and loving advice, and who had intended to give her away at the time of her marriage to Jim, should instead have the ugly prospect of presiding in court where Jim had been so certain to be tried for murder. She had, of course, seen the Judge since then. He had been, as always, kind and fatherly, but they had not talked of Jim.

Yet the Judge would never have interrupted the dinner party tonight, especially a dinner party so loaded with explosive possibilities, without an urgent reason.

She reached the Judge's house. There were lights on in his study which was also, she knew, his lounging room, his book room, his writing room, everything.

She rang and was sure she heard a voice telling her to come in. The Judge lived alone except for rare visits from Lisa. It seemed likely that the Judge had yielded to the prevalent shortage of domestic help. Probably, someone came in to see to his house and his meals and then departed, leaving the Judge alone.

She thrust open the door, and the Judge called to her. His voice had changed since she had seen him last; it seemed weak. She went in; the hall was lighted, the door to the Judge's study was open and light streamed out. "Is that you, Julie?"

"Yes, may I come in?"

"Of course, child. That's why I sent for you—" Definitely his once-resonant voice had weakened.

She went into the booklined room with its heavy leather-covered chairs. The Judge sat or, it struck her oddly, actually huddled near a small fire below the black marble mantel. He had a woolen scarf around his shoulders. But he turned his face toward her, smiling but smiling sadly. "Julie, my dear. Jim very properly came to see me this morning. I had to send for you. You see—" He took a quick breath. "I'm afraid I must make myself tell you bad news."

She crossed swiftly to kneel down on the footstool near him. "Yes, Judge—"

"I knew you were to be at John Wingate's tonight. Celebrating Jim's return. But I couldn't let you go on." He paused to cough feebly.

"You mean—"

"I couldn't let you go on celebrating. I must tell you. I am sorry, my dear. I understand it is the same with you and Jim?" His tired eyes had lost very little of their sharpness.

"Oh, yes, Judge. I'm so thankful—"

Again he caught his breath in a rasping cough. "I know. But I can't do anything for Jim. I mean—" He leaned back, his white head against the chair; something almost like a bird, caught in his throat, was palpitating.

Julie's own heart sank. "I know."

He pulled his head up to look straight at her. The look in his eyes was pitiful, as if it denied the words. But the words came. "I can't change things. A statute of limitations for murder cannot exist. Nobody in his senses would consent to it. So, I am afraid that Jim has made a grave error. He grasped at a perfectly unintentional phrasing of a law of limitations and then stubbornly clung to his hope. Julie, my dear, it is a very fragile hope; indeed, it is none at all. Jim was the only possible suspect if he had been brought to trial."

"Oh, Judge, please—"

"No, Julie. I have already transgressed my duty in permitting Jim to go with Blanche to Hartford. Blanche, Jim told me, has tried to dissuade him from the course he is determined to take. No, only new and convincing evidence could be brought forward even to suggest that Jim is not guilty. As I understand it there is no such evidence. This particular law was never meant to cover a capital crime even though belief in its legality actually inspired Jim to run away and hide for five years."

He coughed, bending over, his eyes watering with the effort. He straightened up, one hand at his chest. "I have known you all your life. It would be cruel of me to encourage you. Believe me, Julie, no matter what anybody says, there is simply no hope. I can't let you go on." He coughed again. "I've thought of nothing else since I saw Jim. His hopes and yours are simply impossible!"

"But, Judge—"

"I can't change this. We are pretty sensible people here, you know." He essayed a weak smile. "You know that we like honesty."

She sought desperately for some lifeline. "New evidence? A trial, then?"

"I can't say. I only know that you and Jim—wait a minute —wait—"

His face had turned a peculiar gray. He leaned forward, one hand at his chest. "Jim has to be arrested on suspicion of murder— My medicine—I must—" He waved toward the desk across the room. "The top drawer—a bottle—hurry— only a few drops—hurry!" Julie leaped up, ran to the desk, jerked open the top drawer, finding only writing paper and checkbooks and what looked like a stack of bills, searched hurriedly, almost frantically as the Judge's suddenly, painfully gasping breaths increased. There was no bottle there. Then the second drawer; she jerked that open and it disclosed papers of various kinds but no bottle.

"I can't find—" she began when the rasping, panting breaths hesitated.

They stopped.

She knew that she whirled around and ran, stumbling, back to the Judge. He lay back in his chair, his mouth slightly open as if he had been straining for his last breath. And it was the last. His eyes were open but did not see her.

It could not have happened so quickly. Between one breath and the next.

But she had to do things, something, what? She couldn't just crouch there, holding a thin, white wrist which had not the slightest movement of a pulse.

Well, what? Call the doctor. Call the hospital. Call somebody. Call anybody. She looked around for the telephone, found it on the desk in which she had unsuccessfully begun to rummage and ran across to it again to take up the receiver. She didn't know the hospital number. She didn't know the doctor's number. But she knew the emergency number and dialed it, her fingers shaking.

A man answered matter-of-factly, his voice quickening

into interest as she explained, said promptly that they'd be there at once and clicked down his own telephone.

It had grown cold in the room; the log fire was dying down.

She had dropped her fur jacket somewhere; she was kneeling beside the Judge, chafing his hands, vainly watching for the slightest flicker of his lips or the slightest gleam of life in his eyes when Chief McClary arrived, puffing and red-faced, followed by two younger men. He said nothing, merely gave her a glance, charged across to the Judge, looked, listened and said to one of his cohorts, "Get the doctor here. But it's too late." He took the fur, put it politely over Julie's shoulders and said, "He's gone, you know. But we have to get the doctor just the same. How did it happen?"

"It just happened. Like that." She was shivering and dimly grateful for the kindness of Chief McClary in dropping her fur jacket over her.

"Didn't he show any signs of an attack coming on?"

"Yes! He asked me to get his medicine. I was trying to find it when—when I heard—I saw— Oh, Chief McClary, everybody loved him."

The Chief nodded gravely. "Sure. Everybody knew him. He stuck to the law and made everybody else stick to it, too. A good man. Comfort yourself, child—I mean, Miss Fan-'um. He had a good and useful life. Everybody in town knew of his illness. Where's the girl, that young cousin, what's her name?"

"Lisa—that is, Maude Munger." This was no time to explain Lisa's change of name. "She is at John Wingate's house."

"Wingate's, huh?" An odd look of speculation came into the Chief's face. "I hear that young Jim Wingate, John's son, has come back."

She nodded.

The chief rubbed his not inconsiderable nose. "I suppose

I'll have to pick him up. He did run away. Makes things worse for him. But today, I thought it better to wait to hear from the Judge."

"Do you think that just maybe the doctor can do anything for the Judge?"

The chief shook his head. "Nope. Sorry. But of course we have to call him anyway. He's our medical examiner. I reckon you've kind of forgotten."

"Oh, yes," she heard herself whisper. Her hands were so twisted together that she was aware of a cramped pain in her fingers.

The policeman came briskly into the room. "I got him on the car radio. Says he'll be along as soon as he finishes seeing to a patient. Oh, it's Ollie's leg or ribs or something, Miss Fan'um."

Chief McClary nodded gravely. "Busted something, huh? Well, that's bad. Ollie's no spring chicken. Still he's pretty tough. Now then—" He went to the telephone. "Do you know lawyer Surton's number, Julie?"

Her own first name, without any prefix, struck Julie with a small tinge of, not pleasure, but satisfaction. The Chief had known her all her life, had indeed once arrested her for speeding. She had been fined and given a warning. Delia had not made it any easier. Delia believed in training a child to be a proper and responsible adult.

"But she's not there. She's at the Wingate place."

The Chief gave her a rather knowing look; he had apparently memorized the number, for he dialed quickly. Julie heard his words; he obviously put his message in as kindly terms as possible. He talked, clearly, to John. "This is McClary, John. I've bad news for you." Bad news just as the Judge had said, wearily, before he told her the bad news.

The Chief went on. "Yes, it's the Judge. He's had a dicey heart for some time. I—" Apparently John interrupted. The Chief said, "Yes, that's right. Well, no, he wasn't alone. Well, sure, Miss Surton too . . . Yes, I've sent for the doctor. He's the medical examiner but he's working on Ollie. Yes. Oh, yes, we'll be right here."

Someone, a policeman in uniform, came in with a blanket, which he adjusted gently over the Judge. Julie huddled in a chair, looking at nothing yet oddly seeming to see everything, even the red leather house slippers the Judge had been wearing, protruding from the blanket. He had always been rather finical as to his clothing. He'd have hated anything so undignified.

He was past hating anything. In a moment, in a matter of a second, like a flame blown out, his long and honorable life had been whisked away. She was going to cry; this wouldn't do at all. The Chief was fidgeting, looking at her, poking up the fire, adding another log, listening for the car.

The car arrived. Two cars, in fact. All at once the sedate and comfortable room was filled with people. Jim saw her, came to her. "Julie, you were here—"

She nodded. Maude—no, Lisa—had flown across to kneel beside the Judge. Clearly her emotional barometer was set for dramatics. She was crying loudly. George Wingate came after her; his sleek, rather plump face was merely a mask half-concealed by the straggly red beard but he put a hand on Lisa's shoulder and muttered something. Julie didn't hear what he said; she didn't want to hear. Jim said, "Take it easy, Julie. I'm so sorry—"

Delia advanced, billowing in her gray silk dress and glittering from a diamond bracelet, old-fashioned in its setting; probably a long-ago Van Clive wife had worn it. She, too, put a hand on Julie's. "I'm so sorry. It must have been very sudden."

John Wingate was standing at the Judge's side and talking in low tones to the Chief. Blanche stood in the doorway, a slender, steady figure in her favorite black. She came forward as the Chief nodded in her direction. "Lawyer—I mean Miss Surton—"

" 'Lawyer' will do," Blanche said quietly. "What happened?"

The Chief made an expressive gesture and turned to Julie, who said unevenly, "Just—just nothing. That is, he had a heart attack. He asked me to get some medicine, over there," she nodded at the desk. "While I was hunting for it he—he gave a sort of gasp and—then he died. I—it was—oh, Jim, we all loved him! Part of our lives."

George lifted his face with its red beard. "He was about to issue some kind of injunction about Jim, though. Wasn't he?"

John Wingate broke sternly into the shocked hush. "Not that we know of, George. Perhaps he sent for you, Julie, to give you good news—"

Julie found her voice again. "No. He said it was bad news and it was."

John came to her. "He felt that Jim had to be arrested?"

Julie nodded. "He said—he said he knew that we were all celebrating, but he couldn't let us go on hoping. He said he had to tell me. He said it would be cruel to let us hope."

"So what did you do?" John Wingate asked.

"He asked for his medicine. He said it was in the top drawer in that desk. It wasn't there. So I was hunting through the next drawer when I heard—I heard his breathing—gasping, difficult and then—" She turned to put her head against Jim's shoulder. "It was just then, that very moment, he died."

Dr. Severe said from the doorway, "If you'll let me in, please." A policeman jumped aside. Dr. Severe came trotting in, his black bag in his hand. He was an old-time Brookboro resident, trusted by all. He couldn't have been much more than fifty but seemed older and very sedate. He lifted the blanket from the Judge. John Wingate and Delia stood between Julie and the little group around the Judge.

But she could hear the doctor's voice, quiet and controlled. "I expected this. Even sooner. He's been going on, sitting on the bench, trying to pretend nothing was wrong. But he promised to take what medication I could conscientiously prescribe."

Lisa lifted her face. She was still kneeling beside the Judge, but Delia had moved a little aside and Julie could see Lisa's beautiful face. "Oh, Doctor! It was so—so sudden!"

"Mercifully," said Dr. Severe. "Come now, child." He yielded, however, to Lisa's beauty and appeal. "Somebody must take you home. I'm sure that—" He glanced around the room, found John Wingate and said, "You'll see that this child is taken care of. Now then, Chief—"

Julie was vaguely aware that all of them except Blanche were being tactfully dismissed. But John Wingate did not take Lisa, still sobbing (with all her might, Julie couldn't help thinking; eyes were red, yes; but fingers could be stuck in eyes and—oh, what a dreadful thought!). But she had never been convinced of Lisa's disinterested affection for her elderly and very remote cousin.

George, escorting Lisa, looked over his perfectly tailored shoulder toward Blanche. "You must have his will, Blanche."

Seven

Blanche lifted her clear eyes to George and blinked once. "Why, yes. That is, I have a copy. I drew it up for him. But the original is in the Judge's safe deposit box at the bank."

Lisa stopped a sob in mid-gurgle. "What was in this will?"

Blanche became all icy dignity. "Really, Lisa. This is no time."

"But I'm his only relation. I have a right." Lisa forgot all about sobbing, thereby ending any doubt in Julie's earlier uninvited and indeed unpleasant speculation. "So I have a right to insist."

"Not on the reading of the will just now," John Wingate said sternly.

Lisa's blue eyes were luminous and beseeching. "Oh, I didn't mean that!"

John said, "Not the time and place. Go on, Lisa. George will take you back to New Haven."

"Certainly. Yes, sir. Come, Lisa, I'll see to you." George put his arm around Lisa, who became very tender and feminine.

Delia rustled. "Then, Chief, can we all go? I mean the

doctor and your—your assistants," she said in a suddenly stately way, which was one way of describing the phalanx of blue-clad policemen who had by now arrived. "That is," Delia added, "we can't do anything here. May we go?"

The Chief nodded to Delia, but stopped Blanche. "You were his lawyer."

"Yes. You mean all the arrangements? Yes, I know what he wanted. You need me, Doctor?"

Dr. Severe replied. "Yes, please, if you don't mind. His wishes—yes. You might facilitate—" He hesitated, glanced at Delia and said, " . . . things."

"Certainly. I'll see you later, Delia," Blanche said. "Don't take it so hard, Julie. He would have wished to go suddenly like—like that."

Julie swallowed past a stiff throat. So she and Delia, Jim and John Wingate left the Judge, the police, the doctor and Blanche, and went to Julie's place, actually in a very handsome vehicle instead of her own little car which would be picked up later. John's automobile was, she heard him tell Delia absently, obviously thinking of other things, a Porsche Carrera. There was a low whistle from Jim. John heard it and glanced back. "I like cars. I can put up the top if it's too chilly."

"He certainly does like cars," Jim said in a low voice. "This is a famous one. Must have cost—oh, never mind. My father can have and ought to have anything he takes a fancy for."

When they stopped at Julie's house, with the one light burning in the hall, and John cut off the engine, they could hear the persistent humming of locusts.

"A fine night, really," Delia said indifferently, as if trying to make conversation while they all got out.

John kissed Delia, who then waited for a marked second, while Jim put his lips to Julie's ear to whisper, "See you tomorrow. Take it easy." Then he moved his lips to her own.

"Well," exclaimed Delia, "well—"

"All right," John said. "All right, Jim. Tomorrow—"

When Julie opened the door, Beau galloped gracefully out of the house, forgetting his usual dignity in his delight. But he stopped cavorting and advanced with quiet self-possession after Julie when she went inside. John's beautiful car left with only a murmur, but a strong and powerful one that suggested the possibility of unleashing a remarkable burst of speed.

Delia stood in the hall, running her hands through her usually carefully coiffed hair. Pyewacket sat on the lower step of the stairs and watched them thoughtfully before she lifted a black paw and licked it.

"Ollie!" Julie cried. "Oh, Delia, I forgot all about Ollie! I must see to him—"

"Not now," Delia said firmly. "Dr. Severe will have taken care of him. Can't be anything very serious. They won't let you see Ollie tonight, anyway. I'm going to fix us some hot milk and—whatever there is in the fridge, and then we'll go to bed. I think the doctor ought to have given us some kind of sedative. This has been a dreadful shock for you. For all of us. And on empty stomachs!"

There was a touch of indignation in her manner that ought to have been weirdly amusing. It sounded quite as if the Judge should have planned better. But she swished off toward the kitchen, pausing only to turn up the thermostat on the way. Julie followed her, shaken and sad, very, very tired and still trembling inside. Hollow, naturally; Delia was right. Nothing should happen on an empty stomach, she told herself with an attempt at self-control, and found Delia already busying herself with eggs and a pan and turning on the electric stove. "Beat these eggs, Julie. Find some bread. I must say, Ollie has left the kitchen and fridge well stocked. How do you suppose he managed to hurt himself?"

"Oh, a dozen ways. He never would admit he was getting a day older."

Beau had obligingly accompanied her, but he couldn't help fixing an interested eye on the food preparations.

The dog's big dish and the cat's smaller one were neatly arranged on a newspaper. Julie found dog food and cat food, opened cans and filled the dishes. Both, however, accepted their handouts with a certain reserve. Probably Julie had not mixed their dinners just as Ollie did.

"I think," Delia said, gazing at her plate rather unhappily, "that we'd better go back to my house right away. In the morning."

"Good heavens, Delia! We are two able-bodied women. Surely we can get along without Ollie! Besides, he's not such a good cook, anyway."

Delia shot her a shrewd glance. "You want to stay around here on account of Jim."

"Of course. Besides, there will be services for the Judge."

"No services. Blanche told me on the way over there from John's house. The Judge specifically stated that he wanted no services at all, not even private ones. He's to be buried quietly in the family plot here. I suppose," Delia said, after a pause, "Maude—Lisa—will be upset about this. But I think Blanche will settle it the way the Judge wanted it. So"—she took a large swallow of milk—"so there's nothing to keep us here."

"Jim—"

"What can *you* do?"

"I don't know. You can't want more," she said to Beau as a paw was placed upon her knee and beseeching brown eyes looked up into her own.

"Don't spoil that dog," said Delia. "Or—" She nodded toward the cat, who had leaped up to another chair and was looking over the table with interest. "Or that cat."

"But if we should go back to your house for a while, what on earth could I do with them?"

"What are boarding kennels for?" Delia said shortly and closed the subject by scooping up dishes, rattling them into the dishwasher and all but shoving Julie out of the kitchen and up the stairs.

Julie was in her room when she realized that she had been followed by both dog and cat, followed very quietly; it seemed that both had taken Delia's measure. There they were, both looking at her with sharp interest. Water, of course. She filled a clean soap dish with water and waited as both put their noses down and lapped. They were like two diplomats from dissenting countries who, however, had fixed ideas of a kind of polite tolerance; dogdom and catdom, no less.

When at last she crawled into bed she almost fell into sleep. It was not as late as it seemed. It was only deep, troubled weariness that had attacked her like a paralysis. Her bedside telephone roused her. The cat had found himself a comfortable nest at the foot of her bed. Beau lifted his beautiful head to listen. "Julie," said Jim as she lifted the receiver.

"Yes."

"I woke you, didn't I! But I want you to know Blanche says we have to go to Hartford again in the morning. The Judge's death may change the situation for me. It's something, not political but important. Anyway, that's what Blanche thinks. So we may have to stay over for a few days. She said, too, that the Judge did not want services."

"I know. She told Delia."

There was a slight pause. Then Jim said, "Have you seen Ollie?"

"No. I couldn't after what happened."

"He's not likely to return to work right away. I've been thinking about it. I don't like you and Delia staying in that house alone."

"But, Jim—"

"You should go to Delia's house in the city. I'll see you there. Now, Julie, you'll do that, won't you?"

"No! I want to stay here near you—"

"Please, Julie. I'll feel so much better about you. I'll come to your aunt's and tell you everything, just as soon as I can."

"But Jim—" She was beginning to awaken more thoroughly. "The Judge said you would be arrested and—"

"I know. He was very upset when I went to see him. But I feel that I just might get another opinion in view of his death. Blanche is going with me. Now, please, promise me, Julie."

"No. I won't."

"But I tell you—oh, hell, Julie! Can't you understand?"

"I'm going to stay right here."

"No, you are not! Oh, have some sense! Everybody knows that I swear up and down that I didn't kill Walker. Now I'm back and everybody who is not a dolt would guess that I hope to find out who did kill him. Can't you see that I'd be more content, honestly, Julie, if you were safely back at Delia's."

"But nobody would hurt me!"

"Are you going to be that kind of wife?"

"I'm going to do what I want to do."

Jim's voice became pleading but also very clear. "I tell you. Anybody who is not a fool would guess what I am trying to do. So you, my girl, should—well, call Brookboro the danger zone. And go back with Delia."

She did give in but not agreeably. But then, later in the night, she could not help reconsidering his words. Brookboro a danger zone? It couldn't be.

It could be.

Delia was still insistent, too, so the next day they went back to the city. But first they made three calls in Julie's car which one of the policemen had driven over from the Judge's house for her. The first was to see Chief McClary, who—luckily, Julie thought—was in his office and very kind and understanding. "Of course you can go. Nothing to keep you here. At least," he said rather shrewdly, "at least nothing that I know of. But just give me your aunt's phone number and address."

The second call was upon Ollie, who was anything but

cheerful, tucked into a narrow white bed, his face unshaven, looking very old.

"Only busted a rib or two. Painful but not too bad. You'd better go to your aunt's place in the city. I can't do anything for a while. But you can't leave the cat and dog at any kennels, Miss Julie. You can't do that!" His main concern was for the two animals.

"Don't worry. We'll take them with us."

Ollie stuck out his lower lip but then nodded. "If you intend to take them with you, there's a white pan, looks like a roasting pan, and a sack of sawdust-looking stuff in the pantry. You'll need them," he said with a glance at Delia. "But she's a very clean cat," Ollie added defensively. "Very clean."

"Ollie, how did it happen? Did you really fall off a ladder?"

Ollie gave her an odd look from under thick gray eyebrows. "H'mm," he murmured and said no more. Aunt Delia said that they must be going and told Ollie to do just as the doctors advised.

"Not much use in trying anything else," Ollie said crustily. "Now, if you're driving, Miss Julie, you take it easy on the parkway."

So, presently, somehow Delia and Beau and Pye (with pan and sack) were in her car with her, the cat in a hastily bought carrier and the dog with a new strong leash. Their third call had been upon the hardware-store owner, Jasper Long, who was eager to talk about Jim and the tragedy of the Judge's sudden death.

This was by no means the first time Beau had gone with Julie for long rides. He stood on his hind legs in the back seat, his forepaws on the top of the front seat, his long nose thrust forward to permit him to watch the traffic. The cat uttered a Siamese oath when put into the carrier but otherwise contented herself with an occasional low mutter and finally went to sleep.

70

With the various calls, the little delays, the stopping along the turnpike for late lunch, and then the crowded traffic as they neared the city, it was almost dark by the time they reached Delia's house. After depositing their varied cargo, Julie drove the car to the garage rented by the residents of the Cove. When she walked back to Delia's house, Delia was still standing in the doorway, sniffing indignantly.

"Somebody is smoking! There's somebody here!"

A very young man lounged out into the hall to meet them. "I'm here, Aunt Delia. Hello, Julie."

It was Peter, of course; he looked a little older than his seventeen years, that or he tried to look older, for there was a fringe of light brown beard on his chin.

Delia said, "Just what are you doing here, besides smoking?" She closed the door behind her with a bang.

"Vacation," said Peter. He put his arm around Julie and gave her a mild peck on the cheek. "Good to see you, pet. What's all this about Jim Wingate?"

"Where did you hear that there's anything at all about Jim?" Delia was on it in a flash.

"Oh," Peter said airily. "I just stopped for the night at Sam Bucknell's in Brookboro. You know, his father is First Selectman. So I heard about Jim. Fact is, the town is ringing with it!"

"Why on earth didn't you come home last night if you were in Brookboro?" Julie demanded.

Peter gave one of his far-too-natural grins. "Oh, I was with Sam. We'd been to a movie in New Haven."

"Why in New Haven?" Julie was suddenly the firm elder sister.

"Because it was showing there! So we got to Brookboro rather late. Seemed convenient to stay at Sam's. Then this morning I heard about Jim. I phoned the house. No answer. So I knew you had come here. That's all."

Delia's suspicions were aroused.

"You went all the way to New Haven just for a movie?"

Peter grinned again with, Julie had to admit, a certain charm, and put his arm around Delia. "Now, darling auntie, don't worry."

"You had no business out of school! Drinking, too, I suppose?"

"Why, Aunt Delia, don't you trust me?"

"No," said Delia, "I don't. You've been told you must not drink."

Peter sighed exaggeratedly. "Darling, look at me. Do I look like a drunk?"

"You look as though your face needs a good scrub."

This touched a sensitive chord in Peter. "That will be a very fine beard. Given time."

"Do you propose staying here for all of your vacation?" Delia shook her head. "Doesn't sound right to me. Well, you can walk Beau."

The dog heard his name and nudged at Peter.

"And by the way," Delia added, with a wicked gleam in her eyes, "there's a cat, too. That is, she's in a carrier in Julie's workroom, but she didn't seem to like the drive."

"A cat, forsooth," said Peter lightly and ducked out the door.

"That boy has been up to something," Delia said.

"I know, but it can't be much."

"Youth," said Delia, rather wistfully. "When I was his age, I could stay out all night and do my share of—whatever there was to share. However," she sighed, "I didn't much. I fell in love with Pieter—my Pieter, at eighteen. Just as you—" She stopped.

Julie finished for her. "Just as I did with Jim. For all of my life—"

"Of course, *my* marriage was exceptional." Delia deliberated. "My Pieter was an exceptional man. Your Jim—"

Julie was stung. "Jim is great."

"Jim," said Delia, turning very sober, "is in danger."

And Jim thinks that I, you, anybody close to him may be

in danger, because he might share any evidence he finds, Julie thought; he had called Brookboro a danger zone.

Peter, followed closely by Beau, came back into the living room with the carrier, which he put down and leaned over to peer inside.

"Why, it *is* a cat! I think."

"Yes, indeed. Her name is Pyewacket," Delia said with another spark of mischief.

Peter stared at the cat, who seemed to utter something unfit for human ears. "Pyewacket?" Peter said, wide-eyed. "Nobody could name a cat that. What does it mean?"

"It doesn't mean anything. Except a character—a cat," Delia corrected herself, "in a play that John Wingate remembered. Anyway, that's her name, Pye for short."

Peter stared at her and again at the cat. "Does she ever wash her face?"

"Yes," said Delia with spirit, "more than you can say."

Peter was not affected this time by the sly reference to his beginning beard. "It's a funny name just the same. Shall I let her out?"

Delia shrugged. "You might as well. I'm sure Ollie has her house trained."

Peter opened the cat carrier. The cat decided not to come out but hunched up inside, examining this new house with wary blue eyes. Beau approached Peter with a polite indication that he'd like a walk. "Okay," Peter said. "I'll take you around the Cove, I mean around the block. Just don't tackle that Doberman three doors down. You'll wish you hadn't."

The door banged behind him.

"Aunt Delia, this is great of you. Letting me bring both."

"Huh," said Delia. "We couldn't leave them alone. Ollie would have got up, somehow, to see to them if we had put them in a kennel. Ollie deserves some peace of mind."

"So do you," Julie said. "I'll see to the cat and hope—"

The telephone rang shrilly. It rang again and Julie ran into her workroom to answer it.

"I'm Sam," said a young and very excited voice. "Is this Mrs. Van Clive's house? Is Peter around? I've got to talk to him."

"I'm Julie, Peter's sister."

"Oh! Well, I guess it's okay to tell you, too. They say the Judge was murdered—"

Julie sank down on the edge of her desk. "What did you say?"

The boy's voice rose. "Didn't mean to shock you. But that's a fact. The way the Judge was murdered. Right after Jim Wingate got home, too. What do you think of that?"

Julie apparently lost her voice. She had to cough and force herself to speak. "Are you sure?"

"Oh, sure. The doctor said so."

There was a sharp click from Delia's extension upstairs. She must have run for the stairs like a girl. Just as well, Julie thought momentarily and weirdly. She wouldn't have to repeat this to her. But Delia's voice came on.

"Sam! I am Peter's aunt. You know me. What do you mean, the Judge was murdered?"

"That's what they all say. I mean the doctor and everybody. It's all over town."

"How was he murdered?" Delia's voice was suddenly different.

"Seems he was supposed to take some medicine for his heart. The bottle was found, broken, along the road by his house. Dated, so they knew it was a fresh prescription. Doctor says so, too."

"But I don't see—"

There was scorn in Sam's young voice. "If he had a heart attack as they say and it seems Peter's sister claims, then she couldn't find his medicine because somebody had taken it away and broken the bottle, and he didn't have any medicine so he died. Got that straight? Now can I talk to Peter?"

Delia sounded very harsh and frightened. "Peter is not here now."

"Well, you might tell him the town is all excitement. Right after Jim Wingate got back and all."

"Thank you," said Delia and hung up the receiver. Julie slowly did the same with her own.

Eight

Delia came downstairs. She was so white that her face looked old and haunted. "Julie, you heard all that!"

"Oh, yes."

"But you told them that the Judge asked for his medicine, and you—"

"I know what I told them. I couldn't find it. I looked and looked where he said it would be but I couldn't find it and then—then he died."

"So now they believe that somebody purposely took that bottle of medicine, that new bottle, all full probably, according to the doctor, anyway it was a fresh prescription—somebody took it and got away with it. Dropped it somewhere so it broke and it has now been found."

"You heard Sam."

"That certainly suggests that whoever took that medicine knew the Judge's condition and thought he might die. Can't mean anything else," Delia said gloomily.

"I *couldn't* find it. He said it was in a drawer and I looked, and it wasn't."

"Yes, you told the police all that. Over and over. Julie, you look white. If you faint I'll just let you faint. I've got to do something about this but—"

Julie said wearily, "What can you do?"

Delia set her lips. "Just now I'll phone John Wingate."

There was, as a matter of fact, no need to telephone John, for the doorbell rang. Julie, nearer, reached the door first, followed by Delia; John Wingate stood on the scrubbed white steps. "Is it all right to leave my car out here in the street?"

"Oh, yes."

Peter, a galloping figure in blue jeans and sweater, tugging Beau with him, came up breathlessly. "Mr. Wingate! Is that a Porsche Carrera?"

John nodded down at Peter's flushed, excited face.

"Wow!" said Peter. "Say, will you let me—no, no, not drive her—I didn't mean that. I'll just watch her, if I may. No telling what can happen on the streets of New York."

For a second a smile hovered around John's mouth, but he said gravely, "Certainly. Very kind of you, Peter."

"Oh!" An expression of utter bliss came into Peter's face. He thrust Beau's leash at Julie. "Here! You take him."

"Come in, John. Aunt Delia was about to phone you. We just heard about the police calling the Judge's death murder."

John put his firm hand on Julie's arm. "That's why I came."

Delia said tensely, "We want to know everything. We heard it was because of the missing medicine, but don't you think it possible that the Judge just happened to drop the bottle himself without realizing it?"

John took a chair in the living room toward which she had absently waved one dimpled hand. He looked very serious. "I don't know, Delia. The Judge still had all his marbles, you know. The doctor said he was fully aware of his condition and accustomed to relying upon this medicine."

Delia had been sitting very straight; now she put her hands

on her knees and leaned forward. "John, he *could* have forgotten."

"Nobody thinks he did."

"What do you mean by nobody?"

"Everybody, I think. It's all over town already. He was well known and well liked. That is, for the most part. There were, of course, a few people who didn't like his sentences. There is always that to consider when a man is a judge and forced by his position and his firm obligation to follow the law. Yes, I expect there are a few people either in Brookboro or nearby who had some reason to dislike the Judge. But the people who knew the details about his heart condition are rather few, I believe. At least the doctor says so and Blanche says so."

Delia was diverted. "What does Blanche think?"

John sighed. "I don't really know. She talked to me for a moment this morning, but then she and Jim started out for Hartford. Also—you'll not like this, either of you. I don't like it myself. But since the Judge's death and Jim's return were coincidental, people are—"

Delia burst in. "We know! They are saying Jim killed him!"

"Well, not quite that. They are only saying that it seems very strange."

"You know what they mean by that."

John nodded. "I'm afraid I do."

"But that's far from being proof," Delia began but John, very soberly, shook his head.

"As you may know, Jim went to see the Judge as soon as he got home. He thought he should. I agreed."

"What did the Judge say?"

"Jim says the Judge said only that he'd have to think it over. Try to discover his own duty."

"He did think it over," Julie cried. "I'll tell you exactly what he said." She repeated the brief and convincing words. "But then he had the heart attack, he asked me to bring him his medicine and then—I couldn't find it—and—"

John nodded. "Take it easy, Julie. But that bottle of medicine, the new prescription, really couldn't have walked out into the road."

There was a long pause. Then Delia said, hopefully, "Fingerprints on the bottle?"

John shook his head. "Not that I heard of. And I'd hear of it."

Delia fluffed up her hair absently. Just then there was a faint scraping sound and the cat emerged from the carrier, calmly, eyed John for a moment, then leaped up on a window seat, curled her tail around herself, and began to lick one paw. John said absently, "Why, that's Ollie's cat!"

Julie stirred. "We saw Ollie before we left Brookboro."

"He told me. I dropped by the hospital. He hadn't heard of the Judge's death. Certainly he hadn't heard that they are calling it murder. And saying that Jim might have murdered the Judge."

"*They* are saying—" Delia began scornfully but John shook his head.

"You know better than that, Delia. What people are saying is very important and in this instance, I'm afraid, very dangerous."

There was another long silence, long but full of thought. Finally Delia said, "In my opinion, Jim was framed."

Julie felt the slightest jolt of surprise. Framed? That was not in Delia's customary vocabulary.

"Oh, yes, I think that, too," John said. "Just about his only defense was his word for it."

"I remember," Delia said crisply, "Jim said Walker himself phoned him. But he didn't really know Walker's voice. It could have been someone else!"

"You are thinking of George," John said quietly. "It might be considered to his interest to get rid of Jim. But you know George had an alibi, that play with Maude, I mean Lisa, in New Haven. He simply could not have been in

Brookboro. Believe me, Delia, I have thought of this until every possible ramification of fact has occurred to me. One thing is true, though. If Jim were arrested, tried and with the evidence against him sent away for a long time in prison, perhaps even life, then George *might* expect to inherit more than half a comfortable sum of money. Not that I intend to pass on, not just yet. Too much to do," said John.

"You mean you really hope to get Jim free," said Delia.

"You are always downright—" John smiled a little. "Yes, I mean that. I don't see how, but I can try."

Julie cried, "You mean find new evidence that would help clear Jim? Jim *couldn't* have gone to an almost stranger's house, on the strength of this very odd phone call—and just shot him."

"Certainly, I don't believe it either. Jim really had no reason to shoot Walker."

Delia said slowly, "There's got to be a motive for Walker's murder. Nobody ever proved that Jim had anything to do with him."

John nodded. "Right."

"This Walker," Delia said, angrily even now, after five years. "Nobody knew anything about him. He said he was trying to paint. He said he was a retired something or other—"

"Broker, wasn't it?" John said.

Julie said, "He seemed to have told people different things. He said he'd been a broker. But he told somebody—I remember! The barber who trimmed his hair and beard, he said he had been in Europe trying to paint."

Delia said, "Yes, and found he couldn't paint—wherever he was. So he came home and tried to find a place near enough to museums but not in New York and then—" She leaned back, proud of her memory. "Then he bought the old Planter place. Small but big enough. He really did try to paint and I use the word 'try' precisely. You never saw such daubs. I said to him, I said, 'Mr. Walker, did a child smear that thing?' and he said"—her remembered indignation was turning her pretty face pink—" 'Now, you are a Philistine, Mrs. Van Clive!' Such impudence! And then he kissed my hand. I almost counted my fingers! He must have thought himself a gift to women, especially old women—"

"Now, Delia—"

"Well, I'm not young. He was what we used to call a dasher. Yes, we did," she told Julie crossly. "And he was. Dapper, dark, slender, with a certain charm—skin-deep that was. Believe me. He was a fake. I don't know what about, but a fake."

A low, musical but penetrating sound came from the street. Julie heard it first.

"That's Peter!"

"Oh, I don't think Peter—"

"You don't know Peter. Can't resist—" Julie ran for the door and she was right, for as she opened it the low but serious warning noise came from the beautiful car.

Peter, unaware (or pretending to be unaware) of his iniquity, looked at her with his wide and disarming grin. "Just to keep the kids away. They want to see this car. Do you know a car like this won in a race—"

"Take your hand off that thing. Come in here!"

"Well, but Mr. Wingate said to guard it."

"I don't see any kids anywhere." A curtain or two moved among the windows close to Delia's house, though. "You are disturbing the peace," Julie said with considerable exaggeration, for she couldn't really think that undue honking was disturbing anybody's peace but her own.

"I'll stay here," said Peter.

"Peter!"

"No, sister. You can't drag me out. I'm bigger than you are now. Stronger—"

John arrived at her elbow. Peter suddenly turned into a boy again and sprang up from the seat. "Yes, sir. I kept the kids away."

John looked up and down the street. "I see no fleeing figures," he said dryly. "All right, Peter. Thank you. I'm going back to Brookboro."

Beau came to the door to see if he was needed. Peter scrambled out of the car and said, very meekly, "Yes, sir."

"Never mind, Peter. I'll give you a ride in it one day."

Peter's face glowed at once. "You wouldn't consider letting me take the wheel?"

"No," said John flatly, took Julie's chin in his hand, and kissed her lightly. "I'll have better—at least some news tonight when Jim gets back from Hartford. I'll let you know."

Julie thought she said thank you. John got into his car with the easy, graceful movements of a much younger man. Then he leaned out and said, carefully but clearly, "I told Delia to stay here. That means you too, Julie. Much better. Brookboro is no place for you just now."

"But there'll be some kind of inquest or inquiry about the Judge. Isn't that so?"

"Depends," said John. "I'll let you know. See you."

He drove away, so silently that the shining car moved like a fully and magically empowered ghost. Peter said longingly, "What a car! What a man! Julie, I'm going to be just like John."

"You'll have to work some." Julie threw sisterly cold water at him but affectionately, too. She put a hand on his too long gold-brown hair. "Come on. You too, Beau. No use in thinking about that cat across the street. He has claws. So has Pye, as far as that goes." Beau seemed to sigh but went beside her back into the living room.

Delia usually pretended to be very cross with Peter; in fact, she loved him dearly. That, however, did not discourage her, or for that matter Peter, from doling out what she considered condign punishment when he needed it. She said, "Go down to the kitchen and see if Mrs. Martine has come back."

"Okay," said Peter cheerfully, but instead of making for the kitchen stairs, which went down just below the stairs to the upper floors, he trotted through the dining room and swung open the door to the dumbwaiter. Delia cried, "No, no, not that way!"

Peter squawked. "Aunt Delia, you've still got this thing, ropes and all! My God, you really are living in medieval times. If not," he added darkly, "Cro-Magnon."

"Peter—" Julie cried but he was not to be stopped. She got to the dining room door in time to see him swing himself into the big, unwieldy dumbwaiter, grin at her as he folded up his long, jeans-clad legs and then touched the electric button. "Cheers!" he shouted and banged the door shut.

Delia was not upset; she actually let a very slight smile show on her face. But then she turned to Julie. "George has an alibi for the Walker murder. Too bad, really. Both he and Lisa were in that play at New Haven. I always wondered if George could have contrived to get Jim to go to Alben Walker's house, just as or just after somebody had killed him. But I don't see how."

There was a shrill whistle from below.

Julie recognized it. "So the whistler is back."

"Yes. I phoned her from your house before we left. Lisa!" Delia snorted in a fine, ladylike way but still a snort. "Now she thinks she's really on the stage! Little theaters!"

"Oh, she is, Delia! She works very hard. She's had a number of roles."

"Oh, really, Julie! I can't see why you defend her. Can't you realize that she was after Jim, hard as she could go? She'd have married him in two minutes if he'd ever given her a chance. Of course that was after John Wingate had made such a success. And after he'd inherited something rather solid in the way of capital. But both those boys! I wonder how his will reads concerning Jim and George."

"Knowing John, I'm not so sure he ever made a will. But he would be fair to each of them!"

Delia gave her a scornful glance.

The whistle was repeated. There was the sound of the

dumbwaiter climbing along, steadily and sturdily. The door popped open and Peter shouted, "Here we are! Food and all. Smells good, too."

Delia said, "That boy!"

But she turned to Julie and said in a low voice, "Ask Blanche about John's will. She'll know. If George had anything to gain by Jim's being sent to prison for murder, then —well, I can't see how he arranged Walker's murder but I still think he did. All right, Peter, you needn't quite bow over my chair. But thank you for pulling it out for me."

"Yes, ma'am," Peter said, beaming, but added, "Did Sam call me while I was out?"

Nine

Delia did not quite freeze but the effect was the same. She gave Julie one pale blue gaze. Julie caught it and rather felt she had frozen, too.

Peter, in the act of sitting, saw both glances. Peter was never slow. "Oh! So he did. Why didn't you tell me? What did he have to say?"

Delia sighed, "Might as well. He'll hear it any way."

Julie nodded. "Go ahead. Use the phone in my workroom, Peter. But don't get excited now."

"Something to get excited about, huh?" He shoved back the chair he had been sliding into, said rapidly, "Excuse me, Aunt Delia," and shot out of the room, a blur in blue jeans and white shirt.

Both she and Delia waited a moment. Finally Delia said, "We couldn't help it. His pal would only phone again—Sam something."

"Bucknell," Julie told her absently. "You know. First Selectman."

Delia considered. "I've never heard anything against the

boy, I mean Sam. And Peter's bound to have friends. Now, let's be cool and calm about this."

In her intention to be cool and calm, she poured coffee on the chicken casserole and took a forkful, not even wincing at what must have been a rather curious taste.

It was only a few moments before Peter came flying back into the room. "Sam told me! The police say the Judge was murdered! Sam couldn't wait to talk. His father wanted the phone." He eyed Delia and Julie stormily, his eyes flashing dark blue. "Why didn't either of you tell me?"

Delia answered. "Because! Eat your food."

"Because why? That's not a good answer."

Long ago Delia had told Julie to call her Delia; she had not yet offered that particular signal of adulthood to Peter. But then Peter was her godson; she had shown affection for both children, but Julie knew that Peter, named but without the "i" for Delia's much-loved husband, was really the pride and joy of her life, however Delia might try to conceal it. Delia said now, "I told you to eat. If I send this back to the kitchen you can go down there and cook for us. Mrs.—" she groped for the whistler's name.

Julie said, "The whistler—you know, Peter, Mrs. Martine, the cook—"

"—will leave," Delia concluded, pouring coffee now on her salad.

That distracted Peter, who stared. "Do you know what you are doing?"

"Don't be impertinent." Delia was at her sternest.

However, she did look with a flicker of surprise at her own hand, holding the coffeepot over her salad. She turned pink and thumped the pot back on the table.

Peter began to shovel food into his mouth and talk between shovelsful. "Sam says the bottle with the Judge's medicine in it was found—"

"For God's sake, stop that talk," Delia snapped.

Peter assumed a most improbable air of reproof. "Aunt

Delia! Swearing! And you promised to see to my religious instruction."

Delia blushed. "I did no such thing."

"Oh, yes, you did. When I was christened, at the altar, you swore to—to— I looked it up. I can't remember the exact words but that was the meaning of it. And I'm pretty sure you've never taken me to church. Let alone swearing. Really, Aunt Delia!"

This, Julie knew, was a discussion that could go on indefinitely. But Delia's natural authority asserted itself. "What else did Sam say?"

Peter put down his fork. His eyebrows were as heavy and golden-brown as his hair; his eyes steely dark blue. "Says everybody thinks Jim did it. That is, they don't say outright that Jim knew about the Judge's dicey heart and the medicine and somehow took that new bottle and threw it away, but they keep saying that it's very odd. You know! Jim coming back and—they say—the Judge discouraged his hope of anything at all. So they figure"—he screwed up his eyes so they were merely blue slits—"so they figure that with the Judge gone somebody else might not know so much about the case and be so determined to put Jim in jail. Or something."

"Finish your food," Delia snapped.

"Sure. I want to get back to Brookboro just as soon as I can. May I borrow your car, Julie?"

Delia rose, her pale blue eyes almost like ice. "You may not! You're too young to drive. Besides, Julie needs her car."

Peter subsided; then hope flashed into his face. "Julie, you are going to drive back home, aren't you? I'll go with you—"

Delia was still icy and sure of her authority.

"You will not. Julie is going to stay right here. So are you."

"Okay, Aunt Delia—when you look like that—"

"Peter," Delia said. It was only one word but it sounded dangerous.

Peter slumped back in his chair. But he was not licked yet. "Don't you want to know what's going on?"

"We know enough," Delia said.

"Okay." Peter ate, thought for a minute and said, "Do you know how it happened that Ollie had that accident?"

Julie stared. "But that has nothing to do with the Judge."

Peter shrugged. "Maybe not."

"See here!" Julie's voice was beginning to sound dangerous, too. "What are you trying to say?"

Peter's face assumed an unnatural innocence. "Why, nothing. Just that Ollie was very cautious about everything. He's worked at our place for years—before I was born, even. So why on earth should he suddenly slip and bust himself! Ain't like Ollie."

"Isn't," Delia said automatically.

"Yes'm," Peter said, with a little too much docility. Julie gave him a suspicious look, but his face was blank and calm.

"Now, Peter," she began, "you and Sam are not to get together on some wild scheme and—and—"

Peter's eyes had a glitter of laughter. "And do what? Try to get Jim out of trouble? You ought to be glad he's got at least two friends who believe in him."

"He has many friends who believe him," Delia said. "Now if you have finished, you can pick up these dishes, put them on the tray and send them down to the kitchen."

"Prehistoric," Peter mumbled but rose politely as Delia got up from her chair. Julie glanced back as she followed Delia toward the living room and saw Peter carefully putting down his plate for Beau and Pye, who, again, with perfectly poised if guarded amity, attacked the chicken casserole that Peter had been too excited to eat.

Julie said, "There's a new movie over on Lexington. I can't remember the name of it, but it's one of those wild outerspace, never-a-dull-moment things. Do you think Peter—"

"I'll tell him he can go," Delia said.

Peter, when approached on the subject, was quite obviously torn between two worlds. He thought of a way out. "It never hurts to take your mind off things, does it! Okay, thank you, Aunt Delia. I'll go now so I can get a seat. Sure to be long waiting lines."

He obligingly slammed the front door when he left.

Delia sank into a chair. "Sometimes I wonder if I ever should have taken on the job of bringing up you two."

"Oh, darling, certainly you should. You have been just great. Besides," Julie added practically, "there was really no one else."

Delia sighed and rallied. "John would tell you to go to work. Nothing like it for the glooms."

Julie didn't have much to do. She forced herself, however, to reopen the package of proofs she had made so long ago, it seemed to her, and to read carefully. She decided that she had written a shockingly bad novel, put the sheets together again, repackaged them and sat back in the one lounge chair. Nothing was interesting just then but real life. What was happening to Jim?

The doorbell rang at that moment and when Julie ran to open the door, Jim himself appeared as if summoned by her thoughts.

Behind him, his modest car stood, in use for the first time in five years. Jim drew her into the hall and closed the door and took her into his arms.

"There, there, don't cry—"

"But Jim—I was so happy, so happy—and now—"

"And now we'll have to go along as best we can. Darling, darling, Julie!"

"Oh, Jim—"

Quite a conversation, one side of her mind said critically. But real life was like that.

"What about your trip to Hartford? Anything hopeful?"

"No. Blanche tried but—no. I had to drive down to see you, Julie. I promise you we'll get out of all this. Put your face up—"

"Oh, Jim," she said again, but a little breathlessly, when she could speak at all.

"Sure, I'm still here. Did you think they had already sent me to prison?"

"Oh, Jim, that boy—that Sam—Peter's friend, phoned and said that people think you must have—"

"Taken that bottle of medicine and thrown it along the road in the hope the Judge would have a fatal heart attack and no medicine." Jim's words were firm but his face was white. "Of course I didn't. But I did see the Judge that morning. You know that. He did his best when he even listened to me."

"He told me. He was sad and grieved."

"I've got to find out who took the medicine if I can. The police may arrest me any moment."

He went into her workroom and sat on the edge of the desk. "I was such a damn fool! So wrong!"

"Wrong?"

"About leaving as I did. Nobody seems to believe in that law—and it was changed or repealed or—in any event, clearly it was not intended to include a capital crime. But just then, sure, I seized on it. There were those pieces, I showed you, in those good Connecticut newspapers. It seemed to me, mistakenly, yes, but at the time it struck me as a way out until some evidence to exonerate me was discovered. I ought to have stayed, let myself be arrested, indicted, anything, but I didn't. And once I had run away I did have the sense to know that that alone was incriminating to me. But now I'm older—oh, I've told you all this: I've got to dig up some evidence and the first step, it seems to me, is to dig further into Alben Walker's past."

Jim swung one leg in the air, studying his neatly shod foot as though he had never seen it before. "He's got to have had more of a past than so far anybody has discovered. None of you really knows anything about it. That is, nobody I know of around Brookboro. My father tried. Blanche tried. But there's got to be something or other in his past which would give somebody a real hard-and-fast reason for shooting him. I've got to dig that out. Fact is, I've got to dig out everything I can about him."

"How are you going to do that?"

Jim's face clouded. "I don't really know, but I can try. I'll start with that guy, that television guy who interviewed my father and found out he had a son. He was really very friendly about the whole thing. He tried to stop my father's talking of a lost son, because he knew what the—call it the harvest, would be. Scores of letters. This TV man was a kind of investigative reporter on some newspaper before he veered into television. I keep thinking that maybe he can give me some notion to start me in looking up all I can about Walker. I may be wrong, but I'll try him."

"Do you remember his name? Channel? All that?"

"Sure. Looked him up. Phoned him. Have a date to see him tomorrow after his late broadcast. Oh, it may come to nothing. But if he's the man I think he is, he'll tell me how —where—to start."

"Oh, Jim, yes! Try, try anything, anybody."

"I will. Stick with me, Julie."

"As if I could help it."

Jim looked at her very gravely. "You really are a darling," he said, as if making a vow.

"I want to be your darling," Julie said candidly. "But you'll have to stop kissing Lisa. So—so fervently. I saw you. The night the Judge—that is, that night."

Jim grinned. "You can't deny that she's a very pretty girl."

"I don't give a hoot about that. Just remember—"

"Oh, now look here! Can I help it?"

"Yes," said Julie firmly.

Jim laughed and put his arms around her. "You can't be my darling or my wife or my anything until I've got out of this. Goodbye, for now."

But it turned out to be a lengthy goodbye, rather as if he

were going on a long and dangerous trip. As indeed, Julie thought after he had gone, was true. A very long and a very dangerous trip. She closed the door and Delia said, "I heard Jim leave. Any news?"

"Not really. That is, not yet."

"Does he know that people are saying it's very strange that his return and the Judge's murder should coincide?"

"We didn't talk much of that. He's still free. And he's going to try to get some facts about Walker that—"

"I see." Delia was no fool. "But Julie, I don't quite see how anything can be dug up about Walker at this late date."

"There must be something."

Delia sighed. "One can hope. It's about time for a nightcap. Where's Peter?"

"Not home yet," Julie began just as Beau gave a pleased bark of recognition and the doorbell rang.

It was Peter, rather flushed and excited. "You ought to let me have a latchkey, Aunt Delia. If you make me stay here."

"I don't make you stay anywhere," Delia said. "A boy of your age with a latchkey!"

"Other fellows have them."

"Well, you don't. Not in New York. In Brookboro, that would be different."

Julie intervened. "How was the movie?"

Peter sparkled. "Terrific. Hello, Beau." He fondled Beau's handsome topknot and asked ingenuously, "Aunt Delia, does your godmotherhood permit a man a nightcap?"

Delia bridled, thought it over and softened. "You are too young for that, too. Oh, all right. Only one now."

The next morning came like any other clear, autumn morning, blue and gold and crisply cool. Peter was apparently on his good behavior and walked Beau and even fed both him and the cat. Mrs. Martine had a few words with Peter about the presence of the pets but he soothed her, probably with the most extreme flattery about her cooking.

Julie pretended to apply herself to work but listened for

the telephone. Delia, she was sure, was listening too.

The telephone did not ring; noon and afternoon came and not even one of Delia's many friends telephoned. However, the doorbell did ring late in the day. Peter answered the door, and Julie heard him say, "What do *you* want?"

"How very rude!" Delia cried, hurrying to the door.

George Wingate appeared. Delia said quietly but rather clearly, "Not rude enough." She fastened a thin smile upon her pretty face. "Why, George! What brings you here?"

"You ought to know. Where's Jim?"

Delia began to sputter. Julie cut her short. "Why don't you ask Jim?" she said shortly.

George insisted; his reddish beard waggled, his chubby face was angry. "You know perfectly well where he is and what he's trying to do. It's no use. He'll be arrested and tried and sent to prison, where he belongs. Julie, I want to talk to you." He turned toward Delia. "Privately."

Julie said stiffly, "What about?"

"Don't say it's none of my business. It is my business. And it's you I want to talk to. What about it?"

Delia looked him over and after a perceptible consideration, merely lifted one blond eyebrow.

Julie interpreted it as consent. "All right. There's my workroom."

"Fine." George had a flash of his usual self-assurance. "Where is it?"

Delia's pretty, plump face now expressed nothing. Peter mumbled something unintelligible. Julie said, "This way."

Once in her small workroom, George looked around with an air of shocked distaste. "Looks like a hole in the wall. Seems to me your aunt could have done better for you than this. Only a desk, books and filing cabinet here, and one easy chair!"

Whereupon he took the easy chair. Julie sat down at the desk and really felt a kind of authority as she did so. It was *her* room. She could order him out of it if she wished.

"That chair seems to please you," she said nastily.

In spite of his weight, George had long fingers and rather thin hands. He stroked his wispy beard, which seemed to give him confidence, and leaned forward. "All right, Julie. You asked for it—that is, you must have guessed long ago. I am very much in love with you and I—"

Julie leaned too far back in her chair, which started to tip over. George jumped up, grasped it, and beamed down at her, with a glow in his pale eyes. "See! You know I've been in love with you all this time. Now Jim is back you feel you can throw me over."

"Wait, George! You really—" She got her breath. "You have no right to say any such thing."

"Right! Why, of course I have the right. You've known it all along. You've pretended that you were waiting in the hope Jim would return—or that you could go to join him wherever he took refuge. But I knew, all the time, that I was the one you really wanted."

"George!" Astonishment nearly choked her.

He jumped up and tried to take her hand. She pulled away and he grasped her by the shoulders and pulled harder until he had her on her feet.

"Of course you knew. Women always know. But I couldn't say anything until I had a job and could support you. Without my father's help."

"But, George—No! Don't! Let me go!"

"You played up to me every time I saw you. Don't deny it."

She thought of the times she had met him casually and had tried to conceal her dislike. Apparently she had succeeded too well. She ought to have allowed for George's immense self-conceit.

"I do deny it. Truly. Now listen to me, George—"

"You listen to me. I know that you—that I am the man you really want. Of course you feel sorry for Jim. Everybody feels sorry for him. So do I. He may not be my father's legal son but—"

"Stop it! John Wingate never—"

"Never had anything to do with any woman except his wife? Don't be a fool!"

"That is not the point. I know that Jim is John's son. That's all I need to know."

He sniggered softly. "John's son—oh, yes, my father knows that Jim is his bastard son. But he doesn't intend anybody else to know it. Sometimes I have wondered who Jim's mother really was. The only person I can think of whom John seems fond of—so to speak—is Blanche Surton. But she's an iceberg, that woman. Iceberg—" A sly look came into his face. "But that's why she is such a friend to Jim. Isn't it?"

Ten

"No! George, please listen to reason!"

"That is reason. You must admit that."

"I don't. I don't admit anything you've said. And I am not in love with you and I don't intend to—"

"Marry me?" George laughed. "Oh, but of course you will. Why, you've been after me all this time—"

She took hold of the edge of the desk behind her and tried to make her voice calm. "George, really, you are entirely mistaken."

"Listen, Julie, I know a thing or two. And now I have a job. Five weeks of winter stock. Now I can promise to support you. And of course you are rich with that silly novel of yours."

This was more than even a young and new writer could take. "Silly, did you say?"

"Oh, dearest girl, I didn't mean that! I think you are very clever. But my father helped you, and he'll be so pleased about our marriage that he'll help us any time we want."

Julie looked at him thoughtfully. "George," she said, surprising herself. "You simply cannot be John's son."

He stared at her; one narrow hand went up as if to cover his twitching lips and flimsy beard. "What on earth do you mean?"

"John couldn't have fathered you! Not John!"

"He is my father! I have proofs. Why, he accepts me. I'm his son—"

"No!" said Julie.

"You little—" He stopped himself with such a visible effort that she was actually touched with an atavistic sense of uneasiness. But he couldn't spring at her with those long clammy fingers and, yes, suddenly wicked eyes. She tried to keep a vestige of self-control and failed. "Get out!"

He stared at her. "Me! Get out!"

"Now."

"But—" He glanced at a very elaborate watch on his wrist. "Of course, I must go. I've got to get to rehearsal anyway. This first scheduled play will be easier because of Lisa."

"Lisa is in the cast? Your special friend."

George smiled. "You see! You are jealous!"

"No, listen to me! I am not in love with you. I never was. Just—get out!"

It didn't seem to touch him in the least. Instead he leaped forward and fumbled for her hand. "Don't talk to me like that! You know you don't mean it!"

"I do mean it. Everything! John's son! Why, he *can't* be your father!"

"Sweet, you are a spitfire! Does you credit. A girl with temperament. Now then, let's have no more argument—"

"That is enough, George!" She went toward the door and realized only then that George, showing unexpected perspicacity, had closed it. She felt, just for an instant, quite cut off from everybody, anybody. He stood between her and the door and smiled.

"Open that door, George!"

"Not until you promise—"

"George, no!" The door might be closed but she had a voice and used it. "Peter! Delia!"

George turned a peculiar greenish color; but he moved away from the door, jerked it open and gave her a smiling bow. "I'll be back. I know you better than you know yourself. Oh, hello, Peter. My, you've grown."

Peter was in the doorway, looking very young and stringy but also very strong. Good for his school's athletic program! Julie thought briefly. Good for Peter's interest in such things as football! George observed Peter's glowering presence, shrugged his handsome jacket over his soft, rather narrow shoulders and laughed. "All right, Peter. You don't need to look like that."

Peter shot one glance at Julie and said, "You'd better go, George, before I throw you out."

"Oh, Peter!" George said as if shocked. "How can you say such a thing! Goodbye, Aunt Delia—"

"Aunt?" said Delia coming into view behind Peter.

"Oh, sorry." George had quite recovered his confidence in himself. "You see, everybody calls you 'aunt.' Forgive me. But I may have a delightful reason to call you 'aunt' myself. Goodbye, darling," he nodded at Julie. "I'll see you soon again."

"Not if I know it!" It was a childish reply but came out.

George rather swiftly slid past Peter toward the outer door. Peter followed him, but the door closed with a thud that resounded.

"I didn't kick him," he said defensively to Delia. "Wanted, to, but I didn't."

"Too bad," Delia said coolly. "I heard almost all of it. You were really shouting, Julie! I don't blame you. The idea!"

"He is impossible! He says I am in love with him! Why, Delia, I never thought of such a thing! I can't stand him!"

Delia frowned. Peter scowled. Neither spoke for a moment. Finally Delia sighed. "I wonder what he intends by that?"

Peter replied, "He intends to get Jim back in prison and get Julie and then get John Wingate's money. Clear as daylight."

Delia said, "I'm going to tell John about this."

"That's not quite all," Julie said. "He says that John is Jim's father, of course, and that Blanche was—is—Jim's mother. He says that's why she is such a friend of Jim's."

After a long moment Delia said, "I didn't hear that!"

"Neither did I," Peter said. "Why, that—" He muttered an expletive under his breath for which Delia should have vigorously reproved him. She didn't. Actually she seemed to agree with Peter's brief but pungent summing up of George's character. She said at last thoughtfully, "We'll think—"

"There's dinner," said Peter. "The whistler is in good form."

Mrs. Martine was clearly annoyed at their delay in replying to her summons and whistled imperiously again.

Silently, thinking hard, they went into the dining room and Peter sat down, remembered his manners and stood awkwardly up again to hold Delia's chair. He let Julie see to her own chair and hurried to the dumbwaiter.

Pye and Beau both sat near Julie, watching her with the patient gaze of canine and feline determination. Food? But surely they had been fed. Peter came back and took his own chair, glancing down at the cat and dog. "I fed them both," he said. "All they could eat. Now shut up, both of you! It's roast beef, very expensive. But I'll save some for you."

Since neither cat nor dog had made so much as a slight noise this was undeserved, but Peter's command had such remarkable authority that the cat retired to another chair and Beau sat down at Julie's knee. Both, however, continued to eye the table.

Delia served, but her hands, as always, sparkling with the diamonds her husband had given her, were unsteady. At last she said, "I don't quite see how that could be." But there was an element of doubt in her voice.

Peter picked it up so quickly that his ears seemed to stand out. "You can't mean that Blanche might actually be John Wingate's—"

"Don't interrupt," said Delia, but mildly. "I'm sure not. There has never been a word of gossip about her and John. Not even a whisper. I'd have known about it," said Delia with a confidence which Julie was certain was deserved. Delia knew everything. "Blanche has been away—I mean, really away, out of the country—only once or twice that I remember."

Peter was all ears. "Where did she go? For how long? How long ago?"

"I'm trying to remember. Yes, once, before her mother needed so much care, she made a trip to somewhere in Europe."

"When?" Peter said.

"Oh, it must have been about twenty-odd years ago. There was some kind of student grant. Then she didn't go away at all until a trip to Bermuda—I think. Perhaps Jamaica— somewhere in the Caribbean. That was only a short trip, about—oh, six or seven years ago."

Peter said sharply, "Would her first trip have been as long as twenty-seven years ago?"

Delia frowned. "Why, yes, I think so. I don't really remember."

Peter was quick, not always a commendable trait, Julie reflected. "That would be about Jim's age, wouldn't it, Julie?"

"Yes," she replied. "But, Delia, I can't believe—"

"Neither can I. Jim resembles John, no doubt of that. But as to Blanche—if that's what you are thinking of, Peter—"

Peter nodded, his eyes glittering with interest.

"No! You are not to make anything of your notion, Peter!"

"George's notion," Peter said.

"That conceited ass!" said Delia with such vehemence that Peter grinned. "Now, George—does look like Elaine. Not much. But some. Same character in a way. Not dependable."

"But Delia," Julie began, "do you think that Blanche— No, it's impossible."

Delia said with spirit, "You were far too young to know. Good heavens! You weren't even born then. Jim is five years older than you. Certainly Blanche is properly concerned about Jim!"

"In love with John," Peter declared through Yorkshire pudding and gravy.

"You don't know what you're saying!" But Delia's reproof softened as always when she looked at her godson.

"Why, sure! So just ask her straight out if Jim is her son. Why not?"

Julie gave a kind of squeak. "*Peter! No!*"

More collectedly, Delia said, "Really, Peter, one doesn't walk up to one's best friend and say—"

Peter went on, however, in an absurd falsetto as if he were speaking for Delia, "My dear friend Blanche, by the way, did you have an affair with John Wingate and, in a reasonable time, produce a son who looks like him?" Peter stopped the falsetto voice and added, looking rather scared, "But that's true. Jim does look like John."

"And George looks like Elaine," Delia said. "That is, as I remember her."

Peter seemed to think that over and suddenly said, "John may have been a very busy man."

That shocked Delia. "Peter! Never let me hear you—"

But Peter had not finished. "Didn't one of you tell me that Blanche met Jim when he came back?"

"Oh, yes." Delia glanced at Julie. "Blanche explained that

to me, that night, over the telephone. Before you took your receiver, Julie, and listened in. He phoned her from Paris. Certainly, because," Delia said with triumph, "he knew he would need a good lawyer. Blanche couldn't stop his coming. So she met him at Kennedy and argued with him and left him in her apartment along with his luggage, while she came to see me and find out whether or not Julie was still—"

"Hadn't he kept in touch with Blanche all the time he was away?" That was Peter, ears sticking out.

Delia shrugged. "Why should he? He sent postcards or something to his father, so his father would know that he was all right and had jobs to keep him busy and supplied with money. You must *never ever* suggest that Blanche is Jim's mother. Understand me, Peter?"

"Yes'm," said Peter. "Honest, Aunt Delia."

"Never! Now that's settled, do you want some dessert? It's pecan pie. I saw it."

Peter's favorite dessert, naturally. Delia relaxed, nodded and looked just slightly smug as Peter removed the dinner service, shot over to the dumbwaiter, sent the big, stacked tray down with his own whistle and pushed the electric button.

Peter's whistle was far too shrill. Julie cried, "Oh, stop it, Peter! Our eardrums!"

Delia took her hands away from her ears but half-smiled. "Boys have to be boys."

"Boys can have good manners," Julie said tartly, wishing not for the first time that she had boxed Peter's ears when he was younger and less able to defend himself. All the same, George had taken himself off rather promptly when faced by Peter, who might still be a little gangling but had certainly developed muscles.

There was a certain amount of thudding and whistling as Peter returned bearing the pecan pie, and beaming.

"Coffee," Delia reminded him.

"Oh, sure. It's on that thing—" He scowled at the dumbwaiter. "I'll put it in the living room. I really think," said Peter all at once very grave and sedate, the man of the house, "I do think we must talk this over and—make our plans." He went back to the dumbwaiter and returned with the coffee tray, which he took into the living room and put carefully down on the table beside Delia's huge armchair.

After they were all seated in the living room, Peter leaned back in a lounge chair, put his fingers together in an arc and said, really quite judicially, "Now then, just what do we do?"

"Oh, Peter," Julie cried. "We can't do anything!"

"Why?" Peter looked at her reprovingly. "You too scared?"

"Why, because—you listen to me, Peter. We'll have none of your hairbrained schemes and you are not Sherlock Holmes, so you needn't try to look like him."

Peter got up, handed her coffee, offered sugar, took his own cup, sat down again, unruffled, and at once got up again. "There's the phone." But on his way to Julie's workroom he tossed a polite "May I—?" over his shoulder.

She didn't reply. It was already too late, for she heard him at the telephone on her desk.

"You don't say . . . not really . . . I can't believe . . . oh, not Jim. He couldn't—" There was a pause. Then he said, "Sure, I'll ask her. But, Sam . . . oh, sure. Yes. Thanks."

He came back. This time he looked seventeen, no more. His face was white and his eyes showed wide black pupils. "Julie, Sam says Jim has gone away again! Escaped! Just as they were about to charge him with another murder. The Judge's this time."

"But that's not possible! Jim couldn't even have known of the Judge's medicine. And Jim has not escaped! He's right here— That is, not here in the house, but I know what he's doing—"

"What? And where is he?" Peter demanded.

"I don't know precisely where he is, but I know what he's trying to do." Peter waited; Julie felt she must explain. "He says he thinks, and I agree," Julie said firmly, "that there ought to be some—well, time spent in tracing back, digging back into Alben Walker's past. Jim is sure there had to be a motive."

"And of course he's right. But he'll have to come back and—" Delia stopped as a high-pitched scream rose from the basement.

It came again in such terror that Delia and Julie ran for the narrow winding stairs off the dining room, leading down to the subterranean kitchen. Peter somehow contrived to get ahead of them and Beau ahead of Peter.

A little, round, black-haired and beetle-browed woman stood in the kitchen staring wildly at the small door that provided her own entrances and exits.

"You—you—" she yelled, "I'm calling the police!"

"Mrs. Whistler!" Delia cried, forgetting herself. "I mean, Mrs. Martine, what on earth is the matter?"

"Out there! In the bushes! Those things you put around the trash cans! He's out there—"

Peter dashed out the open door.

Pye was already munching with determination but elegance upon what seemed to be a scrap of roast beef; she gave Mrs. Martine a cool glance and kept on chewing.

"That cat was here! She came down here and I didn't know it! Oh, Mrs. Van Clive, this is too much! I don't mind the dog. I'm used to him but a cat, too—and a man hiding out there! Waiting for me!"

She waddled to a telephone on the counter near Pye, who gave her a cool look, leaped to the top of the refrigerator and sat there . . . quietly smiling? No, merely licking her paw in preparation to washing her face.

Mrs. Martine had dialed the telephone rapidly, and someone must have answered. "And I was saving all those meat scraps for the dog— What? Who? No, I'm not talking to you. I want the police. Oh, then if you are the police come here, right away! Hurry—there's a strange man!"

Delia took the telephone away from the cook and spoke with reasonable calm. "Police? Oh, Sergeant. I'm Mrs. Van Clive and we've had a scare, a man was apparently hiding near the kitchen door and my cook is frightened and— Yes, I'd like it very much. Thank you—"

She gave her address with a barely quivering voice. Peter came back into the kitchen. "Whoever it was, he's gone now."

The cook started to scream again—at least she opened her mouth—and Delia said, "If he's gone— Oh, it was only somebody prowling!"

The cook cried, "He took my apron!" She fumbled wildly around her neat print dress. "I tell you he grabbed my apron. That is, he grabbed at me and got my apron."

"Then it ought to be out there." Delia was exerting all her self-control, which was considerable.

Peter's eyes were shining with excitement. "There's no apron out there!"

"It doesn't matter," Delia said hurriedly. "You have other aprons, you know. And I'll replace—"

"You can't!" Mrs. Martine shrieked. "It had my house keys in the pocket. How am I going to get into my apartment?"

Delia again tried to take control. "There must be a spare key. You don't live alone. Your husband will let you in—"

Mrs. Martine was simmering down. "Oh, well, it's your loss, Mrs. Van Clive. And the police—"

"Here they come! The patrol car!" Peter cried and ran to open the small door again. The police car shrieked nearer, even more shrilly than Mrs. Martine had, and came to a stop, red light revolving on top and two bright lights showing upon trash cans and shrubbery.

"All the people in the Cove will hear that! Thank heaven, they stopped that alarm!" Delia pulled her chin up, stiffened her back, and went to meet a burly young man in blue.

"Madam?" he said, politely removing his cap. "Prowlers?"

"One," said Delia, cutting off Mrs. Martine, who was probably going to say a dozen.

Peter was at the officer's elbow. "He got away. I ran out to look."

"Well, now, we'll just circle the Cove. We were only around the corner. Guess you don't have many prowlers here. Glad he didn't take anything."

"My apron!" wailed Mrs. Martine.

"I told you. There are others." Delia smoothed back her hair and looked very majestic.

Mrs. Martine gave her a peculiar dark look.

The look alarmed Delia, who turned on her most friendly smile, "Oh, you mustn't let such an incident frighten you! Heavens, it's never happened before—"

"And never will again," said the cook resolutely. "If you'll just pay me up now, Mrs. Van Clive."

"But surely—you mustn't—really, I don't want you to go," said Delia, almost pleading.

Mrs. Martine did not soften. "Fact is, once is too much. You cat, you shut up!" She whirled around toward the cat, who had muttered something. But the cat's fiery blue gaze was fastened upon Beau, who had politely advanced toward a plate of meat scraps on the table, which he seemed to feel ought to have been intended for him.

Delia did not like defeat. There were times when she had to accept it. The young officer looked a little amused.

Making a great effort, Julie knew, Delia recovered. "Very well. If you'll come upstairs. I'll give you a check. Immediately."

The cook seemed to hesitate; perhaps she hadn't counted the cost of her recalcitrance. "Well, but—not many people will put up with a cat." But she put down the plate of meat scraps for Beau, who accepted it as his due but also with a gracious thank you, by way of a pleasant tail wag.

Delia became all feminine warmth and charm. "Captain," she began but the young officer corrected her.

"Not Captain."

"I know, I know. I only want to thank you. So prompt!"

"We were close by, in a prowl car. Now, we'll just take a swing around the Cove. Mrs.—you"—he said to the cook—"might go with us. See if you can spot anybody resembling your prowler."

The cook snatched up a shiny raincoat and said over her shoulder, "Thank you. I must get home. You find the prowler. And you wash and put away that plate, Peter."

"Mister Peter," Peter whispered under his breath, as Mrs. Martine cast a threatening glance around the kitchen and marched belligerently out the door.

Julie said in a low voice, "Peter, you are really getting to be very stuffy."

Peter refused to be affected. "She ought to say 'Mister.' They all do."

"Who all do?" Julie tried briefly to think of anybody at all who still rejoiced in old-fashioned and plentiful cooks.

"I can read, can't I?" Peter said. "Even back to Victorian days."

"See that you read— Oh, never mind." Delia was smiling and thanking the young officer. Mrs. Martine's sturdy figure had disappeared. Then the smooth murmur of the police car moved away. Delia closed the kitchen door. "Well . . ." It was a long sigh. "At any rate I don't think she really intends to leave me. She's such a marvelous cook! And while she doesn't care for the dumbwaiter, she puts up with it."

"Also," Julie said rather sharply, "she enjoys her substantial paycheck."

Delia's light blue eyes flashed. "What of it! If I can pay for what I want, why shouldn't I? Come on, Peter, Beau will follow us. So will the cat."

The cat did not follow them, she led the way: she dropped down from the refrigerator very neatly and went like a swift brown and beige shadow up the stairway.

Once in the living room Pye ensconced herself comfortably on the huge lid of the famous yellow piano. Nobody ever treated it so casually, but Delia gave Pye a hopeless glance and sat down as if exhausted.

Eleven

"Alarms and excursions," Peter said. "I wonder what really did happen?" His long legs sprawled out as he relaxed, altogether too coolly, in a comfortable chair. How could his legs have got so long in a few months, even a year? Julie decided that Peter's school had many things to recommend it, not the least of which must be good food.

However, Peter drew himself up, put his fingers together carefully and said, "Now we must evaluate this situation."

Delia sat up, too. "Evaluate? What do you mean?"

"Just that. Explore it. Decide—"

"What about?"

"Too many peculiar things. Jim's return. The Judge's murder—"

Delia's face took on a marble hardness. "We'll not talk of that."

"Everybody in Brookboro is talking about it. And George's coming here and claiming that Jim is really Blanche's son. Now, you can't say that that's normal, Aunt Delia. Now then, to evaluate—"

"Peter," Julie said. "Go to bed."

"Why?" Peter had got into one of his stubborn moods.

Julie would have liked to slap him, but he was much bigger than she. Her onetime little brother was not now to be sent to bed like a child. Besides, obviously, he wouldn't have gone. However, she had to say something.

"Because you see yourself as a judge. I mean a Sherlock."

"That's what he reads," Delia said. "Would you like a hansom cab, Peter? To take you to collect evidence?"

"Wouldn't mind it at all if you can fetch it up at the door," Peter grinned.

"And while we are speaking of it," said Delia, no mean Sherlock herself, "what have you and Sam been up to, at school?"

"Huh?" Peter came down off his high horse.

"You said something about vacation."

"Well, I—that is—oh, come on, Aunt Delia!"

Delia continued, remorselessly. "It's far past Labor Day. It's nowhere near Thanksgiving. What vacation, then?"

Peter stroked the cat's elegant black head. "Well, you forgot."

Julie had a brainstorm. "Halloween is coming!"

Peter gave her a dark frown. "Smart, aren't you?"

"What did you and Sam do?" Delia was trying to be very stern and almost succeeding.

Peter wriggled. "Well, that is—"

"Don't make up things, Peter." Delia tried for but did not achieve icy disapproval.

Peter sighed. "Okay. We—that is—oh, the guy who teaches history is such a—"

"Peter!"

"Okay, okay. We don't like him much. Has a funny accent and expects us to do a lot of homework and well, anyway—" Peter let out his breath. "I'll come clean. We fixed up a dummy. Dressed it up in a fancy top hat and tailcoat and striped pants and put a pumpkin on its head. Looked kind of—"

110

"And he saw it?"

"Sure. We meant—that is—yes, he saw it, right outside the history class, in the hall—"

"And knew it was you and Sam."

"Must have. I don't see how."

"Where did you get the clothes?" Julie asked, with genuine curiosity. "You didn't steal them, I hope."

"No. That is, we didn't steal them. We only borrowed them. From the Wingate house—"

"The Wingate house—"

"Sure. They belonged to George Wingate. Some role he had. He likes acting and— Oh," said Peter and dug into a back pocket of his jeans. "This is funny. George has been in Las Vegas."

"Las Vegas!" Delia sat up with a jerk. "How do you know?"

"This." Peter showed a blue, rather tattered piece of paper. "It's a cleaner's bill. From Las Vegas. 'Sun and Desert Cleaners.' That's what it says."

He handed the limp paper to Delia.

She examined it slowly. "That's what it is."

"Want to see it, Julie?" Peter offered obligingly.

"No. That is, yes." Peter brought the paper to her, and it was certainly, as he said, a receipted bill for cleaning.

"I wonder what he was doing in Las Vegas?" Delia said. "Is there a date on the receipt?"

Julie and Peter bent their heads over it again. "No," said Julie.

"But it's kind of funny, don't you think?" Peter was clearly delighted at getting away from any discussion of his certainly deserved enforced vacation.

Delia was not deterred. "So you were suspended. The year before you are supposed to enter university—if any good university will have you. How long before you go back to school, if " she added ominously, "they will let you come back."

"Oh, sure. Sam's father and you—oh, sure. We've been let out of stir for only two weeks."

"Out of stir?" Delia was pink-cheeked, trying to conceal a quiver of amusement. "I take it you refer to your school."

"Well, I mean—that is—oh, come on, Aunt Delia! Aren't you glad I was here when George arrived and—"

"Yes," Julie said firmly. "He'll be all right, Delia. This paper—"

"Sure." Peter brightened. "Better show that to the police, huh?"

"Well, I—we'll tell Jim—"

Peter sank back into a chair. Pye leaped down from the piano and up to drape herself around his neck. "What did you do with George's clothes?" Delia asked.

"Oh, Sam will sneak—I mean, return them. Hat, too. Looked funny on the pumpkin."

The doorbell rang. "As if on cue," said Peter. "Probably the police again." He rose, Beau barked. The cat clung to Peter's shoulders with an air of regal ability to cope with anything at all.

Peter ran for the door.

It was not the police again. Instead, Jim came in. "Hi, Peter! Julie—"

"Oh, Jim, tell me!"

"I saw the television man! He remembered the whole thing about my father and the letters that poured into the station. He couldn't have been more interested or more helpful. He said he had followed my father's career with interest and wondered what had become of me. So, now don't look scared, Aunt Delia. He's not going to broadcast a single word of this. At least, not now. Maybe—well, later. But by then—"

Peter cried, "What did he do?"

"Sit down, boy. I'm telling you." Jim too sank down and brushed his hand over his hair. "Of course he knows all kinds of people in the newspaper business. Some are special friends, naturally. He got hold of a reporter. We met for dinner at a place near Rockefeller Center and talked. Then the newspaper man looked at my reports of Walker's murder."

He gave Julie a rather apologetic glance. "I had the clippings with me, you see. Anyway, both men looked at the clippings and especially at a few reproductions of snapshots of Walker. The TV man Brown didn't recognize the pictures of Walker, but the reporter wasn't sure. They weren't very clear. He said Walker must have been camera shy and I think that alone interested him. He said most people love to pose for a camera any time."

"Go on!" said Julie.

"Yes. So after a while he phoned a society reporter, a nice woman, who came to meet us, and we all had coffee and—"

"Something to drink. Go on." That was Delia. Julie wondered, on the fringe of her mind, just how nice the society reporter was and at the same fraction of an instant realized that if she intended to question the attractiveness of every woman Jim encountered, she was in for a hard life. So was he, as a matter of fact.

He was going on. "We kind of struck pay dirt, there. I mean, she did remember Walker. Something about him, that is. Not much, but some. She couldn't remember what it was precisely just then, but she had, she said, tons of notes on file, and she could get at them. But then she thought she remembered him, living in New York for a time and sort of hanging around art galleries and, as she recalled it, he wasn't much liked. However, he wasn't called Walker. He was called, or called himself, Count something or other. She wasn't sure. And she said she believed he had made rather a kind of thing of being very active socially but he was not actually accepted."

"*Count!*" Peter shouted, inducing a sound of Siamese disapproval from Pye.

"A count!" Delia cried. "That handkisser!"

"It figures!" Peter said in a man-of-the-world manner.

Jim sighed. "Get me a drink, Peter, will you. That is, if I may," he added to Delia.

"Get a drink for each of us," said Delia handsomely, but added, "a very light one for you, Peter."

Peter brightened and headed for the dining room cabinet.

Julie said, "First Count something, then plain Mr. Walker! Could that have any connection with all his papers being missing after the murder?"

"Possibly. Certainly there was something in those papers that the murderer was determined to destroy."

Delia put her hands to her hair, pushed it back and said thoughtfully, "Of course, all of us thought that at the time. He had to have some kind of papers. Even if he kept no personal letters, there had to be—oh, records, tax statements, bank statements, something. It seemed so clear that the murderer felt that something in those papers would give evidence as to the motive for the murder."

"Seems so," Jim said flatly. "Hard to prove."

Peter came back with four glasses on a silver tray, ice clinking in each. "Hope I got your poisons right," he said cheerfully.

"Boys!" said Delia in a deprecating but indulgent tone.

Peter sat down, his own glass in his hand. "Now if we take some time to evaluate—"

"Peter!" said Julie dangerously.

"I mean it. Let's get down to brass tacks. Is Blanche really your mother, Jim?"

"What!" Jim didn't drop his glass but it was a near thing. He stared at Peter. "Blanche is my good friend and a good lawyer. What on earth gave you the idea that she could be my mother?"

"George," said Peter nonchalantly. "He was here, you know. Trying to get Julie to marry him—"

"*George!*" Jim turned to Julie.

"Oh, she refused him. Was about to shove him out the door. I," said Peter not really boastfully but proudly, "told him to get out and he did."

"*George!* I thought he was in love with Lisa," Jim said.

Delia intervened as Peter couldn't resist his grown-up drink and his face was hidden for a moment in his glass. "He wants all he can get of John's money. The Judge may have left Lisa nothing. George wants Julie. He knows John likes her, and he wants you tried and almost certainly in prison, Jim, and Julie his wife and—"

Peter emerged, "And a clear field to his goal. Without you to run interference."

Jim shook his head as if to assist clearer reason. "This is preposterous! I mean all of it! Blanche my mother! My God! And George after you, Julie—"

"I—we got rid of him," Peter said again. "Even Beau was upset. About to take a nip at him."

"Beau never bites anybody," Julie began in defense.

Peter laughed derisively. "You didn't see him. You were too upset."

"This," Jim said, "simply makes no sense. That is, I don't really know George. We somehow never—"

"Never were friends," Peter said and swallowed more of his drink.

"That's enough, Peter," Delia said sharply.

"But *Blanche!*" Jim repeated in a stunned way. "*No!*"

Julie took over. "George says that is why she is so firm a friend. But George—"

"Aunt Delia said he was a conceited ass," Peter said smugly.

"Peter!" Delia bristled a little. "The point is right now, Sam, Peter's friend in Brookboro, says that the police are trying to find you, Jim. He says they have orders to hold you on suspicion. They think that you may have got that bottle

115

out of the way, the medicine, I mean, because the Judge told
you he couldn't help you. And then he had that fatal heart
attack and so you—"

"So I may have arranged that," Jim said. "Only logical.
I return and the Judge does not encourage me. I didn't even
know he had any medicine. Or had a bad heart, for that
matter. But I think I'll try to stay out of the way of the police
until I can find something, anything."

Delia said, "This newspaper woman! Perhaps she *can* find
something helpful about Walker—*Count*—" She couldn't
have hissed the remark, but at the tone in her voice Pye sat
up with interest and twitched her tail. "Until you get something—"

"A line on Walker's past," Peter contributed sagely.

"You'll have to stay here," Delia concluded.

Julie welcomed that idea for a moment but only a moment.
"They'll look here first. You'll have to stay at Blanche's
apartment. They may not look there. They may not even
know she keeps an apartment in the city. And if she *is* your
mother—"

"*Oh, no! Not Blanche!*"

"How do you know?" Delia asked.

Jim thumped his hand on the arm of his chair. "It is
simply, completely impossible!" He seemed to hunt around
in his mind for evidence and said, "Blanche likes justice and
thank God she likes me and my father enough to try to find
a way out for me!"

"You haven't got it yet," Peter said, sticking to facts.

"No. But I'll not give up yet!"

"Stay here for the night, anyway, Jim." Delia's invitation
was like a command. "Peter, run up to the room next to
yours and see that there are sheets and all that—"

"Women," said Peter in a denigrating way. But when
Delia spoke in a certain fashion he knew better than to defy
her.

116

"Now, then," Delia said, rising. "It's late."

Jim shook his head. "I can't stay here, Aunt Delia. Julie's right. They'll look here for me, and I can't get you into trouble—"

"I'd like to see anybody forbidding me to have a guest." Delia was icy.

Peter had more to say. "Aunt Delia, you didn't tell Jim about the prowler—"

Jim stared at Delia. "Prowler?"

"Oh, it's nothing." Delia smoothed down her skirt. "Only a notion of the cook's. We sent for the police. A patrol car came. They couldn't have missed a prowler anywhere in the neighborhood."

"But what would a prowler want?"

"Nothing, I tell you. She was hysterical. Saw a shadow."

"Saw a man," Julie said. "Mrs. Martine could not have invented all that."

Delia gave her a scathing look. "That woman could invent anything. She saw a shadow, screamed, ran in the house."

"But where!"

"At the kitchen door, of course. It's that little door not far from the front door. It and the trash cans are supposedly hidden by shrubbery. There's only the streetlight."

"What would a prowler want?"

"What does any city prowler want?" Delia said with dignity. But she waited a moment, her pretty hand, with all its diamonds, sparkling on the back of the chair she had risen from.

"Good night, now, Julie, Jim. Don't stay up too late."

Jim rose and took Julie's hand. "We'll not stay up at all. I'm not going to give the police a chance to bother you. I'll go to Blanche's apartment."

Delia stopped dead still. "But how can you get in? Is she there?"

"No. But I have the key."

"You have the key," Delia said slowly.

"Why, yes. She told me to use it, if I ever needed it. Good night and thank you—"

He took Delia's hand and added with a short laugh, "Trust me. I'll not bite," and kissed her cheek.

He put his arm around Julie and kissed her, but not lightly, called good night, told Peter to be sure to bolt the door and closed it after him. Delia, making for the stairway, turned, her hand on the deeply carved newel post. "How could Jim be certain? About Blanche, I mean. She just *could* be his mother. She did have that trip to Europe—oh, so long ago. We are the same age," Delia admitted, who never, never acknowledged her age. "Forty-seven." Delia caught herself there and actually laughed a little. "Not that she looks it."

"Neither do you," Julie agreed, honestly. Delia always looked fresh as a new penny if a rather plump one; always so well groomed that she could stand as a model. Not a silver-blond hair was ever out of place; never a ragged fingernail, never overdone makeup.

Delia liked the compliment, which was not flattery. "Well, that's the way it is. Of course," she added only a little smugly, "some people grow old more rapidly than others. Blanche is one who simply does not age. Not that forty-seven is very advanced in years. But Julie, do you really think that John Wingate would take in a boy he had no firm reason to believe was his son? I don't. Now let's go to bed. Come on."

Twelve

Delia went first. Somehow she had kept her hips and legs in neat shape, or perhaps she was right, she was one of the lucky people who do not age early. Julie followed her, turning out lights as they went. Beau followed close to Julie.

Pye turned up in her room. How she guessed it was Julie's room, there was no way to know. Oh, yes, there was. A dish of water, probably placed there by Peter, who had a loving instinct for animals and their comfort, stood in the adjoining bathroom. It was a small bathroom, wedged into a half of what once must have been a very large clothes closet. Delia's husband had gone that far in altering his parents' (his grandparents', oh, even some great-grandfather's) original house plan. Pye lapped delicately. Beau looked on rather thoughtfully.

It was hard to sleep. Beau at last turned around his conventional three times before he lay on the rug he was accustomed to in his remembered visits and which had remained in position near the door. Pye sat down and washed her black face.

It was a long time before Julie was ready to turn out the lamp.

It was a longer time before she slept.

Delia's reckoning just could be right. But no! Blanche had been in love with John, Julie was sure, for a long time. So it was natural for her to try to help Jim.

Blanche had given Jim a key to the small apartment she kept in the city. How long she had kept it, Julie couldn't remember; she had simply known that Blanche had a sort of retreat in the city. Blanche worked under great stress at home and at the office. The brief freedom the apartment occasionally gave her must have been valued and certainly earned by Blanche. She called it her hideaway.

Naturally, too, Blanche alone had paid the rent.

That thought so shocked Julie by occurring to her that she sat up in bed, staring into the darkness. The shades and curtains were closed, except for one near her bed; this one was open against Delia's principles. She was very doubtful about the night air. Full of smog, Delia always said. "Smoking chimneys, colds, rain, fog so near the river. But if you must."

A faint gleam of light from the street filtered into the room. She could see Beau, a white, contented curl on the rug. She couldn't see Pye, whose black and beige coat was more easily hidden in the shadows.

She lay back and decided that John Wingate could not be paying the rent for Blanche's city retreat, and after thinking of Jim and the Judge's death and Jim's hope that he could uncover some motive for Walker's murder, after what seemed at least a few years, she did drift into sleep.

It was, however, a troubled sleep. She awoke slowly, groggily, and found herself clinging to the edge of the bed; something warm and rather heavy in the middle of the bed gave a hoarse purr.

She sat up. "Pye! What are you doing there?"

Pye merely settled herself more snugly. "That is a mean,

catty trick," Julie said aloud and indignantly, remembering the days of her childhood and the remarkable talent her various cats had had for somehow, magically, edging nearer and nearer, pushing and pushing, and always ending up in the middle of the bed.

Beau was wakeful, too. He was at her side of the bed, thrusting a cold and urgent nose at her arm, her hand, her knee.

"Oh, Beau! Not now! It's the middle of the night."

He gave her arm a strong shove.

So he meant it. She and Peter had simply been so engrossed with the happenings of the night that neither had remembered to take Beau out.

"All right," she replied to another strong nudge. She turned on the lamp beside the bed, grasped a dressing gown, shoved her feet into slippers, and went as quietly as she could down the stairs. In the hope of not waking Delia she did not turn on lights downstairs but felt her way to the outside door, Beau running ahead in that direction. His leash hung on a chair in the workroom; she groped for it, found it, and snapped it to Beau's chain collar and opened the door. The night air was foggy. Several doors away toward the river a car stood, parked, no lights on. There was usually little if any traffic in that secluded spot; the automobile had to belong to one of the residents, out late and too weary to take it to the garage. She turned Beau toward the nearest lamp post. The light there was haloed with fog. She waited, and Beau as always was very neat and prompt.

She did give a fleeting thought to the cook's prowler as they passed the clump of shrubbery on the way back to the front door.

In a wild, turbulent second the parked car revved up to full speed and came hurtling down toward her.

No brakes, she thought in a flash, and managed to get Beau and herself inside the front door at the instant, really, when the runaway car sped past her.

"There!" She pulled Beau into her workroom and sank down in the lounge chair. "That," she said to Beau, "was a near thing." Beau thought so too; he tugged at the leash, got it out of her hand and edged warily toward the front door. She had closed it; she knew that. It had been an automatic gesture, but she went to look just the same. She had not only closed it but had locked it.

"What's the matter?" Peter called from the stairs.

"Oh, Peter! Go back to bed."

He didn't. He came around the stairs and found a light switch. "What happened? You look awful!"

"I had Beau out."

"Oh!" Peter looked apologetic. "I should have—"

"It's not your fault. I forgot, too. But as I was coming back a car got away, no brakes or something, and crashed at us!"

"No brakes?" Peter looked awful too, at least very white except for two bright red spots in his cheeks. "That's what I heard! The engine was going full tilt. Woke me—"

Peter dashed out of the room toward the dining room. Beau shot after him. A streak of beige and black leaped to her desk and sat down, twitching a black tail and eying her with a vivid blue gaze. Curious as a cat, Julie thought wildly, and Peter came back holding a glass in his hand. "Drink this!"

"Peter!" She must be the calm elder sister. "Peter, you must not get in the habit of drinking whenever anything upsets you or—"

"Or upsets anybody! You! Drink that."

"I—oh, all right—" It was bourbon, neat. "Wow!"

"That is better."

"Peter, I tell you—"

"Shut up," said Peter gallantly. "That car was driven by somebody. And you know who that somebody was!"

"No! No, there was nobody—"

"You are so silly! That was your rejected lover. George."

"Oh, no! Why on earth! It couldn't have been!"

"Who else? Why, Julie, I heard you threaten him."

"I didn't threaten anybody!"

"Oh, yes, you did. You said he wasn't John's son and just as good as said you could prove it."

"I didn't—"

"Not in so many words, but . . ." Peter paused for thought. "Yes, you did almost threaten. You scared hell out of him. Gave the impression that you had some reason for telling him he is not John Wingate's son. What is your reason?"

"And what is all this?" Delia asked from the doorway. "Why aren't you two in bed? What is that cat doing there?"

Pye didn't like the tone and stood, her eyes two blue slits. Beau warily backed a little away from the desk.

Peter said, "Just in time, Aunt Delia, you've got to talk sense to Julie. Somebody just tried to kill her."

"What!"

"Run her down with a car. George, I'll bet," Peter said succinctly.

"George! But how? Why?"

"George thinks she knows something to prove he's not John's son. That's why. You heard them this afternoon, shouting—at least Julie was shouting. George was smoother. Some actor. Says he's got some winter stock jobs. Won't keep him in hair dye," said Peter.

"Hair—" Delia was diverted. "He can't dye his hair!"

"I don't know why not." Peter eyed Delia's own silver-blond hair and said soberly, "Plenty of people do."

Delia ignored that. "A car *here* of all places! It must have had no brakes. There's a very slight slope toward First Avenue—"

"I heard the engine," Peter said. "Come on now, Julie. Are you sure you haven't got something about George that will fix him with John Wingate?"

"Nothing! Really, nothing. I just don't like him!" Julie defended herself hotly. "I never have liked him. Of course I realize that may be because he says he is John's son. He is just not like John. But, Delia, that could not have been George in that car! He didn't try to—to hurt me!"

Delia sat down on the desk, disputing the vantage point with Pye who, however, took it in such good spirit that she snuggled against Delia's pink silk dressing gown. She said soberly, "I don't know. Somehow, George doesn't seem, has never seemed a man of—I suppose one would call it character. It has always seemed to me that he was rather like Elaine. Weak, easily influenced. Not really stable. Yet I can't believe he'd try to—"

"To murder anybody?" said Peter. "Oh, I could believe it! He *could* try! All the books say so. Cowardice! He really is a fool. Lurking around in a car, guessing that Julie might come out sometime with the dog. Tell us again, Julie."

It was a very short tale. She had seen the car but believed that it belonged to some Cove resident. The engine had started with such a sudden roar and the car had sped toward her and Beau so unexpectedly that she had barely managed to get herself and the dog into the house. "But we got here. And I still don't see how it could have been George."

"Well," Delia said after long thought, "we can't do anything about it now."

"Sure we can," Peter said eagerly. "I'll phone Sam and get him to see if George is at home—" He stopped. "No, that won't do. Not tonight. Those winter stock jobs that George said he had, did he say where, when I wasn't listening?"

"Oh, I don't know. I don't think he did—"

Peter leaned against the desk, too, and absently stroked Pye, who liked it and began to purr. "Well, what winter theaters?"

"I tell you, I don't know."

He turned to Delia. "I guess she really doesn't know."

"In any event," Delia said crisply, "it is very late."

But Peter insisted. "Have you got Blanche's phone number? I mean for her apartment."

Delia shook her head. "Certainly. But I'm not going to try

to call her now. You want to tell Jim about this. What do you expect him to do?"

Peter's face expressed the utmost surprise. "Why, beat hell out of George, of course. And then report the whole thing to John Wingate."

Delia said crossly, "Just suppose Jim is not really at Blanche's apartment. Just suppose—"

"It wasn't Jim trying to kill Julie! Don't be so silly, Aunt Delia!"

Delia rose. "I'm silly enough to send you back to bed. Now go. You, too, Julie. I suppose that door is locked."

She tried the door herself, glowing in silk billowing around her. Pye was apparently interested in the rustle of the silk, for she followed, brushing against it.

"The fact remains," Delia said flatly, "that George may not be too sure that he is really John's son."

"Julie made George think she had proof he is not."

Delia sighed. "We'll tell John the whole thing. But if you have any such proof, Julie, why haven't you told Jim?"

"I just feel that George cannot possibly be John's son, that's all."

Delia shook her head. "That's not enough. Well, go on, Peter, Julie. Tomorrow—"

"Hell," said Peter quite audibly. Delia pretended not to hear but swept back toward the stairs.

Peter gave a sudden yip. "Hey! Stop it!"

He was too late. Pye had scrambled by way of Peter's old flannel dressing gown, now outgrown, but still strong enough to give Pye's claws a purchase. She then draped herself again like a boa around Peter's shoulders and looked over one shoulder, pleased with herself.

Clearly she had looked them all over and decided upon Peter as the likeliest friend. A black tail dangled from Peter's other shoulder and twitched slightly. Beau sat down and looked at Peter, whom he had always regarded as his own property, and then moved over to stand close beside Julie, claiming her, but with troubled brown eyes watching Pye.

"She seems to like me," Peter said smugly.

"Go to bed," Delia called back in a tone that had to be obeyed.

"Yes'm," said Peter and started for the stairs, Pye neatly balancing herself.

Beau followed Julie and settled down on his own rug with a sigh, which Julie translated as, "No more of that cat here."

She would talk to Jim the next morning. She could not believe that George had lingered around in the hope that sometime she would have to come out to walk Beau. Yet, of course he could, given sufficient reason. She wished she had not been quite so emphatic about accusing him, in almost so many words, of being a liar and a fraud.

On the other hand, surely that car could not have been driven by George. It must be only a runaway car.

But the engine had not started itself, had it?

Eventually she awoke as Peter bounded into her room, carrying a tray. "Aunt Delia sent me. I'll take some of that toast and marmalade."

"You'll do no such thing." But she relented and drank coffee. Peter crunched toast.

"I fixed breakfast myself." Peter was pleased with himself. "Mrs. Martine hasn't turned up. Aunt Delia is afraid she's gone for good."

The marmalade bowl was empty when he rose, advised her to get a move on unless she wanted to be seen looking like an old hag, and went away. To her surprise, Pye had quietly followed Peter into the room and now followed him out again. Beau, close beside Julie, accepted his own share of toast but gave a worried glance which she knew meant, "Time to go out, please."

"All right, Beau. In a minute."

She did look like a hag in the mirror, hair anyhow, face! After a quick shower and dressing she ran down the stairs,

126

Beau leaping ahead of her, unlocked the front door, seized Beau's leash and went out into another beautiful October morning, all blue and gold, with the river sparkling at the east and no signs of any lurking car—or lurking figure. They strolled along the Cove, turning the corner, going as far as First Avenue. When they returned Jim's taxi was just leaving the door and he stood, waiting for her, and took her hand tight and hard. "Give me Beau's leash. There—now—"

He opened the door, drew her into the house, dropped the leash and took her hard in his arms. "Oh, Julie, I'll get out of this. See if I don't. Once that gossip woman turns up something about Alben Walker we may—"

"All right," said Delia, in the hall. "You can stop kissing for now. Somebody tried to kill Julie last night."

"George," Peter chimed in.

"*Julie!* What happened?"

Peter spoke up. "I'll tell you. Julie yelled at George yesterday when he was here. She said she could prove he wasn't John Wingate's son—"

"No, Peter, I didn't say that!" Julie cried.

Peter was positive. "Yes, you did. You said you knew he couldn't be John Wingate's son. It sounded as if you had proof. So he figured you'd have to go out sometime with the dog. So he waited and waited and—Jim," Peter shook Jim's arm. "Can't you see? This shows that George is afraid. He knows he's not Mr. Wingate's son. He's afraid of what Julie knows."

"But I don't know anything!" Julie cried.

"You sounded as if you did!" Peter all but yelled. "We heard you! Aunt Delia heard it, didn't you, Aunt Delia? Tell Jim how she shouted."

Delia checked him. "You'd better come to the living room and settle down and, yes, of course, Jim wants the whole story. Such as it is," added Delia and led the way into the pleasant living room. She had opened the curtains, so the room was filled with a kind of golden light. Pye was already sitting on the yellow piano top, looking like a judge, her black paws neatly folded.

Beau sat down too, very near Julie.

"Now, then," Jim began, so Delia quieted Peter, shook her head at Julie and told what there was to tell.

In the light from the windows, Julie thought that Jim began to look older. She moved to sit beside him and without looking at her, he put his hand over her arm. "We'll have to see to this. I'll talk to Blanche. My father had proof of George's identity. Father is no fool."

"But I can't see how this links up—or even if it does—with that Walker's murder," Delia said.

"No. Unless of course the society gossip woman turns up something and—oh, I don't know!"

Delia linked her hands together and leaned forward. "Jim, let us go back to the time of the murder for a moment."

"Yes, Aunt Delia—by the way, do you mind if I call you Aunt Delia?"

A lovely smile came into Delia's face. "You always did, Jim. Why change now?"

"Thank you," Jim said. "I wasn't sure about that. I truly didn't kill Walker."

"Why did you leave like that?"

"Because I was scared, if you want to know. I could see no other course ahead of me but arrest, indictment, a trial —and a trial had only one ending. I had read a couple of pieces in very good newspapers. I think now they were either on the missionary side, that is, trying to let their readers know that such a law was unconstitutional, a kind of believe-it-or-not effort which would prevent anybody's trying to escape the law. But the state I was in, I could only think, here is a possible chance. If I can get away—why, in five years surely some kind of evidence will come out."

"You must have seen a lawyer somewhere," Peter insisted.

Jim laughed shortly. "A lawyer! I was lucky if I could find

clean drinking water or a bathroom instead of a pail of water. You don't know the kind of places a young civil engineer can be sent to. Bridges, highways, drainage problems. Anything, except I never dared try a dam. I was not even a graduate. But I worked hard and was paid for it and kept on, from one contractor to another as jobs came up. Oh, yes, I've seen some not particularly pleasant parts of the world. Sometime I'll tell Julie all about it and she can write it." He glanced at Julie, his words half-joking but altogether loving. Then he sobered. "No, there was nothing romantic about any of it. Hard, monotonous work in places I had never heard of and nothing to do evenings but sleep or poker or—" With a twinkle in his eyes, he glanced at Peter, who was leaning forward enthralled. "Ever try spit-in-the-ocean, Peter?"

"But, that—that poker—"

"Peter!" said Delia, stopping such talk.

Jim's words had conjured up vast and empty spaces where there were no such amenities as even newspapers.

After a long pause Delia said, "You must have had a passport."

"Oh, sure. My own. Our consul in England saw to that when I went there. I had it renewed from time to time. But Tanzania, yes, I liked Tanzania. However, by that time I knew I had made a dumb, scared, preposterous mistake in running away. Yet I couldn't help hoping that this peculiar interpretation of that law just might give me a chance. But I suppose I knew in my heart that a murder case cannot be closed until the murderer is found. So—"

Delia sighed. "So that is what you propose to do."

"I hope I can," Jim said.

Thirteen

Then he pulled himself away from thoughts of the past five years. "All this is past history! This car! Julie, what do you think?"

"I'm not sure of anything. Beau and I barely made it to the front door. I was scared."

Jim came to her, drew her up into his arms, and held her against him as if he could impart some of his own physical strength. "If that driver turns out to have been George—"

"Now, Jim," Delia cried, "don't make threats."

Jim gave her a short laugh that did not sound as if he were amused. "If George did that he'll wish he was dead, and then all at once he'll find out he is—"

"Jim!" Delia cried.

"I don't think he is joking," Peter said.

Julie didn't think so either. But Jim laughed again very abruptly, and immediately stopped, for Peter said suddenly, "I hear a car—two cars—" He shot toward the hall. "I'd better look."

Beau sprang up and ran with him, barking. Peter dashed back, again excited, his eyes bright. "Jim! It's the police. One of them is Chief McClary from Brookboro. Three others are in New York City uniforms. One is driving a police car. You've got to get away. Now! Fast! They'll take you to prison!"

Julie was already at the French windows overlooking the enclosed garden.

Delia cried, "Oh, no. He can't get out through the garden. No way. He'd have to burgle one of my neighbors' houses and explain!"

Julie looked frantically around; there must be some place, any place to conceal a six-footer. The dog barked as the doorbell began to give long, unnerving peals. Julie saw a possible refuge and seized Jim's hand. "Hurry!"

Peter got the idea right away. Then Delia. "Of course, he can hide there," Peter cried, but softly. "Show him, Julie!"

Julie pulled at Jim. "I'm sure you can manage to squeeze in. It's old and huge—*come on!*"

But when she swung open the door to the big dumbwaiter, Jim backed off. "I can't get in that thing!"

"Yes, you can. If you'll just sort of fold up. There's plenty of room. They built them big in those days. Peter can fit in it." She pushed at him.

At that unlikely moment Jim began to laugh.

"Shut up," she whispered. "Get in!"

Peter yanked on Jim's other arm. "Go on. It was used before the Civil War. Big enough for escaping slaves, wasn't it, Aunt Delia?"

Delia spoke with pride even then. "Of course. The underground railway. It held many a poor fugitive—"

Julie urged. "It will hold you, Jim. They'll never think of this!"

"Nobody would ever think of it!" Jim said rather sourly. The doorbell pealed imperatively. Finally Jim put one leg into the dumbwaiter. "Are you sure it will hold, Julie? I'm kind of big."

Delia replied, "They made them to hold enormous dinners. Turkeys. Runaway slaves. They built well and, oh, Jim, hurry."

He did at last scramble into the box-like cavern.

"Now, don't touch that button, Jim," Julie warned him. "It's electric and it starts the thing moving up and down. And don't make a sound."

"Where does it come out?"

"In the kitchen, of course. Downstairs. But there's a panel over it. Oh, Jim, you've got to be quiet!"

"I truly don't think anybody is going to take me for a runaway slave or a Thanksgiving turkey. Maybe, however, for a goose."

Julie closed the door firmly.

Peter waved frantic hands from the living room. "Okay?" he whispered.

"I hope so. He didn't like it."

"What do you expect?" Delia said shortly. "Peter, go and open the door, and Julie, make that dog of yours stop barking."

"Yes, yes! Come, Beau."

Beau came to her but reluctantly, casting suspicious glances toward the front door and the now urgent doorbell.

Peter opened the door. "Why, it's Chief McClary!"

"Hello, Peter," said the Chief of Brookboro Police. "May we come in?"

Delia appeared behind Peter, looking all at once a grande dame. "Good morning, Chief. Yes, do come in. Have you brought us any news?"

"He brought us three New York cops," said Peter quite audibly.

"Officers!" Delia corrected him, but really quite graciously if without much breath. Rather as if she herself had been crammed into the dumbwaiter, Julie thought absently.

The Chief nodded at the two policemen, who followed him into the house. Surely none of them had ever seen or perhaps even heard of a dumbwaiter; a vintage dumbwaiter, Julie amended it, a part of the long-ago underground railway.

Delia led them into the living room, asked them (too politely?) to sit down. Julie strained her ears, fearing that Jim might inadvertently make some motion and send the ancient box creaking or thumping as it did when it moved.

"The fact is, Mrs. Van Clive," the Chief said, oh, very politely too, "we are looking for young Jim Wingate, and it occurred to me that he might have come here. So I came myself and had a meeting with a New York captain and—"

"I see," said Delia. "You think Jim is here. I feel you'd rather not take my word for anything." Delia hated to lie. She was obviously bracing herself to tell a real whopper.

But the Chief said, "Oh, now, Mrs. Van Clive! You know we couldn't come here and insist upon entering if we could take even your word for young Wingate's absence."

The older officer added, "Yes, ma'am. Our orders are to search the house. We have a search warrant. But we hope you do not mind."

"I don't think it would make much difference if I did object." Delia couldn't help an edge of tartness in her reply, but then she managed to smile. "Certainly. Go right ahead. Peter, hold the dog."

"Does he bite?" asked the older policeman rather nervously. Probably in the course of his long career he had encountered not only criminals but biting dogs.

Peter, wickedly, didn't discourage the officer's doubt. "Not hard, only a nip or two. I'll hold him. He may sound a little savage but really—"

Beau, savage! And Jim curled up like a croissant in that ancient relic of the past! Julie rather felt as if she had strayed into an Alice in Wonderland world. But the plain fact was that it was neither that nor a nightmare. It was real! Jim in prison! "Would you like to look over this floor first?" Delia said. "Or go upstairs?"

"Might as well start at the top and work our way down," said the rather glum older officer, looking warily at Beau, who returned his gaze with a certain guarded interest. He really looked for a moment as if he might live up to the status Peter and Julie had given him and start biting at any moment. There was no sight of Pye.

At Delia's signal, the three men started trudging, in single file necessarily, up the narrow old stairs. Delia paused at the top of the first flight and Julie heard her. "If you don't mind —at my age—stairs—" She was panting far more than Julie had ever heard her pant, as if gasping for breath. She had no doubt that Delia had pressed her hands pathetically over her heart.

"Peter, when they come down—" Julie said very low.

"Don't worry about that," Peter whispered. "Just hope none of them has ever heard of that thing!" He paused and whispered again. "I never thought I'd be thankful for it. An —anachronism," Peter announced, rather pleased with the fine word.

Julie listened. There was the tread of footsteps, the murmur of voices. No creak from the dumbwaiter. Oh, Jim, be quiet! Don't move! Don't breathe!

Delia came downstairs, still looking the grande dame but also a grande dame who was frightened. She caught Julie's eyes and shook her head. "Now let's get them out." She went to the small door leading to the stairs kitchenward, unlocked and opened it.

Julie agreed. "They can't know anything of the dumbwaiter. But they've got to know that there's a kitchen." She turned to Peter. "Got any ideas?"

Peter shook his head. "Even the dumbest cop in New York knows that a house has a kitchen and I really don't think," he added thoughtfully, "that any New York cop can be called dumb. Honestly, the things they know and do—"

"Here they come." Delia drew herself up.

They thumped down again, still in single file, Chief McClary bringing up the rear. "Now," he said, "there's only the kitchen. I saw a small back door, outside, among some shrubs. The kitchen must be downstairs."

"Yes," said Delia.

An odd thing happened. Delia led the way to the small door to the twisting flight of steps that went so unexpectedly and precipitously down to the kitchen, which prudent Delia kept locked. The stairwell was so dark that an electric light had been installed and a switch for it set in a tiny panel at the top of the steps. First Delia showed the police the stairs, then she carelessly put a white, glittering hand completely over the panel. No one could have guessed that she was in fact covering all means of light on the steps that might help the men see their way downward.

"That way," said Delia. The older, dour and very suspicious-looking officer led. The other two, with Chief McClary bringing up the rear, clumped down and disappeared. But then suddenly and raucously Pye paid for her keep. There was a hair-raising yowl of fury from the cat, followed at once by a strangely mingled cacophony of shouts, thumps, thuds and then some very lively words.

Peter slid to the top of the steps, listened and whispered, "Pye got the first one. The rest of them seem to have got tangled up. They are swearing something awful, Aunt Delia. You ought to hear—well, maybe not. They're coming back."

But first a sleek black and beige figure shot out from the stairs, flew across the dining room and living room, and leaped without apparent effort onto the piano. Pye's tail was twice its normal elegant size and her eyes were blazing red.

"Red!" Julie exclaimed. "But her eyes are blue!"

Peter heard her. "Of course they are red when she is good and mad. Not ruby red," he said with an air of a connoisseur, "more like garnet. Siamese cats' eyes always turn red when they are upset. It's in one of the books in your room."

The police came back, Chief McClary leading the way, since he had been last to go down the steps. He looked rather peculiar, for there was a large red spot on his cheek and he clutched one elbow. The second officer massaged a leg. The third was red, too, but with fury. "What have you got down there, madam?" he began, glaring at Delia. "It scratches and bites. Made us all fall." He said bitterly, "I was first. It attacked me."

"I think it was only a cat," said McClary but rather doubtfully.

"Rabies," said the tall man dourly.

The second officer was limping slightly but said, philosophically, "Ours not to reason why. Ours but—"

"To do or die," Peter chanted happily.

McClary fixed him with a steely eye. "That cat yours?"

"Well—" Peter glanced at the cat, who was muttering to herself, still, and lashing her tail. "Yes. In a way," said Peter.

"Inflicted damages," said the wounded officer morosely.

Chief McClary had by this time pulled himself together. "But we had a look at your kitchen. Everything fine, modern. Thank you, Mrs. Van Clive. Very kind of you. I'm sure. Now we'll be on our way." He became serious and yet he seemed rather friendly, too. "We must find young Wingate, you know, Walker's murderer—we believe. Possibly the Judge's murderer too. You'll be doing yourself and young Wingate a favor if you know anything now or—or later—where he can be found."

Delia bowed, almost too graciously.

Beau wriggled as the three tramped past him. Peter gripped his collar.

The door closed after them. Peter said, "Whew! A good thing Jim didn't try the back kitchen door. There's the police car and driver."

Julie listened for the car's departure and counted to three before she ran to the dumbwaiter and opened the door. Jim crawled out, looked at her with no favor, straightened out one leg and then the other, and said crossly, "I'll never do that again."

"It saved you. Don't be an ass," Julie snapped. "Now, Jim, you must find someplace to go and—"

Peter intervened. "But they've searched this place. They'll not come back, at least not soon. Do they know that Blanche has a place in the city?"

Jim rubbed his shoulder. "I don't know. My God, I thought I'd suffocate and was sure they'd open that panel or whatever it is in the kitchen—"

"They'd have seen only brick walls," Delia said proudly.

Peter picked up Pye. "This is our heroine."

The cat settled down and began to purr. Her eyes took on a brilliant, pleased blue.

Jim said, "So that was what all the ruckus was about. Some fine and fancy swearing, too. What did they do to her?"

"Stepped on her tail, probably. She's not about to permit that, are you, Sweetie Pye?"

"Did you send her downstairs?" Jim asked.

"Oh, no. She just wanted to prowl, I suppose. But Aunt Delia helped!" Peter said with admiration. "You opened the door, Aunt Delia, when you unlocked it; and of course Sweetie Pye had to explore. You thought nobody saw you put your hand over that electric switch by the top of the stairs, didn't you, Aunt Delia?"

Delia did not appear to hear him and Peter assumed his sage and thoughtful air. "Janus," he said gravely. "Tragedy and comedy, two faces—"

Delia came alive. "Stop showing off," she snapped.

She had sunk into a chair and was, in fact, now rather breathless. "That was terrible. Jim, you've got to find a hideout. Blanche's—"

"Yes, I know. I'll go back there. But I can't believe they really suspect me of the Judge's murder. Yes, I'll go to Blanche's place and try to phone her from there and—"

"Listen," Peter said earnestly. "There's got to be some link between Walker's murder and George. Stands to reason. He is the only one to profit by Walker's death. That is, the only one we can think of. George is trying to frame you. He wants Julie and your father's money. He had an alibi, sure. They say an alibi is the easiest thing in the world to break and an inexperienced murderer doesn't know it and keeps arranging alibis and—"

"Oh, Peter!" Delia almost wailed. "Do you ever read anything but—"

"Never mind, Aunt Delia. I tell you, George is somehow at the bottom of this and when you find out more of Walker's background you'll find George in it somewhere," Peter concluded in a very judicial manner.

Jim sighed and brushed his shoulders. "I smell like roast beef, or garlic maybe. All right, Peter. I'm doing my best. This Count—"

Delia broke in. "Count! A handkisser! And probably a fake, too!" She said it so vehemently that Pye sat up and made a peculiar threatening sound. This aroused Beau, who didn't like that sound and suddenly advanced, eyes shining, body held low, upon Pye. Peter clutched at Pye, who leaped to his shoulder. "Now, Beau!" he warned.

Jim said morosely, "All we need now is a good cat and dog fight."

The telephone rang. Peter, Pye clinging to his shoulder with no apparent difficulty, ran to answer it.

"It's Blanche," he shouted back. "She wants to talk to you, Jim. It's about the Judge's will. He's left everything he had to you."

Fourteen

Julie and Delia hurried to listen.

"That," said Jim at last into the telephone, "is simply not possible." He put down the telephone.

There was a long silence. Finally Peter said, "George! George is in it some way."

"No," Jim said. "Doesn't have anything to do with George. Blanche explained it. She had drawn up the will for the Judge."

"But why would the Judge leave his property to you?" That was Delia, also shocked to her pretty back teeth. Julie sat down on the desk near Jim. "Tell us, Jim, exactly what did Blanche say?"

"Just that. She drew up the will. When I ran away five years ago the Judge still believed in me. So—he felt that this might eventually be a slight recompense—his words, Blanche said—in the event I sometime, somewhere needed it. He must have guessed, or even known—he was a very smart old boy—that if or when I returned I would ask Blanche to help me. Blanche and my father. Anyway, he told her he had no relatives—"

"Maude—Lisa," Delia reminded him.

"Oh, he didn't much like her." Peter knew everything, or almost everything, about Brookboro. He added, "She was only some vague cousin's kid. Tossed upon the Judge for some reason. Probably her family couldn't stand her," Peter added.

"Well, she's not a favorite of mine." Delia added, always trying to be fair, "But all the same she's a relative."

"Blanche told me that the Judge said something about blood ties never being as powerful as everybody believes they are. Besides"—Jim did cheer up a little at this—"there really wasn't much to leave, Blanche says. He made a few bequests to friends he's known, some woman who cooked for him, a charity or two, that kind of thing. But he wasn't a rich man. Not at all. He lived simply. He did save some but not a great amount."

"How much?" Delia couldn't help pricking up her small ears a little at the sound of money.

Jim shook his head. "She wasn't sure. Maybe something like a hundred thousand—"

"I don't call that quite nothing," said Delia practically.

Peter whistled and Pye started disapprovingly. "I call it damn rich!"

"Oh, no, don't you see! It gives Jim a motive for killing the Judge!" Julie wailed. "Why, it's as if—as if somebody has been just spinning lies to hurt you, Jim!"

Jim sat up straighter. "It's not quite that bad. Don't give up, Julie."

"I'm not giving up. Ever. But the Judge—Jim, he meant it kindly. He really felt in his heart that to accuse you would be wrong. You could never kill anybody."

Delia asked, "What does Blanche say now?"

Jim turned to Julie. "She says I must leave again. Right away. She'll work up a list of all the places with which we have no extradition treaty." He paused. "You see what that means."

Julie felt as if her knees were dissolving. Again Peter gave a low whistle. Delia just stood blank and pale. But she found words. "It means that nobody can do anything to help you."

Jim set his chin. "I'm not going away again."

Julie ran to him and caught his arm. "You heard the police already after you. There's no possible proof that you killed the Judge but—"

"Public opinion obviously has it that I killed Walker."

"You can't just give in!"

Delia broke in. "What else can Jim do? It's better to follow Blanche's advice. Surely she'll find some way to get him back home."

"She sounded as if she'd been crying," Jim said bleakly.

"It's all because your dear Brookboro friends have made up their minds again!" Peter all but yelled indignantly, "You fight them, Jim!"

"No! No!" Julie had had more time to think. "You must go. Blanche knows. She tried to stop you. She must have seen everybody she could who might have influence and she's given up."

Delia agreed. "Where's your passport, Jim?"

"At home. Blanche said she'd get it for me. She told me to make plane reservations at once. I didn't have a chance to tell her that the police have already been here. I was kind of stunned, I guess. But no, I can't run away again!"

Delia was very stern. "You have to. As soon as you can. Will John bring the passport to you here?"

"I suppose so. Blanche will have told him I am here."

"Jim," Delia said, suddenly making up her mind. "Did your father ever make any definite statement about being your father?"

"Why, of course. He called me his son at once. But there wasn't much, you know, in the way of proof. I was about the age he'd expect. I had been—well, I suppose you'd call it deposited in a sort of nursery, a school, in England. As I got older, money came for another school there. But then I

141

began to realize that I was being kept in school because nobody quite knew what to do with me. I could see that I was an embarrassment. I had insisted, you see, that I was an American. I was old enough when my mother left home to have learned my age, and my name, and that I was an American. So at last when there was no more money, the school headmaster went to the nearest American consul, and somehow I was lent enough money to come back here. But I didn't remember the name Brookboro. I only knew I must go to school, learn how to support myself. So—oh, this is an old story. I got some jobs, worked my way into an engineering school—"

"Harvard. M.I.T.," said Peter. "Why didn't you go to Princeton?"

"Never mind now, Peter. Then I heard my father on the TV and—"

"We know the rest of it, Jim." Delia's voice was definitely soft, as when she spoke to Peter. "You must do as Blanche says. Get out—and do it at once."

Julie decided. "We'll go back to Tanzania, unless Blanche knows of another country which might offer a safer—safer place to wait."

"No." Jim put his hand over Julie's. "Darling, I can't—"

"You can. I'm going with you."

"Julie, darling! No!"

"Certainly she's going with you," Delia said. She appeared to have scuttled her early-twentieth-century morals. "Go and get some clothes packed, Julie. Jim will get a reservation."

"We can't get married," Jim said. "I'll not let her go with me."

Delia said, "I keep a bit of money in the house. Enough to last you for a while, I should think."

"How much?" Peter mumbled as if in an absent way but Delia's pale blue eyes swept him coldly. "I think there's close to ten or twelve thousand, in cash naturally. In the safe in my bedroom. You'll take that, and," she said, with astounding firmness, "it really doesn't matter whether you two marry now. The main thing is to get away."

Jim shook his head. "No—I've got to have a chance to clear myself."

"But Jim," Julie began.

Jim sighed, "Julie, I do love you. But I can't—I won't—" Suddenly, he spoke with an air of pronouncing the ultimate decision. "You couldn't possibly go anywhere Blanche may suggest without a passport. Do you have one?"

"No." Julie felt as if the solid floor beneath her had dissolved.

"I intended to take her on a trip to Europe during the winter," Delia said miserably. "But I hadn't got around to do anything like firm plans, or a passport. Surely, Julie—"

"Of course! We talked of it. But I had my book on my mind and I never even thought of a passport."

"Blanche says you must leave, Jim! Your father agrees," said Delia. "You must let us know where to find you—of course, your father and moth—I mean Blanche—"

But Jim had caught the half-word. "I tell you, Blanche is not my mother! I love her. I believe in her. She's my lawyer! But she is *not my mother!*"

"All right," Delia said peaceably. "Never mind all that. John is your father and you'll keep in touch with him somehow. Arrange it between you. And then Julie will come—"

"There is the doorbell!" Peter yapped. "I'll go. If it's the police again, Jim, I'll give you a high sign." He vanished toward the door, Pye clinging to his shoulders.

It was as if time had stopped for moments, days, weeks before they heard first a feminine voice in the hall, then a man's voice, and Peter came back, his eyes glittering with excitement. "It's the woman from the society column, you know, the newspaper. And I think the guy with her is the TV man. You do want to see them, don't you, Jim?"

"Yes!" Jim shot across to the hall.

Delia followed. Peter's ears were sticking out eagerly as he hurried ahead of the others into the living room. He pulled out a chair for the woman and in general made himself the man of the house.

The woman was attractive, dressed with a certain chic, and obviously very, very curious not only about Jim and Delia and Julie herself, but the house. "Why," she said. "Mrs. Van Clive! How very kind! I've heard of your house. What a beauty! And of course, your gifts to charity, your work on philanthropic boards—"

Delia drew herself up but only a little. "Thank you. I try to help. Do sit down."

"Hattie Town," said her escort, introducing.

"Blythe Smith, really," the woman said, smiling so that two charming dimples came near her lips. "But I use the name Hattie Town in my columns."

Delia lifted her eyebrows a little. "Yes, I've read them," she conceded graciously. "Very well done—and this is?"

The escort was a good-looking man, dark and cheerful and certainly photogenic; he smiled, showing handsome teeth. Television must be a boon to dentists, thought Julie. Such beautiful teeth always seemed to show up on TV. He said, "Anthony Brown. Not a very famous name but—"

Peter murmured, "But mine own—"

Mr. Brown had the accustomed grace to smile at Peter. Then he sobered and leaned forward. "I hoped that Mr. John Wingate might be here. I was very much interested in him and in his effort to find you, Mr. Wingate." He turned to Jim. "Now Blythe, here, has unearthed what she could about your Alben Walker."

Blythe opened an enormous red handbag and drew out a handful of press clippings, fastened neatly together with a paper clip. "I keep files, you know. It's part of my job. But this is all I could find in a hurry about your—well, Count

D'Avray. I'm sure he is the same man who, you say, went under the name of Alben Walker. Same face, anyway."

Jim took the press clippings. Julie, without knowing she had moved, was all at once pressing Jim's shoulder, reading. Delia was there, too. Even Peter stood with them pushing against Delia, Pye still on his shoulder.

The society-column woman said softly to Mr. Brown, "That is a Siamese cat."

"H'mm," said Mr. Brown. "Looks as if she could read."

"Siamese, perhaps," said Miss Smith. "I wouldn't think plain English."

"You never know," Mr. Brown muttered darkly.

Jim read aloud, " 'Count D'Avray among the cocktail guests at a viewing of the new but already known painter'— 'Among the guests at Mrs. Raner's reception was the handsome Count D'Avray.' "

"Handsome!" Delia snorted.

"He seems to have got around—" Jim said, reading.

"Oh, he got around," said Miss Smith dryly. "Especially —I know he was no friend of yours so you'll not mind—if I say where he met people with money and especially," she added, "women."

Delia couldn't resist. "I told you he was a fake! Count, indeed!"

"Oh, he may have been a count," said Miss Smith. "Nobody was sufficiently interested to track him down. We do, here in New York, perhaps everywhere, tend to take a person at his own value. He said he was a count, and he did manage to turn up frequently for a while. But then he vanished. After I noted—it's somewhere there—that he was seen several times with a woman. The same woman. But," said Miss Smith, "I'm sorry I didn't pay much attention to him or to her. Anyway he just sort of vanished from the New York scene." She sighed. "I am sorry. But that's all I could find quickly."

All three read again every single little notice that included Alben Walker's—no, Count D'Avray's—name. Finally Delia went back to her chair. "It's really very kind of you, Miss Smith, and you also, Mr. Brown."

"My pleasure." Miss Smith was looking with quite frank admiration at Jim.

"I liked your father," Mr. Brown said to Jim, "liked him very much. And of course the sequel. I expected a ton of letters. But I really did not expect the son to actually turn up. Makes me feel—oh, I sound pretentious, but honestly, it does kind of warm one's heart. To be, so to speak—"

"The *deus ex machina*," Peter offered.

Mr. Brown's eyes beamed at Peter as if he had made another discovery. "Good for you, young man. No fool, are you?"

Miss Smith rose. "There might be more clippings. But that's all my secretary found. I'll work on it. Surely I must have more information about him and the woman he was seen with. Where he went—well, we already know that eventually he went to—to your town," she smiled at Jim. "And set himself up under another name."

"And kissed hands," said Delia crossly; she never forgave what she considered a blatant fake.

"Did he really?" Miss Smith pondered for a second or two. "Sounds like him. He had a habit of kissing hands and bowing and all but clicking his heels together. Oh, he was too good to be true, if you understand me. Now I've got to get back to work. But I promise you"—she had quickly and accurately guessed Julie's place in Jim's life—"I'll do my best for both of you. I heard—well, I understand that—"

"Yes," said Jim. "I was all but arrested and tried for his murder. Would have been convicted. Not much doubt of that!"

Mr. Brown rose. "You'll get out of it, Jim. If I may call you Jim. Get your father to advise you. That man—" he said gravely and with respect, "is simply great. Give him my regards. Come on, Blythe. No, no, I'll leave the press notices here, Jim. That is, if it's all right with you, Blythe."

"Oh, yes. By all means. I only hope they'll be of some help—"

Peter and Pye ushered them to the door. Beau followed and Peter said, "Come on, old fellow, I know. Time you had a walk—"

Delia, who never gave up, began again. "First, your passport, Julie. It is not the tourist season so it may not take long to get one. During the tourist season they line up for hours. Jim, you must leave at once. Julie can meet you wherever you say—"

Jim said stubbornly, "No use making all these plans. I've got to do it my way—"

"You've got to get away. I trust Blanche's judgment." Delia was coaxing, "You know she'll do her best for you, Jim. Even if—"

She stopped but Jim finished, for the first time with an amused gleam in his eyes. "Dear Aunt Delia, Blanche is *not* my mother!"

"All right. But Jim, do you really remember your mother? I mean, Elaine?"

The amusement left Jim's face. "No, not really. Sometimes when I was very young, I used to think I did a little. But a five-year-old—no, I'm not sure."

"Can't you remember anything at all of her?"

"Oh, I suppose so. I remember somebody, some woman, rather—" A flush came up in Jim's face. "She rather hauled me around by my arm, so to speak. I remember the sea, I think, I remember being seasick and—" He brightened. "Yes. There was a woman in a kind of uniform, I expect a stewardess, who fussed over me in the nicest way."

Delia's lips tightened. Her expression said, not Elaine. Instead she looked at the diamond watch that her husband had given her long ago. "Good Heavens! It's late. We've got to eat. Never decide anything on an empty stomach," she said, repeating her own mandate. "A crisis of any kind is more reasonably undertaken on a full stomach. I wonder where Mrs. . . . Mrs.—"

"Martine," Julie suggested.

"I'll find out." She went to the dumbwaiter and jerked open the door.

Jim watched her with alarm.

"No," Julie said. "I shoved you in that, she didn't. Now, it did work, Jim."

"The back door would have worked, too," Jim said rather bitterly.

"Certainly. If the driver and a police car hadn't been parked in front of the house."

Jim was properly impressed. "Good God! I never thought of that. All the time I had cramps in my legs I thought how much simpler it would have been just to walk out the kitchen door—"

Delia had rung down the dumbwaiter. She emerged, her face a little flushed, and went down the stairs to the basement. After a moment she came back, puffing and angry. "She's still not there. She's left for good!"

"I can't say I blame her," Jim said callously. He'd have to learn a thing or three about housekeeping sometime, Julie thought briefly; if, that is, they ever had a house to keep. It was a sobering reflection.

Delia sat down. "There must be food, though—"

Peter came noisily back, bringing Beau. "Say, that woman —that cook, she's not here."

"Yes," Delia said. "I know."

"I'm hungry."

"Fine!" Delia brightened up. "Then you can go down to the kitchen and fix us something to eat. I'm sure there's roast beef in the fridge. Slice that and—"

"Whoops," said Peter. "There's the doorbell again."

He dashed to answer it. Beau dashed with him and barked.

Lisa came in preceding Peter, who was staring wide-eyed.

And, indeed, Lisa was something to stare at.

Fresh and lovely, the barest touch of mascara on her long eyelashes, the slightest rose tint on her pointed face, the neatest form-fitting dress following the lines of her really lovely figure precisely! How could Peter or anybody help staring!

Delia, however, sat straighter, viewing Lisa with frosty inquiry. "What do you want, Maude?"

Lisa paid no attention to the "Maude." She went to Jim, holding her hands out and looking up at him with probably, Julie thought, the loveliest eyes any mortal ever had. "They'll never find you there! Hurry up, Jim. Come with me."

"Where?" Jim had Lisa's hands. Perhaps he couldn't help it.

"Why, to Darien. It's great. People have dinner and sit around and then have theater. I've got a part, next week, the best, naturally," Lisa said with no arrogance, a simple statement of truth; Julie had to admit that. "And there's a role for you. Nobody will look for you. You'll be perfectly safe until the police find out that you couldn't possibly have killed anybody. But you'll have to hurry. Rehearsals start at three this afternoon."

Fifteen

"But—" Jim began. He gave Julie a helpless glance.

"It's made for you!" Lisa cried exultantly. "That is, not exactly, but it's safe! Jim, can't you understand? Everybody in Brookboro is sure you murdered the Judge, because everybody felt you must have killed that man Walker and then the instant—well, at least very soon after you came back—why, Jim, now everybody knows that the Judge said he could not help you. And then he died. Because somebody—they say it had to be you, and you did see him that morning, the morning he died, I mean—"

"Lisa." Jim drew his hands away and looked very seriously down at her. "I don't think you're making much sense. I know I am a suspect and—"

"But you can't seem to realize how safe you'll be with me! In Darien! Why, nobody will ever think of looking for you there! And Blanche said that you need time." She turned to Delia. "Oh, tell him he must come. I've got a car waiting right outside. Jim must take on a role in the play we're rehearsing. Nobody in the world would look for you there.

And besides, you'll be made up so nobody is likely to recognize you—"

"Lisa, I'm not an actor! I couldn't possibly learn any lines!"

"But there aren't many lines for you to learn. You see, it's a revival of *George Washington Slept Here.*"

Delia broke in. "I saw a revival of that play not long ago. What role do you expect Jim to undertake?"

Lisa did hesitate, just slightly. "Well, there's one role that doesn't require many lines. You could do it on your head—"

Delia could guess like lightning. "The caretaker."

"Only a beard and a little dirt on your face," Lisa began defensively. "You won't mind wearing a false beard and smearing a little dirt on your face, Jim. It's nothing—"

"Wait a minute." Jim was frowning, perplexed. "I do seem to remember that play. Isn't the role you have in mind rather important?"

"No, no! You only enter a few times saying 'No water' or 'the seventeen-year locusts' or something like that. It's practically a walk-on. Honestly, Jim, you can't help learning those few lines—"

"No, thank you, Lisa."

"Now, Jim—"

Delia defected. "It might work, Jim. It will give you a few more days of freedom, and anything might happen."

"Anything *will* happen," Jim said grimly. "But, no."

Lisa was puzzled. "Why, Jim, do you really mind a little crepe hair on your face? And a little dirt. I suppose I could con the manager to let you skip some of it, but, you see, it's a perfect disguise."

"Darling Lisa," Jim said kindly but, Julie was thankful to note, also firmly, "it's very good of you to think of this—but, no."

Lisa flared up in indignation. "Don't you like laborers?

Don't you realize what the world is all about? Don't you acknowledge—"

"I have been a down-to-earth laborer. Very down to earth—" Jim began, but Lisa swept on.

"I have it. If you don't want to take that role—why, yes!" Her face lighted up. "I know another perfect role for you. There's a revival of that old one, *The Circle.* English accent! Why, it's a natural for you. Of course, you'd have to learn more lines, in fact quite a lot of lines, but—"

"Lisa," Jim said with such steel in his voice that Lisa did pause. "Listen to me. You think that hiding in the cast of some play, new or revived, would be safe. What about other members of the cast? What about the stage hands, the manager, the ushers? Lisa, it simply could not be kept a secret. I do thank you for trying to help—"

"George is playing in *The Circle,*" said Lisa. "He will help you."

"No!" Jim did not explode but it sounded like a skyrocket.

Even Delia caught her breath and cried, "No, Maude—"

"Lisa," said she, correcting Delia. "Now, really, George would like to help you. He's your brother—" She did falter a little there, but quickly recovered. "He wouldn't think of telling anybody that the police are after you—"

"Listen, Lisa! I'm going back to Brookboro. I'm going to go to the police myself—"

Delia was stubborn. "You can't do anything under arrest!"

Julie went to stand beside Jim. "No, no, he's right. He's got to go back and face things and I'll go there with him."

"You are both idiots!" Delia was almost crying.

"Idiots!" Lisa said scornfully. "That's a flattering term, I must say. Honestly, Julie, how can you encourage him like that?"

Peter came to everybody's assistance. "Hey," he said to Lisa admiringly, "your driver told me when you arrived that you'd have to get under way soon if you expected to get to Darien on time for rehearsals."

"Oh! Yes, I suppose—Jim, please!"

"I do thank you for trying, Lisa."

"Well—then—then I'll have to go." She touched her eyes with her hand, wiping across them as if wiping away tears, and these might be tears, Julie had to acknowledge that.

Then, however, Lisa looked at Peter, looked again and said sharply, "What is that thing around your shoulders? My God, it's a cat!"

"Her name is Pye," said Peter. "Short for Pyewacket. That's in a play—"

"Yes! I've read the play. Of course I am too young to have seen it."

Pye gave Lisa a disapproving mutter, so very disapproving as Lisa reached out a hand to touch her that Lisa shrank back. "Wear her if you like but she is really not becoming. Why, she looks as if she might fight!"

"Oh, yes, she might," Peter said agreeably. "Come on."

The front door closed and Peter came back, stroking Pye affectionately. He fell at once into his pontifical mood. "I told you. Tragedy and farce have a close relationship—"

Delia didn't like that. "You go downstairs and fix something for lunch. We need a close relationship with food."

Peter shrugged and disappeared. Beau thought for a moment and then followed down the stairs. After a long moment Delia said thoughtfully, "You know though, Jim, Lisa's idea just might work."

"No, it won't," Jim said grimly.

A long, shrill whistle came from the dining room. Then Peter yelled up the dumbwaiter shaft, "there you are!"

There was the bumpy rumble of the old dumbwaiter ascending.

Peter followed but along the narrow, dark stairway, arriving in a very complacent way. "I did a good job. Hurried, too. But the roast beef was already carved and you can make your own sandwiches." He hauled out an enormous tray of bread, butter, beef and pickles. "Didn't have time to make

153

coffee but there's always a drink if anybody wants it."

Delia gave him a look that miraculously silenced him, that or the sandwich he was shoving into his mouth.

"It's better than nothing," Delia said forgivingly, but noticed the jumbled mass of sliced beef, bread, butter with disfavor. "I wonder if Mrs. Martine is *ever* coming back."

Julie went to help her make some more appetizing sandwiches; she had an odd and extremely vague notion that if —a big if—she and Jim ran away and married in some hospitable but perhaps rather primitive country, she would have many such small crises to encounter. Making sandwiches, indeed! They'd be lucky if it were no more than that.

Delia said absently, "You know, Lisa has a real talent. Now, George, I've seen him act. Or try to act. Somehow you always know he's an actor, making believe. And you never believe the character he's playing. Lisa has—has—"

Peter munching, supplied the words, "Star quality."

"Well, yes, that may be the word for it. I hate to say it, but that girl may go far on the stage."

Julie didn't like it either, not really. But she had to acknowledge the truth in Delia's comment.

She didn't need to say anything, however, for Delia offered a plate of very neat sandwiches to Jim. "Now you eat, Jim, and then go to the phone and ask Blanche where you should go so you can make a flight reservation."

Peter jumped up. "There's another car. Bet you it's Mr. Wingate."

"Let him in," said Delia, but Jim was ahead of Peter.

It was John. Blanche came in with him.

There followed what amounted to a council of war, although the warriors were of opposing armies.

Blanche and Delia were of the strong opinion that Jim should take Blanche's advice and get out while he could. Julie said she was going to leave with Jim, whichever way Jim decided.

Jim said he was going back to Brookboro and face the thing.

John Wingate took a passport from a pocket and handed it to Jim, who took it with a low thank you, sir, and shoved it into a pocket. Blanche had a typed list, a rather short list, Julie noted, which she gave to Jim and which he also pocketed without even a glance at it.

Peter was only audience but an audience with the most rapt attention. It fell to John, however, to give the very strong argument in favor of Jim's leaving at once, with Julie joining him as soon as possible. He said he'd get their visas; he thought he could do that very promptly. Blanche said, but in a small voice, that of course they were not married and John joined ranks with Delia, saying that didn't matter. They could take care of it later.

It was then that Blanche asked if the police had come to Delia's home looking for Jim. John looked faintly amused when Peter popped up and explained about the dumb-waiter. Blanche didn't waver. She looked different that day, very tired; her usually clear, tranquil gray eyes were troubled and red-rimmed. She looked at John. "She may as well know—"

John nodded but said to Julie, "Don't let it alarm you. There's not a vestige of proof. It's only because you were there—"

"There—" Julie began but knew the answer.

"At the Judge's," Blanche said, "when he died. Their notion is now that you knew of Jim's inheritance from the Judge."

"But I didn't!" Julie cried and guessed what was coming next.

It came. "So they say, Julie, that even you had a motive for killing the Judge. An easy way, they said. Taking that bottle of medicine away and tossing it out along the road so it broke."

"But I didn't—I would never—"

Jim came to her. "Julie wouldn't kill anybody. Besides, she didn't know about the Judge's will."

"They say I could have told you," Blanche said. Her lips, usually neatly lipsticked, had almost no color. "He told me when I drew up his will that it might seem unusual, but he did not believe that Jim had anything to do with Walker's murder and yet he realized Jim's grave danger following a trial and a jury's all too certain decision." Blanche's usually steady voice wavered. "So he thought that was the least he could do for you. He trusted me to make sure that when he died you had that money as, he said, a slight recompense. He also told me that he hoped sometime that strong and convincing evidence would establish the true facts of the murder."

Peter had kept still as long as he could. "But we have some new evidence. At least we think it may prove to be evidence. About Alben Walker."

John and Blanche listened as Peter eagerly related what the society writer had told them. He performed with zeal but perfect accuracy. Delia nodded approvingly. John gripped the arms of his chair, hard, his eyes dark and grave.

When Peter stopped, Jim turned to Delia. "You have those press clippings that Mr. Brown left? My father and Blanche should see them." Delia got up swiftly.

Julie, however, knew what was about to develop. Delia was almost pathologically neat about herself and her household. The tall wall desk at the end of the room looked polished, neat and dignified. Opened, it was another matter. Even Blanche, who must have seen its interior sometimes, gave a kind of gasp as Delia put down the desk lid and disclosed a mass of papers: letters, advertisements, appeals for charity, everything jumbled together.

Peter said softly to Julie, "No wonder she never scolds me about my school reports. She can't find them. Not that they aren't very good," he added cautiously.

"I doubt that." Julie had an older sister's candor.

Jim had followed Delia to the desk and stood looking stunned at the avalanche that seemed ready to pour out helter-skelter on the floor. Julie could see a wave of crimson spread up over Delia's neck. Her hands, however, were perfectly steady. "I know I have them—*right here*—" In a moment she said triumphantly, "See!"

She waved the press clippings at Jim, who, still looking rather dazed, gave them one glance and handed them to John. Blanche came to John's side. They both pored over the clippings.

Nobody spoke. Delia closed the desk and returned to her chair. Finally Blanche said, "The dates—"

John nodded, "Yes, I saw that. Almost exactly six years ago. Walker was in Brookboro for about a year before he was killed. Isn't that right, Delia?"

Delia nodded. "But I can't see that these clippings tell us much."

John said at last, "May I keep these, Delia?"

"Certainly."

"Anything else?" John asked.

Peter said, "Surely it's enough to encourage Jim to investigate more of Walker's past."

"That's not the only problem," Blanche said. "Julie *was* with the Judge when he died. She *did* try to find his medicine and couldn't." She turned to Julie. "Did the police question you when they were here?"

"No. First we were intent upon Jim, you see, and the hope he wouldn't make a move."

Peter interrupted, giving Pye a complacent look. "And then the cat stopped them." Having the platform again, he related the episode, too. He grinned as he told it.

John suddenly laughed and even Jim smiled. "Sure," Jim said, but ruefully, "I'd have enjoyed it more if I hadn't been cooped up in that thing. I bet runaway slaves shut up there thought it was never like this in the care of ole massa!"

"All the same, the police went away," Julie said crossly,

but also still shocked. She said to Blanche, "Were there no fingerprints on the broken bottle of medicine?"

John replied, soberly now, "Nothing that could be identified. Perhaps the cleaning woman who worked for the Judge broke it accidentally and is now afraid to confess."

Jim stopped him. "Don't you think that a deeper digging into Walker's past is indicated? There's got to be something that the murderer could not permit anybody else to see.

John shook his head. "You mean something to suggest the real murderer—form the basis for a new trial. It's not easy to get."

Blanche said soberly, "At the moment, there's no chance of that. And if the Brookboro police are getting the idea that Julie and Jim worked out the Judge's death together—oh, I don't know!" For the first time in all the years she'd known Blanche, Julie saw her hands clasp together hard. In a moment she was sure Blanche would cry. She did. In a short sobbing breath, she said, "I've tried to help! I've only botched everything! You've got to get away, Jim! And you, too, Julie!" She wiped her eyes hard. "I promise you. Give us some more time. We'll all keep trying to get some fresh and convincing evidence. That could be soon. But I agree with John that you two must get away now."

Peter suddenly piped up. "Don't forget George."

John looked at him in surprise. "But George has nothing to do with this."

"Oh, yes, he has," Peter said, pretending nonchalance. "He tried to run Julie down in a car."

"What are you talking about? *George did what? I can't believe—!*" John was astounded.

"Didn't Jim tell you?"

"No," said Jim. "How could I! His other son!"

But John was on his feet. "You needn't have been quite so considerate, son." But Jim made one long stride to stand beside him. Nobody, Julie thought again, could question their relationship.

158

John said, "No. Oh, no! I'll have to hear the details, but it couldn't have been George. Oh, I know . . . he's not the son that"— he gave Jim a look—"not the son I'd like to have. I had to make allowances about—oh, several things. Small things. But George is—I may as well tell the truth here! I don't understand him. I can't say what or what not he might do. But deliberately trying to hurt—"

"Kill," said Peter.

Sixteen

John went on, "—injure anybody. With a car. Such a foolish way, when you consider it."

"Of course," Delia said in a faraway voice, "George is a bit of a fool."

"Only a fool would wait in the street for Julie. George is the only real fool we know. Therefore it was George. Logic," said Peter wisely.

Delia stopped him. "Julie went out with the dog. A car was parked up the street. It came crashing down. There's a kind of slope toward First Avenue. Peter insists it was driven by George. He did not *see* George. But George had reason to be offended," Delia paused and seemed to debate the word.

Peter said, "Might as well tell them the whole thing. I," he went on proudly, "had to throw him out."

"What did he do?" John fixed Peter with a very stern gaze. Peter wriggled a little. Delia took over again.

"He wanted Julie to marry him. He became obnoxious when she said she didn't want to. She told him to leave. Peter and I heard the whole thing."

"You see," Peter added, "we can't—at least, we haven't really tried to find an alibi for George. I think that a good detective could certainly find out where George was at that time and whether or not anybody saw him there—"

John sighed. "Yes, Peter. That will be seen to."

Jim put a hand on his father's shoulder. "I can't believe that George—"

John turned to Peter. "You say you didn't actually see George?"

"The car revved up and woke me. No, I didn't actually see George. But it had to be him. And there's another thing," Peter added, his face glowing. "Did you know that George was once in Las Vegas?"

"Las Vegas?" John said. "He never said so."

"I'll tell you," Peter offered and did.

It was a perfectly accurate accounting of the discovery in one of the pockets of George's tailcoat. Peter did skip over the reasons for exploring George's clothes but nobody picked him up about that when he said, far too lightly, that he and Sam were fixing up a figure in anticipation of Halloween.

"Las Vegas," John repeated. He turned to Blanche. "You didn't know this?"

"I know that George turned up with some proofs of his identity," Blanche said slowly. "He had a passport. That would show the date of his arrival here."

"Oh, yes, he had a passport," John agreed. "Born in some little town in England. Elaine lingered in England for quite some time before she went on to Europe. I thought she had stayed in England in order to be near Jim. Remember, at that time I had very little money. I sent Elaine what I could."

"But you must have written to her," Delia said.

"Oh, yes. But she only cashed the postal orders I sent and vanished. She divorced me in France. She never mentioned George."

"Ashamed to," Delia said tartly. "But you must have had some idea about where she was living."

"I could never find her. My letters and money by that time were simply sent *Poste Restante*. At last I decided to send her a large sum of money. I had money by then. So I—well, I actually tried to buy Jim. So I sent her the money—"

"I remember," said Delia.

"How much?" Peter asked.

"A hundred thousand."

Delia shook her head. Peter uttered a kind of whoop.

"Yes, I know," John said. "But we had made, I thought, a bargain. She was to have the money and in turn she was to tell me where to find Jim."

Delia always got down to brass tacks. "How did you send the money?"

"To a Swiss bank. And if you want to know"—John smiled rather grimly—"all that stuff about numbered accounts in some Swiss banks is true. I found nobody who could or at least would tell me anything. I went there. I even went so far as to hang around the bank, in the street, hoping to get a glimpse of Elaine. I didn't see her but the money was collected, and after that no word at all from Elaine. She never had mentioned George. I gather that she left George in some school in England, as she had deposited Jim. However, she did keep in touch with George and consequently, when she was not well, she sent for him. He found her in some little place in Italy. After she died he came to me. So! What really *mattered*, convinced me, were the things that only Elaine could have given him."

After a moment Delia said thoughtfully, "John, I can't remember just when Elaine died."

John's eyebrows raised a little. "Why, it was just over six years ago."

"And then George came to you?"

"A few months later. Not long."

"John, did you have any other proof of George's claim to be your son?" Delia asked. "I mean, besides all those papers—"

John said soberly, "I didn't have a blood test, if that is what you mean. Didn't have it for Jim either. I knew Jim was my son. But as to George—well, I knew he was Elaine's son and I owed Elaine a great deal. I hadn't been as good to her as I would have liked to be—had no money—my only thought and aim was to try to make enough money to see to her and Jim. It was obvious that Elaine had given the papers and all that to George. The fact of it is, I would have done anything I could do to—oh, try to make up for my neglect of poor little Elaine. So," he shrugged, "there you have it. He could be my son. I can have two sons if I want to."

Delia smiled. "That's what all of Brookboro believes. But they rather think it possible that Jim is a sort of—"

"By-blow," Blanche said with an edge of steel in her voice. "He's not that."

John sighed. "I am surprised that George seems to have been in Las Vegas before he came to me after his mother's death. He was still living in England. Had some kind of job, selling cars, I think. Oh, I was sure that he was Elaine's son. Perhaps my son. Perhaps—oh, forget it. I acknowledged him. I'm sorry he seems to have taken a fancy to the stage but then, perhaps he inherits that, too. Elaine could—could pretend, you know. Poor girl," John said, "I wish I could have given her more."

Delia patted her hair with two hands, and made a decision. "We are talking about apples and oranges. Chalk and cheese. As far as we know, John's feeling about Jim and George had nothing to do with Walker's murder. I think we should stick to that. And that means both Jim—and Julie if she insists— and I indeed think she is right," Delia interpolated warmly. "She should go away with Jim or follow him, whenever the passport situation and reservations work out. Then we'll have to work on new evidence ourselves." At John's skeptical glance she added, "And I think we can, John. Somebody," she finished, "has to."

There was no answer to that.

At last John said, "Jim can't do anything at all under arrest. He's got to delegate any investigation to—well, to us, of course. And we'll work more on it, Jim, I promise you."

Suddenly Jim thrust himself away from his father, from all of them, plunged across the room, opened the French doors as if for air but then exploded in an exasperated sound which wasn't a roar or a howl but it was loud. Delia looked nervously at the garden below.

"Jim!" John cried. "What—"

Jim turned to face him. "*Stop it!*" Again he didn't quite yell but the effect was the same.

"The neighbors will hear you," Delia began.

"All of you are trying and trying to make me run again! I *simply will not.* So shut up about passports and—visas and whether or not Julie and I can get married somewhere or—or—" His furious exasperation diminished. He said, flatly and miserably, to his father, "You understand, don't you?"

John eyed him soberly and then looked at Blanche. But Blanche, too, had dropped back in her chair; she looked very pale and very sad. "Oh, Jim, I tried!"

"I stay right here. Julie stays with me. So—"

For a moment that just about settled it, Julie thought. Nobody could say anything. But Jim was right. Nobody could expect him to have been on the run for five years, and then return to someplace where he'd still be, so to speak, on the run.

John understood it, too. He said at last. "All right, Jim. But we really tried to do what we thought was right." He put his hand on Jim's shoulder. "We'll do as you say. It's your —that is—"

"Can't be his funeral!" Peter's eyes were bright with excitement. "Not unless there is a trial and the jury—"

"That's enough, Peter!" That was John, still close to Jim.

"Yes, but—" Peter could not be silenced. "Suppose George and Jim—I mean, just suppose that their—situation," said Peter with unusual delicacy, "*does* have something to do with Walker's murder."

"What?" It was now Blanche in her dry lawyer's voice.

Peter wriggled. "Well, I don't know. But it could have."

"Anything could be. Proving it," Blanche said, "is a different matter. Oh, Jim, Julie, give us more time."

John said, "We'll go back to Brookboro, Blanche. But don't you think it would be a good idea for Jim to go to your place in the city? I don't think the police know about it, do they?"

Blanche shook her head. "No, I'm sure they don't."

John added, "Julie might go with him. I'm very much afraid the chief of our police is already planning to question her more thoroughly. I really don't think it would help anybody at all if Julie were, as they say, detained for questioning by the police."

"I go where Jim goes." Julie rose.

John smiled at her, his usual warm smile. "Good for you, my girl. By the way, did I see a box that looked like galleys on your desk as we came in?"

Julie was horrified. "Oh, John! I forgot all about them!"

He gave her a kind and affectionate look but also with a tinge of shock. "My dear, that will never do. Wherever you and Jim go, you must continue to write. Always get your priorities straight."

"My first priority is Jim," Julie said flatly.

"Good. However, I'll take your proofs with me and get them back to your publisher."

"Oh, John, it's my new novel. It's not very good. I am afraid it's not good at all."

John took that kindly, too. "I did not expect the great American novel. I'll take it. Now, keep your chin up, girl—"

Peter muttered. "But don't lead with it."

Jim had sufficiently conquered his storm to grin faintly at Peter. "Julie knows that, Peter."

165

Blanche rose, went to Delia and pressed her cheek against Delia's. She came to Julie and kissed her. Julie felt tears on her cheek. They went away, John with the box of proofs under his arm.

There was not much to be said. Jim did apologize to Delia. "Sorry I made such a fool of myself."

"Can't blame you." Delia was surprisingly matter-of-fact. "Actually I think you may be right. At least I hope so."

The long day had faded into night. Jim and Julie were in Julie's workroom talking and not talking, when Peter yelled. "There's a taxi pulling up to the curb."

The doorbell rang. Peter ran to open the door, but a second later he stumbled back to Julie's room. "She says—says—" he began. "Aunt Delia!"

A woman had followed Peter. "I told him that I am Elaine Wingate." She looked around her, fumbled her way into the living room and then fastened a pale, greenish gaze upon Delia. Peter, Julie and Jim had followed and they heard her speak. "Surely you remember me, Delia."

Seventeen

Delia gave one great gasp and sank back into a chair, both hands clutching at her heart in real shock.

Elaine—Elaine?—stood close to a chair, grasping the back with shabby cotton gloves, very dirty. She wore a black beret, pulled down, but a few red-gray wisps of hair straggled below it. She wore a dark coat, too short for her dress, which disclosed wrinkled stockings and once-white espadrilles, dirty also. Her pale lips moved. "So kind, Delia. Always so kind. So I came to you—"

"But—Elaine—" Delia managed. There were two urgent toots from the street.

Peter recovered himself enough to say, "The taxi."

Jim thrust a hand into a pocket, pulled out a bill and handed it to Peter, and went over to Elaine. Once there, however, he simply stood, face blank and very white, looking at the woman intently. He was trying, certainly, to remember something of his mother—no, no, George's mother. No, their mother.

The woman—Elaine?—didn't shift her pale gaze from

Delia. "Always so kind—no place to go—" Jim leaped forward and caught her in his arms as she tottered, grasped harder at the back of the chair and then simply, completely, collapsed.

Delia said in a strangled way, "Take her upstairs, Jim. The second bedroom."

"Call your doctor," Jim said tersely and swept up his burden gently. She must be very light, Julie thought with pity. Such a little, thin woman. Jim so strong and resolute, far more like his father than Elaine.

But no, she was making a mistake again. George, too, was Elaine's son.

Jim, holding Elaine gently and carefully, disappeared up the stairs.

Delia let out a breath of air as if she'd been holding it. "I don't believe it! She's been dead for—but it is Elaine!"

Jim called down the stairs. "Did you call the doctor?"

"No—no—that is, I will. Now." Delia was still in such a state of agitation that she staggered a little as she walked to the telephone, although she often said she was as strong as a horse. She knew the number and dialed. "Dr. Evans, please! . . . Hurry! . . . Yes, an emergency . . . Thank you, Doctor."

She put down the telephone. "And it certainly is an emergency. Whoever would have thought—but, Julie, she's been dead for years. At least since before George came home."

"She knew you!" Julie said. "She managed to get here somehow! Where has she been? Oh, Delia, Jim acts as if she is his mother."

Delia tottered to a chair. "That's Jim for you. He is just naturally kind to anybody in distress."

"We'd better let John Wingate know."

"John! Oh, dear! Yes. That is, I suppose so."

"You know so," Julie said shortly. "I'll phone him—"

Delia was beginning to recover. "They've not had time to get to Brookboro. Oh, Julie, Julie, it's a shock!" Indeed Delia was shocked; there was only the slightest color in her face, and even her lips had taken on a bluish tinge. Peter came bounding excitedly back into the room. "I paid the taxi. Guess where he picked her up."

Delia and Julie simply looked at him.

"At Kennedy Airport. And she told him your address and then when she got out at the door, she told him she'd have to get some money from you. Or somebody."

"Oh, poor woman," Julie said.

"But where did she come from?" Delia was still distracted. "I can't imagine—where has she been? Why does everybody think she died years ago? Even John Wingate believes she is dead."

"Well, she's not," Julie said. "I hope your doctor will be here soon."

"Oh, he'll be here. You remember Dr. Evans. He lives in the Cove. The house at the corner. Oh, Julie, this is so unexpected, so—so—I can't seem to—to do anything."

Peter's eyes were sparkling. "And guess what! The cabbie called her 'Countess.' What do you think of that?"

"Countess—" Delia leaned weakly back in her chair.

"Countess what?" Julie asked.

Peter shrugged. "The cabbie didn't know. Just said she took his cab and gave him your address, Aunt Delia, and when they got here, she told him to wait. She hadn't any money but she was Countess something-or-other and a friend of yours and you would give her money for him," said Peter. "What do you think of that?"

Delia paid no attention. "Elaine! Oh, yes, it's Elaine, but terribly changed."

"So would you be if you'd been dead for years," Peter interjected, rather too obviously enjoying the drama of the moment.

Delia didn't so much as look at him. "She was such a pretty little thing. Not much sense. She did drink and carry on and leave John and her son—that is, she did keep in touch with George—but she was so very pretty. And now—"

"I'll go up and help Jim." Julie started for the stairs as Delia suddenly came alive and all but shouted at Peter, "Did you say she said she was a countess?"

"Sure—I mean, yes'm."

"*Countess,*" Delia shrieked. "That awful man's wife!"

"Oh, no!" Julie tried to reason but stopped. It was barely possible that she *had* been Walker's wife. And if that were true then, why, then she might have had a motive for killing him. But oh, no! That would be stretching imagination too far. Yet suppose it was not imagination. She caught at Delia's shoulder. "Do you really think she could have been married to Walker?"

"Yes," Delia flared. "Yes—*Countess!*"

"But then—why, then—"

Peter finished. "Where has she been? Walker was murdered over five years ago. Did she just come to Brookboro and take a shot at him and vanish and—" Peter shook his head. "Can't be." He changed his mind with dizzy speed. "Yes! It could be. I told you. *Cherchez la femme!* She got back to Brookboro and found him and shot him, probably for some very good reason," said Peter judicially, "and then vanished and—"

Julie tried to rein in her wildly galloping thoughts. "But how could she do that, Peter? How could—"

"Julie!" Jim called down the stairs. "Come up here, will you?"

"Countess," Delia muttered as Julie ran up the stairs. "Walker—"

Jim had placed Elaine on the bed in a small guest room. He had removed the heavy silk bedcover, and taken off her black beret, disclosing pathetically thin but certainly onetime red hair. He was trying to get her coat off when Julie came in. "Good, Julie! Help me. I've got to get her as comfortable as I can. She really is in a state of collapse. Is the doctor coming?"

"Yes. Right away. Here, let me take the sleeve."

It was a shabby kind of raincoat on the outside, worn black cloth on the inside.

Jim pulled off the dirty espadrilles, disclosing men's socks, wrinkled down over some very pathetic ankles. Together, as gently as they could, they eased Elaine out of the battered raincoat. "We'll leave her dress on till the doctor gets here," Jim said. "He may not want us to move her. She looks—why, Julie, she looks starved. Really starved. Look at her hands and—and her face—"

It was better not to look but she did and hoped the doctor would come soon and do something, anything for the woman who lay here. Her sunken eyes were closed, the bones of her face startlingly accented.

Elaine had been so pretty, Delia had said.

There were no faint remnants of beauty left. But there was the direct, stabbing appeal of helplessness.

"Jim, she can't be Elaine!"

"I don't know," Jim said oddly.

The woman on the bed stirred slightly, lifted heavy eyelids and said, "Delia—"

"She's here," Julie replied quickly, leaning over. "Delia is here. The doctor is coming—"

At the word "doctor" the woman began to shake; it was like an ague. She struggled to sit up. "No, no! Not a doctor! Please—not a doctor—"

John took her bony, seeking hands, "It's all right. No doctor you ever saw before. He's Delia's doctor. Nearby. Now please be quiet. He'll see to you. Trust me."

Elaine's pale green eyes flicked up toward his face, then toward Julie. There was an inquiry in the gaze. "Yes,

171

Delia's doctor," Julie said. "You will be perfectly safe here. Safe."

She straightened the crumpled-up folds of a dark gray, shabby and sagging dress; it was machine knitted and too big for the emaciated little body. Jim went to a chest of drawers, opened one, then another, and came back with a light blanket, which he put gently over the figure on the bed. "There, she'll get warmer."

"Don't you think a brandy—"

He shook his head. "We'll wait for the doctor."

"Here he is," Peter called. "This way, Dr. Evans—"

"Thank you, thank you—" said a cheerful voice and a man walked in; bounced in would be a better description of his entrance. He was short, plump and efficient-looking; even his short dark moustache and neat beard seemed efficient. However, his pleasant face sobered as he looked at the woman on the bed. "Now, then. What's all this?"

"We don't know," Julie began, but Dr. Evans advanced to the bed and took one thin wrist in his hand. He counted—he seemed almost to listen—and his usually cheerful face became very grave. "I don't know. She looks half starved." He turned to Jim and Julie. "Perhaps you'd better leave—"

"I am staying," Jim said.

The doctor gave him one look and apparently believed him. "As you wish. I'll just get out my stethoscope."

He was digging in a pocket when Julie edged past him and then, going down the stairs, simply sat on the lower step. She felt utterly drained of energy and of any reasonable conclusion. The living room and dining room were very quiet and the quiet began slowly to impinge upon her awareness. Jim could be this woman's son. George had to be her son. Elaine? she thought again and then heard voices from the kitchen below. The door to the narrow stairway was open. Neither cat nor dog, nor Delia nor Peter, was visible.

All of them must be in the kitchen. One shouldn't try to cope with anything at all on an empty stomach, Delia always said.

So Delia had gone to the kitchen; Peter, always hungry, had gone with her. Naturally Beau and Pye had followed.

Julie did manage to stir; she went to the stairs and looked down. Lights were on in the kitchen, spreading upward to the stairway.

"That woman—" Delia said clearly. "That Mrs. Martine hasn't been here at all! What—Peter, oh, yes, of course, in the freezer and—that's right. Now what are you doing?"

"Feeding the livestock."

Julie got to her feet and, feeling rather wobbly, made her way down.

Delia saw her first. "What does the doctor say?"

"I don't know. Jim is staying with her."

"What does Jim say?" Peter asked.

"There wasn't anything to say. Delia, is she really Elaine?"

"You asked that before! Yes, she is! I recognized her. Changed, of course—oh, sadly, tragically changed. But she's Elaine. And I don't—I really don't know what to do," said Delia, and sat down on a kitchen chair and began to cry.

Peter gallantly patted her shoulder. "There, there, Aunt Delia. We'll see to things—"

"I'll try John's number." Julie went to the kitchen extension of the telephone. Delia lifted her head, tears streaming down her cheeks, and listened. There was no answer.

Delia forced herself to seem natural and in control. "We'll do whatever the doctor says. You and Jim must go to Blanche's place. Right now. You *must do as I say.* If the police come here again and find Jim—"

"I'll stay here until the doctor tells us what to do."

Delia watched her for a moment. "It's like Jim," she said as if reassuring herself. "George would never have bothered with anybody, no matter who. But Jim is different."

Peter said practically, "You said we'd better see to some food, Aunt Delia."

"Oh, yes. Anything you can find . . ." Delia sighed.

Pye was already tucking into a saucer of food that Peter had put down for her; she didn't eat daintily, as cats usually do; she gobbled voraciously, uttering tiny growls in her throat as she did so. Beau stood by but looked wistful, and at Julie's word came to her and pressed his head against her knee; it was his way of asking for something. She went to the shelf where there were cans of food. He waited while she opened a can with a most efficient can opener, and scooped out his choice liver scraps into a dish. He settled down to that.

Delia said, as if to herself, "A menagerie, that's what. And now I'm afraid Mrs. Martine is gone for good."

"Go and find her," Peter suggested blithely, having discovered a bowl of pâté and some crackers. "*Cherchez la femme,*" he said again.

Delia glowered as adequately as she could glower. "Don't keep showing off your French. How about your Latin? And don't give me any of that 'all Gaul is divided' or *amo, amas, amat—*"

There was a spark of mischief in Peter's blue eyes. "How about *tigna bigna sesquipedalia*?"

Luckily for Peter, the doctor and Jim came down into the kitchen just then. They were both very serious. Delia jumped up. "How is she?"

The doctor settled himself wearily into a chair.

"Half starved, I'd say. She needs hospital care, constant nursing. I've sent for an ambulance. It will be here in a moment. Meanwhile I'd better get some information—" He drew out a small notebook. "Now then, you know her, Mrs. Van Clive?"

"Of course. I haven't seen her for over twenty years. But I do know her! Terribly changed but—"

"Name?" said the doctor, getting a pen uncapped. "Jim says her name is Elaine Wingate—"

Delia began. "She thinks—that is, she was."

"Where had she been?"

"We don't know. Somewhere in Europe, we think. A taxi picked her up at Kennedy. Brought her here."

"She didn't say where she has been?" the doctor asked.

"No, she collapsed too quickly," Jim said.

The doctor shook his head so that his neat small beard quivered. "Wherever she's been she has been treated very badly. Indeed, this seems preposterous, but I wondered if she has escaped from—from somewhere."

"Escaped!" That was Delia.

The doctor nodded. "After I had given her a small injection she did mutter a few words. Something about stealing money."

"Stealing!" Delia cried.

"That's correct. I can't help thinking it possible that she may have been in some sanitarium, held there for—oh, for any reason. But she seems to have used up the last of her strength in getting here to you."

"Well," Delia said weakly, "she knew I was her friend. That is—but she is terribly changed. I know she's Elaine, but one time"—tears were in Delia's eyes again—"she was very pretty."

"Yes, too bad. If, in fact, she has been in some sanitarium, I'll do my best to find out which one. Did she have any sort of identification, a handbag or something? She had to have a passport if she came in from Europe."

For a second nobody moved. Then Peter flashed up the stairs to the living room and tumbled down again, holding a handbag, worn but of good leather. "Here it is."

"Thank you, Peter. How you've grown," said the doctor, glancing at Peter. "Remember when I had to give you a quarter to take medicine?"

Peter sidled up to Julie and whispered, "Bet Aunt Delia gave him the quarters."

"So." The doctor opened the shabby handbag and emptied the contents onto the table.

Everybody looked, fascinated, while the doctor took out a little stack of paper tissues, an empty change purse, no keys, no letters, but what was certainly a passport.

He opened it and looked quickly at Delia. "Didn't you say you knew her?"

"I did. I do. She is—was—Elaine Wingate."

Dr. Evans shook his head. "Passport says she is Alice Parget. Age forty—height—well, here's the photograph."

All of them bent over the gaze at the photograph. After a long moment Delia leaned back. "It could be anybody."

"Not quite," Dr. Evans said. "There could be the faintest resemblance to the woman upstairs, but it is a dim photograph. Not a very good light or perhaps too good a light, so the eyes flare. But, no, I can't say if it is the woman upstairs or not."

"But I tell you, the woman upstairs is Elaine Wingate. I knew her at once."

Peter piped up again. "The taxi man said that she said she was a countess."

The doctor scanned the passport again. "There's no mention of being a countess, or anything, really. Place of birth, New York. Why do you think her name is really Elaine Wingate, Mrs. Van Clive?"

"I knew her—that is, it's been—how old are you, Jim?"

"Twenty-seven. At least that's what I've been told, and I believe—"

"Yes. Well, then. I knew Elaine when she lived in Brookboro. My—hometown. And she was married to John Wingate, you've heard of him—"

"Not only heard of him. Read him," said the doctor. "But go on."

"John was then having a hard time. Hadn't got started on his career—hadn't any money to speak of, and Elaine was very pretty and very—very—I don't know how to put it—"

The doctor guessed. "Do you mean, say, easily influenced?"

"Why, yes! Yes, that was it! And so she—she left John and took their son with her and—put the boy in a school, a kind of nursery school in England, and John sent her money to keep them both for years. After he became famous and also rather rich—"

Peter was irrepressible. "An uncle died. Left him dough."

"I see. Yes, but now his wife. Were they divorced or what?"

"Oh, yes, I know they were divorced. I don't remember when. She may have married again. It's possible that a man named Walker—"

"Wait a minute." The doctor began to make small notes. "Elaine Wingate. Disappeared—" He glanced up at Delia, who nodded. "Returned to New York with a stolen passport."

"Stolen!" Delia cried. "And on stolen money! Oh, why didn't she write and ask me! But if Elaine—she said she was a countess—if she had married this—this fake count by the name of Walker and then—" Delia checked herself in horror.

"She did not come back to Brookboro and kill him." Jim stood at the end of the table. "She did not take a shot at Walker, although if by chance any of this notion is true, he deserved it. But she would not—"

The doctor stood so suddenly that he seemed to face Jim across an unseen arena.

Jim looked at him and then at Delia. "Let's stop all this nonsense about Elaine. She is my mother."

Delia stared at him with shocked, blank eyes. "Jim! How do you know?"

"I know," said Jim and looked as if he dared anyone to deny him.

Nobody did. After a long moment the doctor sighed. "You are perfectly sure of that?"

"Yes," said Jim and meant it.

Eighteen

Delia sat down, put her head in her hands on the kitchen table, and began to sob.

The doctor looked at Jim again. Jim looked at the doctor. The doctor finally repeated, "You are very sure of this?"

"I am sure."

"But as Mrs. Van Clive has said, how do you know?"

"I know," Jim said with tense finality.

The doctor waited again. Delia continued to cry. Peter put a consoling hand on her shoulder but kept his gaze glued to Jim and the doctor. At last the doctor shut his notebook. "Well, whoever she is, she must have been quite desperate. She must have used up the very last of her strength to do what she did. She's here, and we can't question her now. Certainly the ambulance will arrive soon. She'll have the best possible care. Intravenous feeding may help. But I must insist that none of you question her or upset her in any way. If you try to I won't be responsible for anything."

"We'll not question her until you give your permission." Jim was solid as a rock.

The doctor said thoughtfully, "Odd. Doctors have two

sides. One, he is a doctor, trained, and does his best to follow every aspect of his training. The other is—I can only call it the humanist side. And sometimes we deceive ourselves. We think we know so much but there are things we simply do not understand. This woman's name—well, if she stole the passport that is explained in a way. But you, Jim, are so certain she is your mother—"

"Yes," Jim said.

"I see. That is, I don't see but I believe you. Doctors can't diagnose everything. There are things we can't explain but have to accept. Nature, yes, nature's law does work. Now then, Peter, there's the ambulance, I think."

Peter dashed up the stairs. Jim ran after him, the doctor followed at a more sedate tread, as if he knew just what to do, and when, which was probably the truth. Delia was still sobbing. Julie reached the top of the steps in time to see a little procession heading up toward the bedrooms.

In a few moments it came down again; two paramedics, she thought from their uniforms, carrying Elaine wrapped in a blanket. Her eyes were closed. The men maneuvered their slight burden carefully through the hall and out the door. An ambulance stood at the curb, gleaming white. The doctor said, "I'll just go along and make sure of my orders," and pulled himself into the ambulance after them neatly as a boy. But Jim said, "I'm going, too," and put out his hand to Julie as if he needed her: they were always to share life's difficulties. She snatched her red coat from the hall closet and draped it around her shoulders.

Not sables this time, she thought irrationally and went with Jim. The three of them crowded into the ambulance, the doctor beside Elaine, Julie beside him, somehow Jim squeezed into the seat between the two young paramedics.

It was a rather long ride, it seemed to Julie, before they reached the hospital. Lights were still on in the great apartment buildings along the way. The traffic lights shone red and green. The ambulance drove very carefully, stopping so gently at the red lights that she barely felt the motion.

After a while the ambulance came to a complete halt; the two paramedics swung down and opened the wide door. The doctor got down to the pavement before the enormous doors of the hospital. How many people had approached it in just this way, Julie thought, and stood back to permit the paramedics to lift Elaine's stretcher down and then followed them. Jim was at her elbow. She was grateful for that; the entrance was so big and so frightening in a strange way that the touch of Jim's hand on her arm was comforting.

"Now, then," Dr. Evans said, "you and Jim stay right here." He gave a quick gesture toward the nearest bench. "I'll call you, Jim, if there's any need. But in the meantime, just wait here, please, both of you."

So they sat and waited in the cathedral-like hush around them. Other benches were occupied by other people, not many but enough to offer a subtle but unnerving kind of apprehension about the news for which they were all waiting. One woman kept going over and over her rosary, her eyes fixed upon a bank of elevators. One man lighted a cigarette, gave a rather scared glance around him at the small click of his lighter, and instantly dropped the cigarette in a tall vase, like an umbrella stand, nearby. The doors to the street opened now and then, permitting someone to enter, and swung together again. Occasionally a doctor hurried in, carrying a bag. Another pale and apprehensive man came in, searched for and apparently found a telephone, for he vanished; his voice became a low murmur in the vast entrance. Then he came out, took a place on a bench and, like the others, fastened his gaze upon the bank of elevators.

Jim simply sat beside Julie but once he put his hand over hers; it was warm and steady and unbelievably comforting. "She'll be all right," she whispered.

"Sure." But Jim whispered too. One didn't speak loudly in that solemn hush.

Time passed and passed. There was no way to guess what was being done for Elaine.

Suddenly, when a door to the street swung widely open and brisk footsteps crossed to them, Julie looked up with a start. It was, of course, John Wingate.

"How is she?"

"We don't know yet," Jim replied. "We're waiting. The doctor is still upstairs."

"Delia phoned Blanche in town. I was there. Delia said that she is Elaine."

"Yes. Yes, she is."

"Delia says you knew her at once."

"Certainly. She's my mother."

There was a pause while John and Jim exchanged a long and serious look. Finally John said, "Yes. Children do remember without knowing that they remember. How long will she be here?"

"We don't know. The doctor seems to think that she needs complete rest. No questions."

"I understand that. All the same—"

"What else did Delia tell you?"

"Said it appears Elaine stole some money and somebody's passport and—and came back." John's face was like a rock.

"Here's the doctor," Julie said.

He came across toward them. There was no sign of anything on his face but he gave Jim a slight nod. "I think she'll make it."

Jim said, his voice rather shaky, "This is my father. I wonder—just for purposes of—of clear identification—"

"H'mm, yes. I see." The doctor and John shook hands.

John said, "One brief glance, Doctor. I'll not try to talk to her."

The doctor didn't debate long. "Fine. Come with me. Jim, you and Julie stay here. I must ask you only to look from the door, Mr. Wingate. Don't try to speak. I've got a fine nurse for her. She's getting intravenous feeding. My God," said the doctor, "she was starving."

The two men walked back to the elevators. The other watchers and waiters seemed to shift slightly as if the appearance of a doctor, any doctor, with news, had both lifted their spirits and frightened them, wondering what news a doctor might have for each.

Actually both Dr. Evans and John were back in not more than ten minutes. John was suddenly older; there was none of his usual buoyance and certainty.

"Yes," he said to Jim, "she's Elaine—" John put a hand upon Jim's arm, as if to steady himself. "Thank you, doctor. Thank you—" He pulled himself together with visible effort. "It's a—a shock you know."

The doctor nodded and very carefully laid a hand on John's wrist.

John gave him a half-smile. "Oh, I'm all right. Just—just shocked. Horrified! Little Elaine—but there, I was going to say that my car is outside. May I take you with us back to Mrs. Van Clive's? I believe you live near her in the Cove?"

"Thank you, yes."

They went back again through rows of what were by now largely darkened apartment houses. A light was on in Delia's doorway. The doctor got out of the car with them. "It's shorter for me to cross the garden," he said.

Delia opened the door and stood firmly in their path. "It is Elaine?"

"Oh, yes, yes." Even John's always firm chin and nose seemed different. His deep-set gray eyes were shadowed.

"Jim said so," Delia began and put her hand on John's arm. "Come in—"

Peter rushed to open the French windows for Dr. Evans. "Good night," the doctor said. "I may have better news by morning."

Blanche, marble-white, black hair slightly disheveled, was

standing in the living room near the piano, waiting, too. "She really is Elaine? I couldn't believe you, Delia. I couldn't—what happened to her, John?"

"I don't know. May I?" he said to Delia and nodded toward the dining room. Peter guessed what he wanted and ran ahead to show him the liquor cabinet, but John knew his way around Delia's house. "Thank you, Peter. I'll pour it."

Blanche said unsteadily, "It's a shock. A terrible shock. Poor John—and poor Elaine. Has she much chance, Jim?"

"I hope so. I believe so," he said firmly, but afraid, Julie knew.

Delia said, "I kept trying Blanche's apartment until John answered. She had switched off the telephone so they could talk. When she turned it on again, I told her. They both came at once."

John came back. "First, yes, she is Elaine. And yes, the doctor thinks she'll make it." He drank slowly, as if taking time to get his thoughts together. "Second, I'll tell you, I think—I am afraid—" He looked at Julie. "I am very much afraid that George may have—have tried to run you down. No, stay where you are, Jim. I'm not perfectly certain it *was* George. I can't"—he swallowed more from the glass in his hand—"I cannot believe that George would do anything so —so cruel—"

Delia said, "What did you discover, John?"

"Oh, after considerable phoning around from Blanche's apartment, I found the theater where he is supposed to be playing this week and next. Woodedge. Not far from New Haven. He rented a room but his landlady says she has not seen him at all since he paid in advance. So I had to stop there. I haven't the least idea where he is now."

"And that may mean that he has no alibi for the time when the car tried to run down Julie." Blanche's lawyer's voice was trying to return, Julie felt, but it was shaken and forced. "Finally I turned off the phone. That's why you couldn't reach John."

184

"But George's lack of an alibi does not mean automatically that that affair with the car was a deliberate attempt to hurt you, Julie." John put down his empty glass. "I'll get at the truth eventually. Blanche, may I stay in your apartment tonight?"

They went away, companionably, both very thoughtful. Once Julie had almost believed that Blanche was in fact Jim's mother. There was nothing evident except a firm friendship between her and John.

It was a wakeful night. Even the dog could not seem to settle down comfortably on his rug but repeatedly came to Julie's bed and nudged at her arm.

There was too much to think of and too little to decide.

However, sometime after midnight Jim came quietly to Julie's door, knocked lightly and came in. She could barely see him through the slanted rays of a streetlight from the windows. "Jim—"

"Oh, Julie, my darling." He sat down on the side of the bed.

"She will be all right, Jim."

"I'm not sure. She looked so—so gone. If only we knew what has happened to her. All this time, shut up somewhere probably. If this Walker fellow did it I'm thankful he's been shot. Otherwise I'd—"

"No, you wouldn't! And you know Delia. She took such a thing against him that the moment anybody mentions the word "Count," she thinks of him."

"All the same, it could be. Remember Miss Smith's file of newspaper clippings? What about the woman Walker had been seen with? She could have been Elaine."

"But that was in New York. Over six years ago."

"Yes. And if she did come here over six years ago, she'd have tried to find me. She'd have asked my father. I know she would have. If she could."

Julie put out her arms and caught his shoulders. "Jim, we'll make things up to her. Somehow—"

185

He held her closely. He put his cheek against her face. "You don't know what it's been like these five years, knowing all the time that the newspaper stories about that law mightn't be entirely right. That I was still virtually under sentence for murder. Julie, I sometimes couldn't really remember how you looked, I only hoped you were still—well, my girl. I didn't even know that you tried to interest yourself in anything, everything, even—" There was a small chuckle in Jim's voice. "Even trying to learn to cook."

"That didn't last long!"

"You are sure you want to stay here?" Jim held her hard against him. "There's no safe place to run to, Julie. Believe me. I know—"

Julie said as firmly as she could, for her heart was thudding and her throat seemed choked, "We'll fight it out here."

"If it takes all winter?" Again there was a kind of smile in Jim's voice. He sobered, however. "No, Julie. It will take more than a winter—or— oh, I don't know. I cannot believe that my mother was ever married to that Alben Walker. I know that Delia thinks so. But I can't see how—" He lapsed into thought.

Julie waited.

At last he turned her face with his cheek so he could reach her lips. "I've missed you so. By this time, Julie, we'd have been an old married couple."

"Now they want us to elope—"

"And in some ways," Jim lifted his mouth from hers, "that seems a fine idea. But, no, my darling. There are things to do first."

A sharp hiss came from the doorway. A sepulchral voice whispered, "Aunt Delia is on the prowl. Her bedroom door is open. Better make it snappy. Kiss her, Jim, but hurry up and get out."

"All right," Jim laughed and kissed her so hard and so long that Peter whispered again, "Hurry up. I can't stave her off. Right now she's coming. Good night." He was gone.

186

There was a kind of rustle, as of Delia's silk dressing gown.

Jim said, low, "Dear, Julie. Go to sleep—"

He bent over, tucked her in. Touching her hair, her face. "You are so dear," he said and went quietly across the room.

But in the hall he met Delia. Julie could hear their voices.

"Aunt Delia! I thought you'd be asleep by now!"

Delia's silk robe swished indignantly. "What are you doing?"

"Saying good night to Julie."

"Now look here, Jim—"

"But Aunt Delia, you urged us to elope—"

"That," said Delia with great dignity, "is quite different!"

Both the rustle and the sense of their presence died away. How like Delia and how contrary! Julie smiled and loved her and loved Jim and eventually, feeling warm and comforted and yet lonely, slept.

Morning brought a curious problem. Indeed two rather curious problems. Both were initiated by Peter, who had got on the telephone early to his friend Sam and came bursting into the kitchen to tell them what he had heard.

Nineteen

Delia and Jim and Julie were all stirring around, knocking into one another, getting something like breakfast assembled.

Peter galloped down the steps. "Guess what! I talked to Sam. He had seen Ollie. Took him some cake."

"Oh!" Julie felt a quite justified wave of compunction. She had scarcely thought of Ollie. Peter went on, "And Sam says that Ollie says he fell over a ladder. He told Sam it was that light aluminum ladder from the garage. He always kept it there. But it wasn't there. It was lying just below the steps into the house and he didn't see it and fell over it and busted a rib. What do you think of that?"

He saw some bacon on the table and snatched a slice.

"I don't think anything of it," Julie said stubbornly.

Jim, however, was looking serious. Delia said, "Go on, Peter. Are you trying to say that somebody left the ladder there intentionally, hoping Ollie would hurt himself? What nonsense!"

Jim said, "Wait a minute. If somebody wanted to get Julie and you, Aunt Delia, out of Brookboro, one way might be to get rid of Ollie. Anybody who knows you—that is, anybody in town—might guess that you wouldn't stay in the house alone and see to the menagerie and—no, if the story about the ladder is accurate, Peter, and not some exaggerated notion of Sam's and yours, I suppose it might have occurred. But it would be a very long shot. Nobody could be sure that Ollie would trip at all, and certainly not that he'd break a rib and have to go to the hospital and—no, Peter!"

Peter was determined. "Okay, okay. A long shot. But it came off, didn't it? So who would take such a chance at getting rid of Aunt Delia and Julie?"

"Nobody." Delia sat down heavily.

"But it worked!" Peter repeated and added with an air of shrewd perception, "It got you both out of the—danger zone."

"You simply don't know what you are talking about!" Delia said.

"Maybe not. But all the same—okay, I'll say no more. But you might be glad to know that Ollie is better. He enjoyed the cake. But he told Sam not to tell anybody about that ladder. So Sam told me," said Peter.

"I think Ollie could have been right," Jim said slowly. "I hope you and Sam keep your ideas to yourselves."

"Oh, sure, we don't tell people our ideas, as you call them. But we think all the same. And," said Peter, "that's not all. Look at this—" He dug out a bulge from under his sweater and showed them a crumpled, once-white but now bedraggled and dirty garment, and flung it down on the end of the table. "It's her apron. Mrs. Martine's apron."

Delia stared at it.

"And look at this. Blood," said Peter ghoulishly and pointed.

There were indeed some long streaks of a kind of reddish-brown. Delia stared for about a second and fainted.

A certain amount of confusion followed. Jim lifted up Delia and told Julie to get cold water. Peter thudded up the stairs to the dining room liquor cabinet with Beau after him.

Pye, who had quietly appeared, took advantage of the confusion to spring to the table, help herself to a slice of bacon, and leap with her treasure to the top of the refrigerator.

Julie shoved a cold wet towel at Jim and took paper towels to try to mop up a lake of coffee that Delia had spilled when she fell.

Delia struggled for breath and sat up, but leaned against Jim's arm. Peter tripped back down the stairs, carrying a glass of what proved to be brandy. Delia took it, sniffed, wavered an instant between disapproval and gratitude, and sipped it. A little color came back into her face.

"I found that apron," said Peter, "out there at the next corner. Behind some shrubs. It is Mrs. Martine's, isn't it?"

Delia nodded.

"I don't think it is blood," Jim said, but looked rather pale himself.

Julie was thinking back. "Didn't we have roast beef that night? Didn't Mrs. Martine carve it?"

Relief flooded Delia's face. "Julie, of course! What a fool I am!"

"I still think it's blood," Peter insisted.

"We'll soon find out." Jim took Delia's hand. "What's her phone number?"

"I don't remember. I—oh, yes, I have her address. Up-stairs—"

Rather to Julie's surprise, she did unearth a quite neat address book. "Here it is. Phone number and address. Second Avenue; it can't be far away. She always said she liked to walk to work."

"It's not far. I'll just go over there and talk to her," said Jim.

But Delia had pulled herself together. "You've got to be here in case the doctor calls, you know. I'll walk over there and talk to her myself. You stay here, Jim. Julie—"

Julie had already snatched her red coat from the hall closet. She adjusted Delia's walking coat over her shoulders.

Peter, of course, went with them. Neither even tried to stop him.

Actually the address was within walking distance although by quite long east-west blocks. The three of them walked steadily along, stopping for traffic lights, pausing when they turned to identify the number of the apartment house. The name was on the plate in the lobby of the rather old but well-kept apartment house. Mrs. Martine did not answer the bell. Instead there was a rumbling of hasty steps on the stairs beside the elevator shaft and a big, dark, tousled-looking man glared at them suspiciously. "What do you want?"

Delia was polite. "Mr. Martine?"

"Sure, sure. You're Mrs. Van Clive."

Peter couldn't resist. "How do you know?"

Mr. Martine gave him a half-amused but still unpleasant look. "Why, kid, my wife has described Mrs. Van Clive to me many times. Highfalutin, that's what I say. She only said a good lady. So, if you're so good why did you hit my wife?"

"Hit!" Delia stood back, almost as if Mr. Martine might retaliate and hit her with a rather hard and heavy-looking fist.

"That's what I said. Hit her on the back of the neck, right there at the street crossing and leave her lay on the sidewalk. Why, a car could have hit her—"

"Not on the sidewalk," said Peter.

This time Mr. Martine's fist really doubled up. "Not another word out of you, kid. Yes"—he transferred a black gaze to Delia—"she could have died. But she didn't." Mr. Martine was triumphant. "A kind man driving his own car stopped and picked her up and brought her home. And the next morning she tried to go back to your house, Mrs. Van Clive. But you had locked her out. A fine way to treat her!"

"I didn't lock her out. She had her own key."

"She said you locked her out. So—" He was now smug. "So right away she got another job. My wife is a great cook.

She never needs to go ten minutes without a job."

"I'm sure she'll come back to me if I can talk to her. Explain—"

But Mr. Martine was adamant. "Nope! I mean, no ma'am. The lady she's working for now is paying her more than even you paid her, which," he said with an air of giving credit where credit was due, "was a very good salary. No, ma'am. She made sure of her new place. Somebody on Park Avenue and—"

Delia was really quite desperate. "Will you tell me where? I mean, what name?"

He considered it but shook his head. "I'll tell her. But I don't think she'll come back. You see, there was a prowler. And then being knocked on the head like that, right at the corner near your house. No, I don't think she'll come back. If you'll excuse me," he said very politely, but looking at a watch on his wrist, "I've got to get to my own job. My restaurant. If I'm not there long before noon, I never know what may happen."

After a moment, lady to the last, Delia said, "Thank you, Mr. Martine. When you talk to your wife will you tell her I'd like to have her back and I didn't lock her out. I'll send her a check for last week. And—I'll be glad to increase her wages. I mean salary."

"Yes, ma'am. Good morning, now—" He was not to be outdone in politeness but was very firm.

Dismissed, politely but dismissed all the same, the three of them started walking back toward the Cove. Presently Peter said, "That corner, where she got her head bumped. That's the corner where I found the bloody—that is, the apron."

Nobody replied to that.

When they reached the house it was immediately evident that Jim was not there. Beau sprang to meet them, joyously. Even Pye condescended to lower herself from a chair back and brush against Peter's legs.

"Jim has gone to the hospital," Delia guessed. "I hope no—bad news—"

But he hadn't gone to the hospital. There was a note on Julie's desk. "Heard from the doctor and my mother is the same. Doctor hopeful. See you later. Love J."

Twenty

There was no way to know with any degree of certainty where he had gone or what he meant to do. But Delia said angrily, "He's gone to Brookboro, I know it. Just putting his head into the lion's mouth."

"No," Peter said sapiently. "My guess is he's gone to find George and settle his hash."

Delia looked hard at the scrap of paper in Julie's hand. Finally she sighed. "Wherever she's gone, Mrs. Martine is certainly gone for good. I'll order some groceries. You'll have to cook for us, Julie."

"Well, I—I'm not sure—" She was thinking only of Jim's note.

Delia said crossly, "After spending all that money on lessons in cooking! I agree they didn't last long. Or you didn't last long. But you must have learned something. No matter what happens people have to eat. I'll order the groceries. Then I have an errand or two."

After Delia had ordered what seemed to Julie an appallingly long list of groceries, she trotted off to get a taxi. Peter took Beau for a walk; Pye sat on the mantel this time, having arrived there without in the least disturbing any of the ornaments that were strung along it.

Outside, the sky was changing subtly; it was no longer a gold and blue October day. The telephone did not ring. Jim would let her know what happened—if anything had happened. Jim or John or Blanche.

Waiting is hard. She had learned that over five years. She let herself out the French windows and down a couple of steps into the neatly plotted garden.

She strolled along the carefully raked paths; it was an enormously protected and quiet place, perfect for thinking, but she couldn't produce any very valuable thoughts. She wanted only to sit in the quiet and—well, wait. What else was there to do?

The gardener, employed by all the residents of the Cove, was very good. He was old enough and kind enough to remind her of Ollie, dependable, too, and an excellent gardener. He was then tying up some of the tea roses and carefully wrapping them in burlap.

He greeted her cheerfully when she said good morning.

"Good morning, Miss Farnham—" Getting her name right, too, but then he had known her for years. "Fine morning, but I don't like the weather. Anything can happen in October. I'm ordering some marsh hay—that's good for bedding the peonies."

"The garden looks lovely at any time." Julie noticed the neat paths and expert clipping of vines over most of the balconies that lined the garden. There was a sense of seclusion and safety there. The windows that looked down upon it were friendly ones, she knew that, and sought out Dr. Evans' windows but they, too, were merely clean and shining; no sight of the doctor, who was probably in his office.

How many times she had sat on exactly that bench, near Delia's house but at the same time isolated, in the quiet of the garden! It seemed to her now that always, during those five years, she had had a stubborn, illogical certainty that sometime Jim would return, that Jim would be cleared of the monstrous charge against him, and that he would not have forgotten her. Perhaps John Wingate himself had given her a sense of hope.

Yes, John had encouraged her; he had suggested trying to write. He had told her practical things, like not to put too many characters in your novel; it confuses the reader and leads the writer astray, far from the path of narrative. He had given her many bits of advice. They were not rules; there were few rules about writing, he had said. Just write the best you can, as lucidly as you can.

So she had done her best but she had scarcely expected her novel to be published. That had been a rosy kind of dream, but it had taken her out of her brooding as John had known it would. It gave her a hard task. But certainly she had not expected the success (modest, but still a success) with her first book. The present one: she wouldn't think of that yet!

She couldn't think of anything, really, but Jim and what he might be doing or where he had gone.

The gardener had worked nearer to her. He nodded at one of the houses. "She's gone west again," he said. "Got a big job in television. Two, three million dollars, they say."

"Good!" *She* had been an idol of Julie's, of the whole world, probably. She was no longer young, certainly, but an actress of great gifts.

"Yes'm. And he"—he nodded at another house, neatly kept as were all the encircling houses, windows shining, curtains drawn just so—"he's gone to Washington again. Seems they can't get along without him. Wife went with him."

"Good!" Julie said again, for "he" was a respected figure in government.

"And now Miss Delia says she's going away soon, too bad."

"What's that?" Julie sat up.

"Oh, I thought you knew. Fact is, I thought you'd be going with her."

"No, I—no, I didn't know."

The stocky figure in the clean blue shirt and blue jeans bent with the ease of youth to dig up an impertinent bit of crab grass. "They will come in the fall," he said. "I thought I'd got them all. Well, this one is gone, roots and all." He looked at the sky. "Weather is not going to last. Fact is, looks like a storm to me. But haven't heard any radio warnings. Oh, well, we are safe here." Beau came running down into the garden. The gardener looked at him thoughtfully but with favor. "A good dog. Never digs up anything."

Peter called to her. "Hey, Julie. The Gristede's man is at the kitchen door. He can't get in and he's got what looks like a truckload of groceries."

"Why don't you unlock the kitchen door?" Julie rose, however, sensible of the call to duty.

"Can't unlock it," Peter said. "No key."

"Of course there's a key."

"Okay. You find it," said Peter and stood back for her, politely. She waved a hand at the gardener, who nodded in his usual friendly fashion, and led the way into the living room, dining room and down those wickedly steep steps to the kitchen. Here Peter apparently had already put on blazing lights. There was no key in the lock of the kitchen door.

"I don't think—surely Delia wouldn't have taken it. Never mind. I'm sure she keeps a spare somewhere."

The deliveryman outside whistled morosely as if to remind her that he was waiting.

Peter went delving into drawers. Julie searched shelves and called to the deliveryman to wait, please, just a moment.

And in a moment Peter unearthed a key, hidden under the paper lining of a shelf. "This it?"

"I don't know. Try it—"

He was already trying it in the kitchen door, which gave

a creak and opened. The deliveryman marched in and unloaded boxes and, Julie saw with dismay, boxes and boxes.

"Anything else?" he said cheerfully.

"There can't be." Julie did not add a question as to whether anything at all was left in the branch of Gristede's where Delia was accustomed to trade.

The deliveryman nodded cheerfully and left. Peter, interested, helped her unload and find a place for all the groceries. He brightened when he saw that the boxes had included numerous bottles of soda water, tonic and other accompaniments to whiskey or vodka.

There were also, Julie saw with gratitude, some packages of frozen food.

She hurried to get them in the freezing compartment of the refrigerator. Pye, obeying an instinct, appeared softly on the table itself.

However, Delia was just, even when she disapproved; she had also ordered food for what she called the menagerie. Peter opened a couple of cans for Pye and Beau to the intent interest of both cat and dog, who fell upon the contents Peter served them.

Julie watched absently. Surely there was something odd about the necessity to hunt for what she was sure was an extra key.

Those domestic chores attended to—with her ears tuned all the time for the telephone, which obstinately refused to ring—Julie left Peter, who was watching Pye's voracious gobbling with approval, and went back to the garden, thinking to rediscover some of its peace. She did not.

While she had been in the house the whole character of the world seemed to have changed. The garden was strangely still. Not a leaf quivered on the red of the dogwood trees, placed at advantageous spots around the enclosure. It seemed eerie for the dogwoods to be such a startlingly clear autumn-red.

But at the same time the colors in the garden were all at

once strange, rather more vivid than when she had left them.

The sun had gone, too. So the gardener was right. It must be going to storm.

The sky had become a low, yellowish gray. Hurricane weather, she thought; October was always a month for hurricanes, sweeping up along the Atlantic coast, growing in violence strangely as they passed Cape Hatteras, then far too often falling upon the land. They were also madly capricious in spite of weather bureaus.

The Van Clive house had stood through many a real hurricane, solidly and perhaps stolidly.

Her own house (or rather her house and Peter's, for it was a joint inheritance) had not been so lucky or perhaps so firm. More than once trees had been shoved over, their roots shamelessly exposed. After one such hurricane the tops of the maples had gone and, sadly, never grown in again; the tree surgeons had slid here and there, dangling perilously, Julie had always felt, from ropes as they sliced away at the trees. After another, Ollie had reported gravely that there were so many trees down, which he had reduced to so many cords of firewood and neatly stacked.

The garden seemed to be brighter now yet at the same time shrinking into itself.

There was not so much as a breath of wind from anywhere. It had always been a sheltered spot but just then it had changed so swiftly that it did seem possible that a hurricane might strike through all the protection of solid walls. The gardener had gone, so she could not question him, and he had cannily gathered up all the implements of his occupation. But the gardener had felt and expressed a kind of uneasy weariness.

Probably, she decided, the odd light of a coming storm had not only changed the colors in the garden but also the color of her thinking. She began to feel a tremendous pressure, not of the possible weather coming, but from some outside influence that she could not identify.

With a quirk of fancy, Julie said to herself: I feel like Eliza, leaping over the ice and the hounds after me.

There was no more reason to feel hunted that day and hour than at any other time since Jim had returned and since —yes, since the Judge had died so swiftly and, it now seemed certain, by murderous design.

She wished Peter would come out. She wished Delia would return and bring Julie's fancies into sensible order.

It must be time for Delia to return.

She heard the French doors open. She heard a woman's voice but it was not Delia's. It was, instead, Lisa's happy trill; she was tripping down the two steps to the garden followed by Peter, who wore a supercilious grin. With a certain fury Julie recognized that look: the man of the world, flattered by Lisa's attention. She wished she could box his ears. But again, the time for that was past; now she barely came up to Peter's ears and it was a question as to how much boxing he would permit. He said to Lisa, smiling and admiring her with frankness, "I told you she'd be out here. Here's Lisa, Julie. She is looking for George. Or," he added as if it were merely a postscript, "Jim."

Lisa gave a perhaps practiced but graceful wave of her hand and came toward Julie.

She looked, Julie had to admit, perfectly lovely in a pinkish-brown suit with her hair tucked up into a shining roll at the back of her head. Even her handbag was neat, very correct leather. "Hello, Lisa," Julie said.

"Hello." Lisa sat down on the bench beside Julie with the greatest calm. She wore some perfume which was a little too heavy to associate itself with flowers, yet attractive. No getting around that.

"Where is George?" Lisa asked.

"I don't know. He's not here."

"So Peter told me." Lisa lavished a smile upon Peter, who suddenly stood on one leg, lost in admiration.

Lisa lowered her voice, "Peter told me that George's mother *is* here."

Peter rather abruptly abandoned his nonchalant pose and stood on two feet, in really a quite threatening manner, and glared at Julie. Julie didn't know what the glare meant but did not tell Lisa that Elaine was in fact in the hospital, mainly because Lisa's dramatic sense would almost certainly drive her to the hospital and to see Elaine. Dramatic sense, yes, but also curiosity.

Lisa's voice was low, in consideration of her understanding that Elaine was in the house, but also clear. "I really must find George. You see, Mitchell Basom got sick and can't take his role and I know that George can fill in. George really is reliable"—(Was there a slight pause there?)—"in the theater. He learns quickly and doesn't have to be told all the moves and—oh, call it tricks of playing to an audience. He's good at that, although—too bad," Lisa said, with what struck Julie as thoroughly honest regret. "He could have been quite an actor if he'd really put his mind to it. I think," Lisa added soberly. And then as soberly but rather surprisingly added, "Not as good as I am. And as I will be."

Peter quickly shifted to complete admiration and stood on the other leg, so near Julie that she could have kicked him, as she secretly wanted to.

"I'm sure you will be, Lisa," she had to say and, indeed, as she believed.

"I promised the stage manager that I'd bring George back with me. But now George is not where he is supposed to be. So I thought he might be here." Her voice lowered again and she gave a quick glance toward the house. "I suppose he is simply beside himself. His mother back here!" Her lovely eyes did narrow slightly as she looked at Julie. "What is John Wingate going to do about that?"

"I don't know." That was easy.

Lisa, however, had to pursue it. "But weren't they divorced—oh, ages ago?"

"Yes."

Lisa looked at her with wide, speculative eyes. "Sounds like a play," she said. "Poor Elaine! Everybody says she was fascinating. Or at least young and very pretty. Returning now! John Wingate has been so successful. It would be a happy ending, wouldn't it?"

"Do all plays have happy endings?" Julie said crossly.

"Well, no. Certainly not. Depends upon the kind of play. Look at—"

"*Macbeth,*" said Peter, "*Hamlet—*"

"Or for that matter, *Romeo and Juliet,*" said Lisa. "But I do think it would be wonderful for George. And of course for Jim. By the way"—she was a little too casual—"what happened to Jim? I haven't seen him in days. Where is he? What is he doing?"

Planning to give George the trouncing of his life, Julie thought. But she had to say, "I don't know."

"Really! Why, I thought you and Jim were going to be married. As soon, of course, as Jim is fully exonerated."

Could Lisa's wide eyes be seeking information? Certainly, a very good, natural actress could suggest anything, even entire innocence of any hidden meaning.

"I think Jim will be back soon," Julie said.

"Then—then I think I'll just wait. I'd like to see him. He might know where I can find George."

Peter saw something in Julie's face and said swiftly, "The doctor said we had to be very quiet. She is George's and Jim's mother. They have first claim."

Lisa opened her eyes. "Jim's mother? Elaine? Why, everybody believes that only George had the proof."

"Everybody is wrong." Julie rose and Lisa had to rise too. "It's very good of you to come, Lisa. If George happens along I'll tell him—"

Lisa was reluctant but had to stroll with Julie toward the

Van Clive steps. "It isn't a very important role. But George can do it if he can get out of whatever he's doing now. Frankly, I've lost track of him—that is, I can't get any information as to where he is now."

Peter looked off into some dreamy distance and puckered up his lips to make a small whistle. Lisa said, "It's going to storm, isn't it?" She gave a little shiver, a very pretty little shiver, but an uneasy movement just the same. "Everything looks different. As if it's—well, waiting for something. Yes, yes, I'll go now." She walked along beside Julie and up the steps into the house. "Thank you," she said then in a whisper. "Let me know—"

"Yes."

When the outside door closed behind her, Julie turned to Peter. "Why didn't you tell her that Jim's mother is in the hospital, not here?"

"Oh, you know Lisa. If she knew that, she'd stage a dramatic scene right there in the hospital. Of course, I didn't give her such a chance." Peter was indignant but also admiring. "Lisa is quite something," he said. "A beauty, but not," he added with brotherly affection, "half as good-looking as you are."

"Why—why, Peter!" Julie was stunned at this unusual tribute.

"Don't you ever look in the mirror? It's time you did. Of course," Peter added, rather pleased with himself, "we have the same goldy-brown hair and lots of it. You cut yours too short, by the way. I let mine grow—a little. But the same blue eyes. Same kind of chin, not too prominent but still kind of determined. Nice eyebrows, too. Yes," he said, considering her, "I'd say you're a damn good-looking woman."

"Well," said Julie, taken aback but deeply pleased, too. "Well."

"Oh, don't thank me," Peter said.

"I wasn't—that is, yes, I was going to thank you. At least I am glad you appreciate—"

"Our common heritage," Peter finished the sentence wisely and Julie couldn't help a kind of gurgle of laughter.

"Laugh if you feel like it," Peter said. "But where's Jim? Have the police got him? And where is George? Where is Mr. Wingate for that matter?"

"And where is Delia? She should be home by now."

"Getting her hair done." Peter put his hand down so Pye could more easily climb up to his shoulder.

"Most likely. Peter, did she tell you anything about going away, I mean taking a trip anywhere?"

"Nope." He caressed the cat's lovely, small head, and Pye gave forth the hoarse rumble that passed for a purr.

"Delia told the gardener she intended to go away, soon. I suppose she wanted him to keep an eye on the house while she was away."

Peter's eyebrows lifted. "Oh, well, she doesn't tell us everything, does she? Maybe she's got a man somewhere? It's a possibility, isn't it? She's a very attractive woman. Money, too." Peter listened, and added, "Oh, hell! Here's the police again!"

Twenty-one

It was the police. At least it was Chief McClary and another man who remained in the driver's seat, looking like a statue in khaki-colored uniform, while Chief McClary came up the steps. "Sorry to bother you, Miss Fan'um. Mrs. Van Clive here?"

"No, not yet. She'll soon come home."

"Doesn't matter. May I come in? It's you I have to talk to."

She opened the door wider and Chief McClary thanked her with a nod; he acknowledged the cat, who had draped herself around Peter's neck. After a second or two McClary allowed himself a slight grin. "So that's the fighting demon we met with on those kitchen steps! Dear me," he said moderately. "I'm rather afraid she got her tail stepped on."

Peter said, "I'm very sorry about that, sir. I didn't know she had gone down those stairs."

"Oh, I'm sure you're sorry." There was a twinkle in the Chief's eyes. "Just don't let it happen again, Peter. I've still got a bruise on my ankle. Now then, Julie—I mean Miss Fan'um—"

"Julie is all right," she said. "Good heavens, Chief, you've known me—yes, and arrested me—"

He shook his head. "Not arrested you. Only suggested you drive less speedily. Good thing, too. Very dangerous to sail around like you were the only car on the road. However, that's not what I came to see you about. Do you know where Jim Wingate is?"

"No. No, I truly don't, Chief."

"Or John Wingate?"

"No."

"Well, then, how about George Wingate?"

"I don't know that either."

"H'mm! Not very helpful." He sat in the lounge chair in Julie's workroom. She didn't remember having invited him in, but of course she had, automatically. Finally he said, "I hear that John Wingate's wife has returned from—from wherever she was."

"Yes. She's very ill. Dangerously ill."

"You mean I can't talk to her."

"Nobody can talk to her yet. The doctor prescribes absolute quiet. I'm not sure she's even conscious, anyway. She arrived in a—a terrible state, Chief."

He brooded for a moment, seeming to search back in his memory. "I remember her. A very pretty woman, willful and impatient but very pretty. George takes after her in looks. But then," he sighed, "of course, it has occurred to you that George may not be John's son."

"It has occurred to John."

"Mm, yes. It might be that George was born after she left Wingate, but by a different father. Right?"

She had to nod.

The Chief said slowly, "Then John took him in, out of chivalry to his wife? Divorced, I believe. And believing that she was dead. However, it must surely have struck John Wingate and Jim that there's a third alternative."

Peter perked up, his eyes shining. "You don't mean—"

The Chief nodded but with a kind of reservation. "Oh, yes, George could be an impostor."

Julie stared at him. "But he had all those proofs of identity."

The Chief nodded again. "Sure. But things can be stolen. Now, Elaine Wingate would have papers of some kind, say her marriage certificate, pieces of jewelry that John Wingate recognized. Suppose she gave those to somebody—"

Julie thought hard. "But she couldn't. She's been in a sanitarium, the doctor thinks. The doctor says she used up the last of her strength to get here. She apparently stole some money and a passport, and she got here and then just—"

"Collapsed," said Peter.

"I see," the Chief said in a voice that indicated he didn't see much. "However," he added, "I'm afraid I have to question you, Julie."

She took it as a sign of friendliness when he used her name, Julie. But she felt suddenly cold and frightened, just the same.

"Now, then, I have no dictaphone, no way to transcribe anything you say. No official witness. Don't be afraid. Just tell me the truth. I believed you the night the Judge died—was murdered," he amended the word with a dreadful respect for its dreadful meaning. "You told me what had happened and I believed you. But now, since the Judge's will is known as well as the fact that he left what property he had —and being a very honest man there wasn't much property to leave—anyway, he left it to Jim Wingate, so now suppose you and Jim—"

Julie had been sitting at her desk. She rose suddenly. "No, Chief! We didn't get together to—to kill the Judge. Truly we didn't. We didn't even know about his will. We only were afraid—"

She stopped but not in time. The Chief said slowly, "Yes. You were afraid, you were sure, in fact, that he was right that Jim's arrest would inevitably lead to an indictment, a trial and a verdict against him. Now, I want you to tell me again, the entire account of that evening when the Judge asked you to come to him."

"But I told you—"

"Tell me again," said the Chief inexorably.

The room darkened as she told it again, as clearly, as factually as she could remember. There were tears in her eyes, her voice grew unsteady as she told of the Judge's plaintive, dying words. "I loved him, Chief. He was part of my life. He was going to give me away when Jim and I"— she had to cough a little here—"when Jim and I were to be married. But instead—"

The Chief nodded. "Yes, instead, impending arrest, a trial —it was hard for him. Hard for you, too. Well—" He stood with a precise motion that reminded Julie of something she had known in her childhood: that the Chief had been in the Navy. Its marks still showed in his erect bearing, his neatness of uniform, his unending yet resolute courtesy.

She said, "How did you know about Elaine, Chief, I mean about her return?"

"Oh, that. John Wingate told me. Phoned me as a matter of fact, good of him. But now he seems to have disappeared. He and George and Jim, too, and I'm sorry to tell you that I have orders from topside"—(Navy again, Julie thought)— "to arrest Jim at once. Hold him for questioning at least. If Jim is trying to find somebody else who might have murdered Walker, as I guess, then that could be a very dangerous thing. However, we'll have to see about this. Thank you. Good afternoon." He opened the door and a hot swirl of wind came in, startling them all. "Dear me," he said. "I do hope we're not in for even the tail of another hurricane. Julie, remember this; I want to know where Jim is and what he's doing. And where George is. And where John Wingate is."

Peter, with some difficulty because of the wind, closed the door after him and said, "If George is not nursing the results of a pretty fine beating, I miss my guess. Jim had a look in his eye that would scare the hell out of me."

"You still think it was George driving that car."

"Sure. Only a damn fool would do it. You have to admit that George is an idiot. Didn't it ever occur to you that he could be a very well-informed impostor?"

Julie stared at him. "No. John—"

"It occurred to Chief McClary. John Wingate could be deceived, couldn't he? He's not omniscient. Just a man," said Peter airily, "like other men. Capable of being deceived."

"Oh, Peter, shut up! Do stick to what we know!"

"What we don't know, you mean. I'm going to turn on some lights."

The rooms had become desolately dark. The sound of the wind penetrated even those thick walls. Julie wished uneasily that Delia would return.

Beau indicated politely that he wanted a walk.

"Oh, Beau! Not now!"

"Oh, sure, now." Peter was interested. "This storm will only get worse. Come on, old fellow." He deposited Pye on Julie's desk and took Beau's leash.

Both of them staggered back a little as he opened the street door and the wind was so strong, with sudden hot puffs, that Julie had to help him close the door.

Julie was still sitting in the chair the Chief had left when Peter came hurtling back into the house. "A storm," he shouted. "Lucky to get inside again. Delia home yet?"

"No."

He shook himself. Beau shook himself. Peter said, "It's not raining yet. But when it comes it'll be a humdinger." He went into the living room and turned on more lights, which, however, did not diminish the feeling of something very like fear, an atavistic sense of being the prey of something outside that was determined to get in.

Delia did arrive, however, her hair blown; she was grasping her handbag and panting as Peter ran to help her close the door.

At the same time the telephone at last rang. Julie ran to answer. It was Jim.

"Oh, Jim!"

His voice was a little jerky as if the wind and weather affected it, too. "Everything all right?"

"Yes. That is, no. The police were here. I mean the Chief. He's trying to find you. Did you hear me, Jim?"

This time his voice sounded very far away. "Sure, I heard. I know. I saw that newspaper woman this morning. Then I—" There was only a mumble; a voice but no distinct words.

"Jim, I can't understand."

His voice came on full, with a jerk again, "—and so I'm in New Haven. George—"

His voice died away again. "What about George?" She shouted into the telephone. "Where is he? Lisa was here looking for him—"

There was a long silence and when his voice came again it was clear that he had been speaking for a moment or two. "—so I'll do my best. But I must say I was—" It faded again but this time she thought he had said "surprised" or "astonished" or some such word; it was expressed in what she could hear, which wasn't much.

She yelled, "Can you hear me? I couldn't understand!"

Dead silence! Complete silence! She shook the telephone, she rattled it. Only blank silence!

Peter at her elbow said, "Line is out. Storm must have really hit. Where is he?"

"He said New Haven. I think he had some kind of information that—that surprised him or upset him or something. Oh—" She put down the telephone with a bang. "The line went out at just that moment. What shall I do?"

"What can you do?" Peter said coolly. "I'll tell you something. You can cook dinner. Aunt Delia has gone to fix her hair, I expect. She looked a little wind-blown."

The storm didn't quite shake the house; it had been built too strongly. Yet they could feel the onslaught of the wind, which came at unnerving intervals. After they had finished the rather scrappy meal Julie had contrived, Peter quite calmly stacked the dishes in the dishwasher. "Don't turn it on now," Delia said. "We may need all the electricity we can get."

"I don't see how," Peter said. "If the electricity goes it goes anyway. Wouldn't matter really how much we were using. Has it ever happened here, Aunt Delia?"

"Oh," Delia said, adjusting her hair with an absent gesture, "I suppose so. Yes. I remember. But the house stands," she added proudly.

Twenty-two

So far the storm had not so much as touched its reservoir of strength. The windows on the garden side were rattling, not much but enough to induce a definite uneasiness. Peter spoke to the cat, who was fully aware of the storm outside and had curled herself with instinctive aplomb upon a chair back that was almost in the middle of the house. Peter approved. "She's got good sense. They always say, get in the middle of the house or, better, below a doorway. Protects—"

He was at Delia's desk, fiddling with a tiny battery radio that stood upon it. After some squeals a voice came on: "Going out to sea. Unexpected swirl in storm, back toward the land—forecaster could not advise in time—no storm warning—assure you that—" The voice stopped, with finality.

"The forecaster looked out the wrong window," Peter said disgustedly. He strolled to the sacrosanct piano, daringly lifted the lid over the keys, tossed aside a strip of felt with which Delia had protected the ivories, and began to touch the keys, beginning what Julie recognized dimly as his school song. Delia lifted her head. "Not now, Peter."

"Okay," Peter said agreeably. "Now, would you like a little hard rock?"

His hands came down unmercifully on the keys. Delia gave him one icy look and rose; Peter paused at once. "Okay, I'll not touch these things of beauty." And indeed the piano was beautiful in its gay-nineties way, yellow and garlanded with all its painted flowers—its big triangular top offering a fine platform from which Pye could safely observe anything that caught her blue eyes.

"Well," said Peter, "we've got to do something. How about a little cutthroat?"

Delia gave him a blank look. Peter rather patronizingly explained. "Each of us keeps their own score. We bid for dummy. Count as you used to do in auction. Back, say, about the time of Lincoln's inauguration. A friend's grandmother taught him. We don't count as in contract."

Unexpectedly, Delia did not fire up. Yet Julie could not possibly ask her what was wrong and if she did, Delia would not give an answer she didn't wish to give. Delia said absently, "Get out the table and cards. And score pads. We can try it."

Peter found the card table. It, too, was a holdover from some Van Clive. Looking like a handsome side table, it opened to disclose a green-felt-covered top and a drawer beneath which provided cards and score pads. Peter arranged it and pulled up chairs. Beau sat down and put his head on Julie's lap, while his ears perked up a little, listening.

The lamps were still shining; indeed the light wavered only once, when Peter got the gambling spirit in his blood and bid wildly for the as yet unknown possibilities of the dummy. "Three handed," Peter said musing. "Really a betting game, isn't it? Raises one's gambling instincts."

"Three no trump," said Delia coolly.

Nobody denied it; Peter looked with interest upon the score card that Delia had taken over. She had recovered sufficiently to bid and spread out the dummy, which provided some fine honor cards. Peter groaned. "Do you always win, Aunt Delia? By the way," he said conversationally, "that story about runaway slaves being sheltered by the dumbwaiter, is that really true?"

"I guess so," Delia replied, looking at the exposed dummy and arranging her strategy. "At least my husband said so. Of course," she added, overtaken by honesty, "stories sometimes are only that. Part of family tradition."

"You missed that," Peter said triumphantly and took a trick.

Delia bit her lip. "All right, Peter, now! Ah, I thought you'd play that." She took the next trick, relaxed and added, "There! Made my bid. And by the way, Peter, how do you find much time for playing bridge? You shouldn't."

"Why, Aunt Delia? And me doing my best to get into university!"

Delia didn't believe his unsaid but tacit denial. "Never for money, now, mind me."

"Oh, Aunt Delia! What an idea!"

How he pulled the wool over Delia's bright eyes, Julie thought meanly. Peter said promptly, "Your deal, Julie."

So, dealing four hands as if there were in fact a fourth person playing, and wishing there were a fourth player and that it was Jim, Julie dealt. At the same time she noted that Delia's hands were shaking just a little, so the diamonds she habitually wore were trembling and shooting forth red, gold, blue lights.

"So Jim only said he was in New Haven?" Delia said.

"I told you. We were cut off just as he was trying to tell me something."

"Can't you guess what? Have you no idea what he was trying to say?"

"No."

"But what did you think?"

"What could I think? He seemed—I can't describe it—astonished, perhaps, certainly upset."

Delia gave her a sharp yet uneasy look, as if trying to pierce every scrap of Julie's memory, not only of that provokingly cut-off conversation but of Julie's impression of it. Julie answered it, a little troubled. "I told you. It was only an impression."

Peter was dealing when the lights went out.

"I knew it," Peter cried. "I knew it!"

"They'll come on again in a minute." Delia's voice sounded unlike herself, uncertain, nervous perhaps, something not natural to her, not right.

The dark house (dark everywhere, no lights anywhere) was not at all pleasant; Julie suggested candles.

Delia's voice came again from the darkness, and it sounded again curiously unlike Delia. "Ought to be some in the buffet. In the dining room, Peter. Don't fall over the menagerie."

"The menagerie has got sense enough to get out of the way," Peter said cheerfully. However, his progress could be followed by the sounds of a few thuds and a few words of which, normally, Delia would have keenly disapproved. Delia didn't speak but Julie could hear a little thump of her fingers, beating a kind of tattoo on the table top. If Delia was nervous about the storm, then Julie had a right to be nervous, too. But, thinking hard there in the complete darkness, Julie decided that Delia was not at all nervous about the storm. There was a clatter as Peter dropped something.

Julie said, "Where were you all afternoon, Delia? I expected you home much sooner. You must have seen the storm coming."

"Oh, I heard about it. I mean, there was a radio where—where I was. Some hurried storm warnings. But I—oh yes, I came home. As you see." She raised her voice. "Any candles, Peter?"

"Nope." Peter's voice came back through what then seemed a very long distance. "Lots of forks and spoons and knives and—oh, hell!" Another clatter came. The wind burst hard against the windows.

"Probably my husband's grandmother's coffee pot. Well, can't be helped. All right, Peter." Delia pushed back the table. "Might as well go to bed."

There was obviously nothing to do *but* go to bed. Peter had found some matches somewhere and lighted their progress upstairs. The flares from the matches lasted only a short time but the bannister for the stairs helped. At the top Peter said, from behind a small flare of red light, "I locked the kitchen door. You know you lost one of your keys, Aunt Delia. I locked the front door, too." The small glare went out.

A cold, uneasy nose pressed against Julie's hand. "It's all right, Beau," she said. "Good dog."

Delia said from the darkness, "If you find any candles or matches in your room, Julie, better not light them. Those curtains—the storm—"

"No. I mean, yes. Delia, I forgot to ask you. The gardener, you know, for the Cove, said that you expected to go away."

There was a silence except for the wind hurtling against the house. Then Delia's voice came again out of the blackness. "Oh, that. Of course. I thought I might go with you and Jim. When or wherever you go. Now—oh, I might take a little trip, myself. Good night. Don't let the storm bother you. This house has withstood many a storm—" Delia's door closed with finality.

It was strange, though, how complete darkness affected the impression one had of another's voice. In a lighted room Julie was sure she would never have detected a kind of uneasiness, haste, perhaps too much haste as if Delia was intent upon hiding something.

But that couldn't be. The storm was also plucking at Julie's nerves, urging her to entertain unreasonable notions. There was a steady purr from Pye, somewhere very close. Knowing Peter was there, she said, "Delia—"

"I know," said Peter very close to her. "What's she got on her mind?"

"I don't know. That is, probably nothing special."

"She's got something on her mind, she doesn't want to tell us. And whatever it is—" Peter paused for a moment and whispered, "It bothers her. Like everything. You know Aunt Delia. You can tell—"

"No! No, I can't tell! It's only the storm and the winds and the— What could she have on her mind?"

"All sorts of things," Peter whispered after a moment. "But I think something about the murders." A soft rustle, a kind of sixth sense told Julie that Peter with his cat had gone on to his bedroom.

What could Delia be thinking about so intensely that so troubled her mind that she refused to admit it?

Peter just could be right. Murder?

But Delia had nothing to do with Walker's murder. Certainly nothing to do with the Judge's murder either. However, Delia was not herself, no getting around that.

Julie put her window up the barest fraction and such a torrent poured through the open space that she had to close it. Rain was coming down now, beating upon the house, the city, the country, including, certainly, her own special world of Brookboro. She hoped that no trees would be downed. She hoped that the roof would have no damage and that the pump house would not suffer. She hoped that Jim had gotten himself into a safe place where he could wait out the storm.

Beau was uneasy, pacing around, pausing now and again to nudge at her hand. The night seemed much darker than usual and indeed it was, for always there had been faint streaks of light coming from the streetlight on the corner. The corner where Mrs. Martine had been mugged.

That was not a cozy night-thought either.

However, she thought that she was asleep when Beau gave a very soft growl.

Beau rarely growled. His best effort was merely a matter

217

of form, a kind of soft talk. He growled again, though, and this was neither talk nor soft. He seemed to be across the room near the door.

Delia might be having a restless night; she had certainly acted strangely earlier.

Peter might be roaming the house, after more food, probably; sometimes Julie thought he had hollow legs.

It might be nobody.

If she didn't move at once she would so frighten herself she couldn't move. So she was out of bed; she was trying to find Beau, who had disappeared into the darkness the moment she opened the door. She couldn't even hear him. But what she did hear was strange. It took her only a few seconds to identify it for she had heard it often, before Delia had installed such very convenient electricity, inconvenient now since the lights were gone in what New Yorkers calmly called an outage.

But the sound was perfectly identifiable. It was not the thud and thump of the wind, hurling itself inexorably against the house. It was not the fierce onslaught of gusts of rain. It was something within the house itself and she knew what. The dumbwaiter was thumping, thudding a little, very distantly and jerkily. So—so someone was pulling it up by the ropes that still dangled beside the wooden box.

Jim, she thought.

Of course, Jim. He must have come back, but he didn't have keys to the house. How could he?

She remembered as if a light had flashed on for just one illuminating second: Mrs. Martine had lost her apron. She had worried that she would not be able to get into her apartment because her key was in that apron pocket. The back door key for Delia's house had been in the apron pocket, too. When Peter found it there had been no keys at all, merely an ugly stain.

Then she heard a soft tinkle of the piano keys being struck lightly. Pye! And Peter!

Fooling around in the darkness, first with the dumbwaiter, then letting Pye explore the piano keys, which Peter had not covered. Delia would be beside herself.

The idiot! There were things Delia did not forgive!

She had to stop it. She wrapped a dressing gown around her. In the hall the tinkle from the piano was faintly clearer. That Peter! She fumbled her way down the stairs. She emerged into the living room and all was blackness.

"Peter!" she whispered. Then she started across the room, feeling her way. "Peter! Stop it! You'll have Delia down here!"

The light notes from the piano stopped.

She could barely see a figure standing beside the piano in the darkness.

But it wasn't Peter. A voice said with a chuckle, "I thought that would bring you down." It was a voice she knew. The dimly black figure came toward her.

Something came out of the darkness and clutched her shoulders. Unbelievably strong hands moved to her throat. She made a kind of dive to one side, cannoned into the bridge table, which crashed over with all the cards. In the clatter, the hands released and she screamed.

Twenty-three

She screamed and screamed and thought desperately of a refuge; the cavern under the big piano? She tried to crawl that way, groping in the darkness. A chair went over with a thud. Suddenly everything happened at once. The lights came on, brilliant in her eyes. The doorbell rang. The voice she knew shouted, "Call your dog off!"

Beau was growling and snarling through closed teeth; she heard that. George disentangled himself from the table and began to dance, a most peculiar activity, it occurred to her wildly. Then she saw that Beau had him by the leg and was holding on.

Peter dashed from the stairs, fell, scrambled up, seized George by the arm and dragged him (and Beau, who wouldn't give up) halfway to the front door. He must have reached out one hand to the door. George kept on yelling at the top of his thin and certainly scared voice. Jim came running into the house, throwing the door wide, telling Peter to get out of the way and falling upon George. Delia descended the stairs, wrapped in pink silk, wearing hair curlers and contriving to look outraged and majestic at the same time.

George howled. "He's killing me! Call him off—"

It was not a moment for giggles; nevertheless, Julie felt a kind of dreadful laughter welling up inside her throat. George trying to strangle her! That could not be!

But it was. Somehow Peter and Jim between them induced Beau to release his hold on George's leg but he stood between them, still growling as if, when they let George go, he'd finish the job.

George interpreted that growl quite correctly. "Shut up that dog! He tried to kill me!"

Jim's face was stony white. "What are you doing here, George?"

Peter cried, "He tried to kill Julie!"

"No, no!" George cried. "No! I didn't know it was Julie."

Julie at last found her own voice. "George had his hands on my throat!"

Delia came to look at her throat. Peter forgot to hold the dog, who launched himself at George again. George emulated Pye and shot to the wide top of the piano, where he looked completely ridiculous.

How could she have been so frightened, so terrified, when it was only George!

George began frantically, "I came to see my mother. Everybody knows she died years ago. I saw her myself just before she died! Now Lisa says she's here! I can't believe it. I've got to see her!"

After a moment of packed silence Delia said firmly, "Why didn't you ring the doorbell, George? I gather you got here by way of the kitchen and the old dumbwaiter?"

"I had to." George kept a frightened gaze upon Beau. "That damn dog nearly took my leg off."

Jim said, "It's still there. What do you mean, you had to?"

"I did ring at the doorbell." George was very slightly recovering his usual self-satisfaction. "The electricity was off.

So the bell didn't ring. The kitchen door was not locked. But when I tried the stairs up from the kitchen the door at the top was locked."

Delia said sternly, "That little door is never locked at night—"

"It was this time." Peter looked sheepish. "Pye. I was afraid she'd get down in the kitchen. It suddenly dawned on me that she's very smart."

"About door knobs?" Delia asked coldly.

"About any crack. She lies on her side and claws at it. Want to see?" Peter replied with even then a certain pride.

"No!" said Delia.

Jim said quite coolly, as a matter of fact, "The electricity *was* off. I tried to ring the doorbell several times. I was just trying to decide what to do when the lights came on all over."

Delia weighed that. Peter scowled. George rubbed his leg. Finally Delia said, "We'll sit down and talk this over."

"I'll stay here," George said. "Until you chain up that dog."

"Fine," said Delia. "Stay there. I must say you look a little odd. But what makes you think your mother is here?"

"Why, isn't she? I saw her—she was dying then. She gave me her papers. But Lisa told me she is still alive and here. I can't believe—"

"Where did you see Lisa?"

"Oh," George looked unusually evasive. "Just a little bar I sometimes visit."

"In New York, I take it. I was looking for you all over New Haven," Jim said.

"I can come to New York if I want to."

"Oh, certainly. How did Lisa know about my mother?" George blinked.

Peter wriggled. "I told her. I let her think that your mother was here in the house, Jim. I didn't want Lisa to go to the hospital and put on a big scene. It would have done your mother no good."

"Right, Peter. But you could have waited till tomorrow morning, couldn't you, George?" Jim demanded.

"Certainly not." George had so far recovered as to assume quite an impressive air of eager affection. "My mother! Alive! Here!"

Jim's black eyebrows rose. "Why did you try to hurt Julie?"

"I didn't know it was Julie."

At this Julie had to insist. She had never suspected that wispy George could have such lethal strength in his hands. "He did see me! He said he thought the sound of the piano would bring me down. Oh, he knew I was here!"

"I tell you I didn't know it was you!" George all but yelled. "Would I have hurt you, Julie? Never!"

"But you did."

Delia intervened. "Jim, what do you advise?"

Peter, however, replied. "Call the police at once. Let George cool his heels in jail. Breaking and entering!"

Delia and Jim did not exchange a look, a word, anything. Yet curiously at that moment Julie felt some kind of communication between them. She didn't know how she felt it or why; she only knew that it existed, like an unseen, unheard means of exchanging thought.

Jim stood very close beside her; Julie was thankful for that. She also wondered, oddly, if George had really meant to kill her. It didn't seem likely, not George. And yet George's hands had grasped her throat. George had known what he was doing.

Pye came discreetly into the room, cast a glance from red eyes at Beau, as if to tell him not to take advantage of her presence, and leaped up onto the piano beside George. George leaped, too. "What in hell is that?"

"Never you mind," said Peter. "Here, Pye—" He took up the cat, whose eyes were beginning to turn blue again. "Don't let George contaminate you." Jim grinned.

It was a very brief grin, however. He said to George, "It

is breaking and entering, George. You did get into the kitchen and the—that thing." Even then Jim gave a distasteful glance toward the dining room and the big old box whose door still hung open.

"I—that is—yes, I told you. The kitchen door was open." He took a breath and went on. "So you see, after trying the street doorbell and seeing that lights all over were out, I felt my way to the kitchen door and it was not locked, so I came in. Then when I tried the steps and the dining room door and that was locked—" he shot an accusing glance at Peter, who looked inexcusably smug—"I remembered that old dumbwaiter. I didn't expect it to make so much noise." He, too, gave a baleful glance toward the poor old dumbwaiter, certainly an innocent participant in the family scene.

Peter perked up. "The kitchen door *was* locked! I locked it!"

George, except for keeping a pale green eye on the dog, had quite recovered his usual self-confidence. "You couldn't have locked it, old fellow."

Peter turned bright red. "Don't call me 'old fellow'!"

"Why—why—certainly, old—I mean, Peter. Why don't you chain up that dog?"

"You came to see your mother?" Jim said. "You couldn't wait till morning? Even in this storm?"

Suddenly, everyone listened. The wind had gone down. There remained only short gusts. The rain was no longer slashing hard at the house. The house itself seemed too quiet.

"Why did you touch the piano?" Jim said. George only swallowed hard and watched the dog.

"No reason." George felt his leg and looked at the range of Beau's attack, which was really quite evident. Red scratches where George had tried unsuccessfully to escape Beau's teeth showed through tears in George's otherwise neat gray trouser leg. "Hydrophobia," he said dourly.

Julie was beginning to recover herself. "Not unless you gave it to him!"

This drew half a smile from Jim and a whoop of laughter from Peter. George glowered. "I ought to see a doctor right away. Get rabies shots—"

"Seems to me you already have rabies," said Peter irresistibly. "And I did lock that kitchen door, Aunt Delia. So how did he get in?"

"I told you!" George began to straighten his legs, which Beau did not approve of, for he gave a leap which nearly ungripped Peter's hold on his collar.

"Might as well put Beau in my workroom," Julie told Peter. He looked unhappy but marched off, tugging at Beau, who gazed longingly back at George.

Delia sighed. "I think we'll leave all this till morning. George, your mother is alive. It was very surprising to us all. But she has been very ill. The doctor says nobody can see her until she's better. However—" Delia drew herself up. "You must stay right here. Until I see John."

Jim said, with cold anger, "George *did* get into the house and *did* attack Julie."

"I did no such thing!" George cried.

"You are lying," Jim said. "Julie tells the truth. Another such word out of you, George, and I'll give you the beating you've been asking for."

"Why, Jim! Your own brother!" But George's round cheeks turned slightly green.

Jim's face took on a kind of expressionless mask. So, oddly, did Delia's.

"In the morning," said Jim, "Aunt Delia. We'll have a chance to find my father—"

"Our father!" George showed rather long teeth. "Don't forget that."

Jim paid no attention to him. "Aunt Delia, do you have a room with a good strong lock? One that can resist any attempt at"—Jim paused and said deliberately—"breaking. We really have to keep you here, George, until—well," said Jim rather strangely, "until."

This time the unspoken communication between him and Delia operated at once and visibly.

She nodded. "Certainly, Jim, you are quite right. Peter!" she called.

Peter banged the door of Julie's workroom and ran back to the conference.

"But, Aunt Delia! The police—"

"No, not now. That room above yours, hasn't the door a key? Go and look."

"Oh, I know it has. You're going to lock him up?"

Delia said, "This is too much for me. After we talk to your father tomorrow, Jim, it is barely possible that the doctor will let us speak to Elaine. That means—well, never mind. Take George upstairs, Jim. And, Peter—"

"At least give me some iodine," George whined.

"Sure," Peter's eyes brightened. "I'll put it on for you. Of course, it'll sting like blazes but—come on, George."

"You're sure that dog is shut up."

Jim put out a hand and yanked George off the piano. "We said, upstairs." Julie had never heard Jim speak just like that.

But Peter lingered a moment, eyes still brilliant. "How did you like Las Vegas, George?"

"Las—Las Vegas! I was never in Las Vegas in my life! What are you talking about?"

"The cleaner's tag in one of your dress-suit pockets. Said Las Vegas. I only wondered." Peter looked with the pretense of great innocence at the ceiling.

Jim whirled around to stare at Peter. Delia tried to smooth her hair, encountered curlers and looked slightly embarrassed. "Better explain to him, Peter."

Peter explained, briefly, still with a very innocent look on his face but very shining eyes.

George laughed, wriggled, laughed again and finally said, "Oh, that! I lent the clothes to an actor friend of mine. I didn't realize that he'd been in Las Vegas. On the road, I expect. Really, Peter, don't you think I know where I've been?"

"I think you were in Las Vegas and—" Peter paused.

Delia said abruptly, "That actor friend was yourself, wasn't it, George?"

"No! Why, have you cooked up something or other to tell my father? Believe me, this is something you can't possibly prove!"

The telephone rang sharply. Nobody stirred. As it repeated itself urgently Julie said, "I'll go—" and ran to answer it in her workroom, where the dog greeted her with pleasure.

It was Dr. Evans on the telephone. "Saw your lights. Glad you got electricity back on again. May I speak to your aunt, Julie?"

"Yes, she's right here."

Delia had followed her and again put an absent hand to her hair and again looked faintly embarrassed. Delia, rarely in all her life, to Julie's knowledge, appeared without every single silver-blond hair in place. What could she have been doing all that long afternoon? It was a brief question. She heard Delia say, "Oh, thank you. Yes, everything is working now. The telephone was off for a while, and our lights were off, too. I expect everybody in the Cove had trouble—what?" There was a long pause. Then Delia said slowly, "Thank you. Thank you very much. Yes," and hung up.

She turned to Julie and said in an oddly low voice, as if it were a closely held secret, "He says Elaine has improved so much that she's quite conscious. We can see her in the morning. That is, Jim can see her. And—I suppose George—"

"Did *he* say George?"

"Oh, no, I say it. After all, George must be her son."

Delia's pink silk dressing gown rustled as they passed Beau and returned to the living room.

Beau, left behind in the workroom, gave a frustrated yelp,

as if longing to get his teeth into George's leg again. Julie would have liked to open the door and let him out.

Back in the living room, Delia said, "Now, Peter, Jim, please take George upstairs."

Another interruption came; it was the doorbell this time, rung over and over.

Twenty-four

Jim went to answer it. George merely huddled up tightly against the piano.

John Wingate came in, his arm around Jim's shoulders. This time, it struck Julie that their likeness was somehow rather strangely exaggerated; perhaps it was because John seemed so much younger than he had for a long time. He was almost exuberant. He hugged Jim's shoulder and said, "Delia, glad your lights are back on again. Oh!" He saw George and said in surprise, "What on earth are you doing here, George?"

Explanations came from Delia and Peter. Jim said nothing. Julie leaned against a chair and listened but saw the change in John's face. The sudden youth and glow which had been in his eyes changed, too. He said, "Well, we'll have to wait until morning, Delia. You are quite right. I'll talk to you later, George."

Delia interrupted. "The doctor says we can see Elaine in the morning, John."

"Oh?" John thought for a moment, then clapped his hand on Jim's shoulder again and brightened almost as if nothing could dim the new eagerness that wrapped him like an aura of good feeling. "You'll have to stay here, George."

Neither Jim nor Delia had mentioned George's attempt to strangle Julie. Peter did. "He broke into the house. He tried to strangle Julie. He—" A flood of perception swept upon Peter. "Hey, listen! George had the key to the kitchen door. Sure, he had it. He hit that cook and took her apron and she had her own key in it and your key, too, Aunt Delia!"

He turned back to John and burst out in full spate. "Before he came here, he tried to make Julie promise to marry him —or something—and then he tried to run her down with his car—oh, you know all that! But also he scared hell out of the cook and got her apron and the kitchen key and—isn't that so, Aunt Delia?"

Delia had frozen. "It sounds reasonable. We almost believe it could be true. What shall we do, John?"

John was suddenly very grim. "You'll settle with me, George. But let it go now, Delia. It's late. Tomorrow I'll see to things, I promise you. For God's sake," John added, "stop hanging on to that piano, George. Come on."

George did move, cautiously looking at the hall. "That dog still shut up?"

"I am about to let him out," said Julie wickedly and started for her workroom door. George did not merely scramble, he nearly fell in his haste. "Stairs, huh? Sure. You'll see, father. I'm not as bad as they are trying to make you believe—"

"Go upstairs."

"We'll lock him in," Peter said eagerly.

"Then do," said John. "I promise you I'll see to all this tomorrow. He didn't really hurt you, child, did he?" he said to Julie, came to her, lifted her chin, looked at her throat and turned pale. "Thank God it's no worse." He kissed her lightly and turned to Jim, "Take care of her, Jim. I'll go now."

But he paused to give Delia a long look. He was all at once

the John whom Julie had grown to know during the past five years, guarded, careful, never permitting his emotions to show if he could help it. He said gravely, "I'm afraid you are right, Delia. George is a—a very weak and—and—well, be that as it may, he is Elaine's son. It must have been a shock for him to hear that she is alive and here. If you feel that all this should be reported to the police at once and charges brought, then I do understand."

Delia this time really shoved at the curlers in her hair. Her lips trembled. "John, I don't know what to say. He'll have to be—" She paused and finally said, "Made to see that he can't steal and try to kill anybody and—"

"Yes, Delia," John said. He turned toward the street door. Yet somehow, strangely as Jim went with him, his voice, even the alert and vigorous way he moved, seemed to recapture that youthful glow. "Good night, Jim. I'll be back in the morning."

Peter and Jim thrust George toward the stairs. He did not, however, require much thrusting, for Julie let the dog out. Beau tore into the living room for the piano before he discovered that George was on the stairs and Peter and Jim were behind him. At which, for once in his life, Beau growled, sat down and let out a small but dismal howl. "His prey escaped," Delia said, with a flicker of her usual self.

Julie, rubbing her throat cautiously, thought of the transformation in John. That transformation had been altered, blotted out like a cloud over the sun, when he was told of George's most recent behavior. Yet it seemed to Julie that it had returned when he went away, as if he were going somewhere where there were no clouds at all, nothing but sunshine and everything a man could want. Delia dropped a curler and Julie said absently, "I thought you had to be at the hairdresser's this afternoon."

"Oh?" Delia's pretty face took on its blank I'm-not-going-to-say-a-word look. "No. No, I had to put these curlers on because I hadn't time to go to the hairdresser's. Do you

231

suppose they'll lock George up? I mean, when we report to the police?"

"I don't know." Then where were you all that time? Julie couldn't help thinking but didn't dare say. As a matter of fact, a question would not be answered, not when Delia looked blankly stubborn. And, indeed, it was merely a small, unimportant question.

Delia said very soberly, "Something's got to be done about George. If he really tried to run you down—and then got into the house by that key and tried to strangle you— Yes, something will have to be done. Attempted murder. That's what it was."

"He tried to explain it."

"Don't defend him. He's not worth it." Delia flashed a hard bright glance at her. "I think the storm has gone."

It had, as swiftly as it had come. "Out to sea, I hope," Delia added. "I suppose you'll have to take that dog out."

"Yes. Come on, Beau." Julie took out her raincoat and put it on over her dressing gown.

Delia was right. The surge of wind and torrents of rain had slashed their noisy and indeed destructive way on. When Julie opened the door, the street lights were shining, the street was cluttered with broken branches and leaves. But the wind and rain no longer swept their terrible way through the world, at least through their little world.

She put Beau on his leash and Delia stood in the doorway watching until they returned. "Good night, my dear." Delia rustled her way upstairs to her room, and Julie turned out the lights, all but one in the living room, and followed.

She did wonder just how Jim and Peter had contrived to put George neatly and swiftly and, of all things, quietly into one of the several bedrooms on the third floor, but she discovered Peter on the bottom steps of the second flight of stairs, munching a banana. Pye sat beside him, blue eyes mere contented slits. Peter's face lighted up. "Think Mr. Wingate believed me?"

"Oh, yes, Peter. I think he did. But George is his son. It's very hard for John."

"Didn't look like it!" Peter swallowed and pulled down the banana skin. "Tell you what he looked like. Looked as if he had a date. Some dame."

"Oh, now, Peter."

"Looked that way to me."

"Where is Jim?"

"He's got a chair outside George's room. George didn't make a sound. Well—" Peter paused, an impish gleam in his eyes. "I told him—that is, I didn't lie, I just suggested that I had left the dog free to roam the house. So," said Peter smugly, "George went quietly."

Jim peered over the railing of the landing above. "Why don't you go to bed, Julie?"

Peter swallowed the last of his banana, rolled up the skin and threw it up at Jim, who caught it deftly, rolled it up again and tossed it back at Peter. Unfortunately it struck Pye, who gave a most startling yowl. That brought Aunt Delia into the hall beside Julie, and a torrent of kicks and yells from George behind the bedroom door. Jim's face lost its momentary grin at Peter. He said, in real compunction, "Sorry, Pye, I didn't see you."

Delia brought a certain order into the scene by telling Peter to pick up the banana skin and Julie to go to bed. Everybody always obeyed Delia.

Julie couldn't possibly sleep. There was far too much to think about, reason about, try to find some clear way through the contradictions and the unanswered questions. But there was one incontrovertible fact: George *had* crawled up into the house by way of the old dumbwaiter, he *had*—yes, he had caught her by the throat. He had recognized her. She was sure of that. George could have been upset, confused to the point where he'd have seized anybody in his path. But, no, her throat was still painful.

No, she couldn't sleep. She could never sleep until—all at

233

once she awoke and the sky was blue and sunshine was coming in the window.

The trip to the hospital was accomplished most dexterously by John and Jim. Somehow together they all but forced George to accompany them. John's car went ahead with George wedged securely between John and Jim. Delia, Peter and Julie followed in Julie's small car. It was a silent ride except for Peter, who came out with the information that he had talked to Sam and Sam had said that Ollie was leaving the hospital, was okay. Ollie had said that he intended to go home at once.

"Then he can see to your cat," Delia said, but absently. "When you go back to school."

"Oh," Peter said in a small voice. "Well, about that, Sam, that is—"

Delia came out of her abstraction to pick it up. "What about school?"

"Well, seems somehow it was fixed. That is, the headmaster is going to permit us both to come back."

"When?"

"Right away. But not today. I think Sam said next week."

"Oh," said Delia and added, but with no perceptible interest, "that Latin word—something about *sesquip*—well, what does it mean?"

Peter shot a smug glance at Delia. "It was part of Caesar's bridge. They made us draw and describe that bridge. It was so silly that I memorized some of it. That means two-foot timbers, six feet across. Silly."

"Ah," said Delia, losing all interest.

"Anyway, it has come to mean 'a long word.' Of course," Peter added handsomely, "I may be mistaken."

"Sesquipedalian—" Julie said, absently too, and turned into a parking space.

The doctor met them in the entrance. He was unusually cheerful. "She's really doing very well," he told them.

They followed him, without speaking, any of them. Yet it

234

was quite a party to visit a woman who had been so very weak. At the door of her room, the doctor stopped them. "You, Mr. Wingate. And her sons. That's all, I think."

So Julie and Delia and Peter waited outside in the wide hall, behind a brown covered screen. Peter was all eyes, and, Julie was sure, all ears. Delia looked hard and firm as a rock. Julie's heart was pounding.

From behind the screen came the voices. The doctor's was very cheerful and encouraging, Jim's was very low. John said firmly, "Elaine, I've brought your sons, Jim and George. It's great you are looking better. Do you feel like just opening your eyes and taking a look? We'll not bother you."

Elaine apparently did open her eyes. Her voice came thinly but clearly from behind the screen. "Jim! My boy! How you've grown and—but, I'd expect that, wouldn't I?" Elaine tried a feeble laugh. Jim said, "Yes, mother."

But then Elaine's voice rose. "Who is *that*?"

There was a swift motion behind the screen. The doctor cried, "Take it easy now."

George shouted, "Let me go!"

John said, "Look hard, Elaine. He says he is your son George—"

Elaine's voice rose again, shrilly. "I never saw that man in my life! Take him away! My only son is Jim."

Twenty-five

Pandemonium is simply not permitted in a fine, well-run hospital. It nearly occurred then. First, George thrust the screen aside so that it fell upon Delia and Peter. Then the doctor must have pushed some button or given some alarm, for two hefty orderlies came running, their white coats swinging, to grasp George. Another man, a guard in blue with a bright badge on his shoulder, came to help and in a second, it seemed to Julie, George's hands were caught behind him, clasped there by a glimmer of steel and chain and he was neatly removed, completely removed, out of sight around a corner.

The doctor was bending over Elaine, his stethoscope in his hand. Jim stood beside her, holding her hand. John stood at the other side of the bed, his face deeply troubled, and yet, there was still that air of vigor and youth which Julie would have said, if she had thought of it, had vanished forever with Jim's involvement in murder and his long absence but now had returned.

Delia had got herself upright. Peter stared wide-eyed into

236

the room. Julie said, "I think we'd better go home." But her voice shook.

"No." Delia had fully righted herself. "We'll wait for John and Jim. The doctor can't let them stay until Elaine is all right. She's had a shock, of course. Poor darling!"

So like Delia: years of thinking hard thoughts of Elaine but now soft as butter with pity.

There was a low-voiced conclave near Elaine. Both Jim and John seemed to disagree with the doctor. The doctor was quite accustomed to family disagreements, apparently, for all at once both men appeared to yield and came into the corridor.

John stared at them as if he didn't see them. Jim took Julie's arm. "It's all right. She'll be better. Dr. Evans says we must let her rest—"

Again they separated for the journey home. Not a word was spoken by Delia, Peter or Julie herself. Broken branches, huddled clumps of autumn leaves were being busily gathered into enormous hoppers. The machines had considerably edged around Jim's little car, which stood stubbornly before the door of Delia's house.

The house, strangely, looked exactly the same. Jim and John were waiting for them. Beau greeted them politely as always, too, and pushed his nose at Julie. Peter saw it and offered to take him out.

John went into the living room and at Delia's invitation, uttered rather breathlessly, sank down into a deep chair.

Peter shouted through the open street door. "Don't tell anything till I get back."

John did smile a little at that. Delia tried not to. Jim said, "Please, father—"

"Yes. Yes, I know. But I had to do it this way. Somehow I had to prove it to all of you. George," he said wearily, "is an actor. You were right, Peter—oh, he's gone. Well, Peter was right when he suggested that George had been in Las

Vegas. Probably pursuing his acting career. It was there that Walker met him."

"But Walker—the Walker I knew was a fake?" said Delia.

"Worse than a fake," John said. "Is that Peter already?"

Peter bounced in. "Yes, sir. You didn't tell anything—"

"Only that Walker met George in Las Vegas and George was an actor—"

"Lisa said that!" Peter cried. "She said he'd helped her about odd bits of stage business but he wasn't a good actor."

John leaned back in his chair, frowning. "You all know something of my efforts to find Jim.

"Delia and Blanche know that when I had the money, I made a bargain with Elaine. Her agreement was to tell me something about Jim. She didn't. She spent the money as she chose to spend it. She attracted the attention of a man calling himself Count Alvary."

This time, remarkably, Delia said nothing at all.

John went on. "Naturally the way poor little Elaine was spending money, he believed she was another rich American and very pretty in addition. We were divorced by then, so Elaine was free. So he married her. However, it wasn't long before he discovered that the money was not endless, not by any means. After some time he contrived to get her into a shoddy kind of sanitarium and left her there while he traveled to New York, seeking another rich wife."

Again there was utter silence on Delia's part. Curiously, it was shared by Jim yet they did not exchange so much as a glance. John went on, "He didn't, at that time, find one so he went on to Las Vegas! He had run short of money and was trying to cook up some scheme when he happened on George —I really don't know yet what George's real name is. There was, however, a slight resemblance to Elaine's reddish hair, rather weak face and yet he could be charming. About the right age, also. So the Count's—that is, Walker's—scheme must have seemed like an inspiration. He offered George a part to play. Walker had secured all of Elaine's papers; her first marriage certificate and some communications from me. George had lived in England: he had a passport which I can only suppose Walker later managed to doctor—name, date and place of birth, all that. Dangerous, but George got by with it. He simply approached George, who was easily approachable, I think, and hired him to act out the part of my second son. Or, if I questioned that, Elaine's son by another man.

"All this developed as Count Alvary—call him Walker, which may or may not have been his real name—had planned. So, he sent George to me with the story that Elaine had kept in touch with him in England and had sent for him on her deathbed to give him all those papers as proof of his identity before she died. Of course I believed him, because not long before George came, I had a letter from the sanitarium, telling me that Elaine had died. I'm not quite sure how Walker managed that, but he probably bribed someone at the sanitarium to write the letter, which is why I never heard from them again. Meanwhile, Walker came back to New York, still in search of a rich marriage that might offer more money than George could supply. He met a charming and beautiful woman, but, simply because she was a charming and intelligent woman with a demanding career, she had had little experience with such men as Walker. He married her after a swift courtship. On their honeymoon he had a letter from the sanitarium wanting more money for Elaine, who, of course, was not dead at all. His new—call her wife, for she certainly believed herself to be his wife—happened to see the letter, which proved her to be a bigamist. An unintentional bigamist and—oh, yes, an easy mark for Walker. She left him at once. So he came to Brookboro to fasten himself upon George. That was barely a year after George had convinced me that he was Elaine's son, no matter who his father was. George didn't like Walker's arrival but couldn't help it; he was George's senior partner, so to speak, in this miserable game. But the woman was by no means without feelings. She had learned all that I have told you. In the meantime I told her that Elaine died, for I believed it. So she faced Walker. She knew that only Walker could have supplied George with what I had to accept as proof! Thus George had to be an impostor. So she demanded that both of them stop this business of mulcting me for all they could get. A—violent scene developed."

Again there was the most complete and utter stillness between Delia and Jim.

John went on, "Walker, defying her, actually phoned Jim. He was sufficiently cautious to phone from another room. So his brief talk with Jim was not overheard. Then he was bold enough to tell this woman that he would ruin her reputation by accusing her of bigamy if she insisted upon telling what she knew of him and George. It was a foolish act of defiance. She—this fine woman—lost her head. She had the gun. She threatened him with it. There was a gunshot."

Neither Jim nor Delia moved.

Julie heard her own whisper, "Blanche!"

"Blanche. She was distraught when suspicion developed in such a way that in the end Jim was sure to be judged guilty of murder. But then Jim took matters into his own hands and ran away and"—John said firmly—"I don't blame him. He was right at the time. There was simply no other way he could see. Once he was gone, how could she confess? Jim would be all right; she was sure of that. She knew that the time would come when she would have to confess. She is a brave, deeply grieved and—conscientious woman." John put his hand over his eyes for a moment and said. "She told me all of it last night. The whole night," he said gently.

He glanced up, his eyes piercing. "You guessed that, Delia. And you, Jim—"

At last Delia and Jim exchanged a look. Jim said, "I went to that newspaper woman, Blythe Smith. She had had her files more thoroughly searched and had come upon a photograph, one of those party snapshots. I recognized Blanche with Walker."

Delia nodded. "I saw Miss Smith myself. Later in the day. She showed me the photograph, so I knew you had seen it too, Jim. But I couldn't believe—"

"I thought Blanche might have told you of her marriage, Delia," John said. "Apparently she didn't." Delia thought for a second; then she exchanged an odd, almost conspiratorial look with Julie. Julie said promptly, "Oh, but John, you had turned her down—"

"No! No! I didn't—"

Julie went on, "You don't understand. Women—well, to put it bluntly, Blanche must have felt hopeless about you. She wouldn't tell anybody, even Delia, about that marriage until she could come home with a handsome husband and—"

"A title!" Delia cried. "Fake, but a title!"

Peter whispered into Pye's black ear, "I'll never understand women."

Delia took a breath to prepare for saying something scathing, Julie was sure, but John rose.

"I have some things to ask you to do. Here is a letter written by Blanche. It must go to McClary. It's the whole story. It was for her a tragic kind of balance sheet. Her mother would have died if she had known the truth. Her highly respected firm would certainly have been compromised. Jim wrote to her. He quoted a newspaper clipping" —(the one he showed us later, Julie thought)—"that he thought at first just might offer him a way out. Later, of course, his common sense told him that a capital crime like murder could not have any limitation. However, he put in the requisite five years in the rather dim hope that the wording of that law, plus his own voluntary return, might provide some lenience. At least he might be given time.

"Meanwhile, Blanche's mother was failing, yet somehow clinging to life. Blanche had to hope that her mother's life could go on comfortably, day by day to the end. But then, against her strong advice, Jim returned. She still had to bear the heavy burden of her own conscience for a time. McClary will understand all that—and the district attorney, state's attorney, the governor. But she can never come back."

Peter said, "But it *was* murder, sir."

John looked at Peter. "Yes, Peter. Nothing can change that. Unless, of course, it was actually Walker whose hand pulled the trigger. But she supplied the means and motive. She'll bear the burden all the rest of her life. And in a rather close degree, Delia and Julie and Jim and you, too, Peter, will have that burden. But that is the way it is. We can't change it."

"But she *could* have confessed. Perhaps not just then," Peter said in a low voice.

"Peter, life sometimes takes its own course. If you get in deep water you struggle to get out of it and sometimes you only find yourself in deeper water. Now"—he turned to Jim —"now Jim, you'll see to this letter to McClary. Also, you'll see to your mother. I'm leaving money in your account."

"Leaving," Julie whispered.

John turned to her. "And you keep on with your writing. You have a gift. If you don't use a gift you lose it. Now I really must go—" There was suddenly again a glow of warmth and happiness in his face.

Julie cried, "Why, John! You're in love with Blanche!"

"Of course. So—"

Delia intervened. "But the revolver! That belonged to you, John."

"Oh, yes. Remember at that time few people locked doors in Brookboro. She walked into my house, got the gun without being seen. She went to her own home with it and thought and the more she thought, the more mandatory it seemed to her that this fakery of George's and Walker's must be stopped. So she went to see Walker. She meant only to threaten Walker with it. But when he came back from phoning Jim and saw the gun, a struggle followed and in the struggle—oh, yes, he was shot. And whether it was Blanche's hand, intentionally, or Walker's hand unintentionally, the fact remains. There was barely time for her to scoop up the briefcase with his papers and get out the back door before you arrived, Jim. It never occurred to her then that he had phoned Jim and that Jim would be accused. Remember, she was simply not in command of herself. She was terrified, distraught, I understand that. A woman of such intelligence, such control, placed in so tragic and unintended circumstances. Now then, I *must* go. The weather is good enough—"

Julie cried, "You are going with Blanche!"

"Oh, no." John smiled happily. "She's already gone. Her plane got off this morning as soon as the weather permitted. I'll meet her. I'll not tell you where. But we'll keep in touch with you. For heaven's sake, you needn't look so surprised. I've been in love with her for—" He looked at his watch. "Forever. At least it seems so."

Peter had been silent. He now said, "Sir—"

"Yes, Peter."

"That ladder!"

"Oh," John actually smiled, but sadly, "I'm afraid George must have done that merely from some idiotic notion of confusing things. It was like George. Jealous of Jim perhaps. Uncertain of his own claims."

"That was very cruel of George," Delia said.

"And not very bright. Like him," Peter muttered.

"Yes. I'm afraid like him. Same with the Judge. Although we'll never be able to prove it, George had to have taken the medicine, hoping the Judge would have so severe an attack that he would die, as tragically as he did. But his death would remove a certain and perhaps legally valuable friend of Jim. It doesn't matter now, anyway. Since Jim's innocence in Walker's murder has been established, his motive for killing the Judge won't hold water either. I have to go, I can't miss that plane. Jim, my son, Blanche has suffered from this more than you."

"But, John, how about her mother?" Delia said.

"Her mother died peacefully night before last. I went with Blanche to see to the quiet services in their family plot upstate. If Jim had returned only a little later, Blanche would have been free to tell the whole truth. Now, goodbye, Delia. Julie." He took her swiftly in his arms, kissed her, shook hands with Jim and was gone.

Jim followed him to the street door. He came back, looking rather as if the storm had more or less torn him apart. Probably, certainly, all three of them felt the same way.

Jim said, "She—they are going to one of those places she hunted out for me."

Delia nodded and wiped her eyes. Peter gave a long, low whistle. "Ladder—medicine bottle—we ought to have guessed George. The kind of thing he would do! Just like attacking the whistler."

Julie said, "But it's over. They will be together."

Out in the garden, Julie had a glimpse of the gardener raking the path, tying up shrubs that the storm had torn down.

The doorbell rang, short urgent bursts. Peter went to answer it and with a whirl of dancing feet Lisa rushed in. "You'll never guess! I've got a Broadway role. My big chance!" She twirled around on tiptoes. "I'll be great! By the way, if you see George tell him he is not needed. The role I thought he might take over has been filled." She flung herself at Jim and kissed him warmly. "Now, then," she said triumphantly, "you can always say 'the great actress, the great Lisa Carlyon kissed me.' Goodbye, everybody."

In another second she was gone. Peter had had the sense to go to the door with her. He came back. "Didn't kiss me," he said glumly.

Delia said, "What can we do about George? What will happen to him?"

"I don't know," Jim said. "Breaking and entering. False identity, fraud. Attempted murder. That is what he meant to do: First kill Julie, who had denied his claims. Then kill my mother, who would denounce him. He really thought she was in the house that night. But it would be hard to prove and—my father said, just let that take its course. McClary will see to it. Julie, we have got to get blood tests and a license."

"Shouldn't take long." Delia was back in the saddle, her eyes sparkling with energy. "Why, Julie dear, you can wear my own wedding dress."

Peter grunted and sauntered to pick up the cat.

"You cats have so much sense," he muttered. "It's only humans who get themselves in so much trouble."

"But all the same there are rewards. Now, Peter, will you take Sweetie Pye and *get out!*"

About the Author

MIGNON G. EBERHART'S name has become a guarantee of excellence in the mystery and suspense field. Her work has been translated into sixteen languages, and has been serialized in many magazines and adapted for radio, television and motion pictures.

For many years Mrs. Eberhart traveled extensively abroad and in the United States. Now she lives in Greenwich, Connecticut.

In the seventies the Mystery Writers of America gave Mrs. Eberhart their Grand Master Award, in recognition of her sustained excellence as a suspense writer, and she also served as president of that organization. She recently celebrated the fiftieth anniversary of the publication of her first novel, *The Patient in Room 18*.